HUNGRY
for
HAPPINESS

Also by James Villas

Dancing in the Low Country

Hungry for Happiness

Published by Kensington Publishing Corp.

HUNGRY
for
HAPPINESS

JAMES VILLAS

KENSINGTON BOOKS
www.kensingtonbooks.com

KENSINGTON BOOKS are published by

Kensington Publishing Corp.
119 West 40th Street
New York, NY 10018

All Kensington titles, imprints, and distributed lines are available at special quantity discounts for bulk purchases for sales promotion, premiums, fund-raising, educational, or institutional use.

Special book excerpts or customized printings can also be created to fit specific needs. For details, write or phone the office of the Kensington Special Sales Manager: Kensington Publishing Corp., 119 West 40th Street, New York, NY 10018. Attn. Special Sales Department. Phone: 1-800-221-2647.

Kensington and the K logo Reg. U.S. Pat. & TM Off.

ISBN-13: 978-0-7582-2848-2
ISBN-10: 0-7582-2848-1

First Kensington Trade Paperback Printing: November 2010
10 9 8 7 6 5 4 3 2 1

Printed in the United States of America

HUNGRY
for
HAPPINESS

1

THE CURSE

I reckon I do love my mama, but I gotta say sometimes she can be the most spiteful human being on earth when she pitches one of her hissies. You know, a real bitch. I mean, what I could use at this point in my life are just a few kind words of encouragement from my own mother, and what do I get but the same ridicule she's been dishing out ever since I decided to have the surgery—and before. I figure any other mother would be proud of a daughter who's determined to improve herself and overcome what I can only call a family curse. I also figure Mama's just envious of anyone who gets sick and tired of looking like a tub of lard and has the guts to finally do something about it.

Yeah, I used to be fat and make no bones about it. None of this wishy-washy crap about being full-figured and curvy and having a weight disorder. I'm talking about fat, disgusting fat—pure and simple. Like five foot four and 280 pounds. Hell, I was fat my whole goddamn life till I took the bull by the horns. I ate when I was happy. I ate when I was sad. I ate when I was disappointed or scared. If there was any reason to eat, I found it. And diets? You name it, I tried it. Weight Watchers. South Beach. Atkins. Nutrisystem. Tubular pasta. Even a stupid sugar-water diet I read about in *Reader's Digest*. Fat pills? Whatta joke! Also tried a MultiFlex for two months I ordered on the Internet, then weeks of purging, then some stupid support group, then heaven knows how much counseling and therapy. Nothing worked, and I hated myself, and all Mama could say was "Loretta, you're nuts," or "Sugar, why can't you just accept the way the Good Lord made you?" or "Loretta, nobody's ever gonna mistake you for a bathing beauty"—awful things like that.

Fat. As I say, it's always been like a plague on my whole family. Maybe it's partly genetic, but the truth is, we all love food more than life itself, and, myself, I love to cook and fool around with food and watch the Food Network almost as much as I love eating and blowing the sax and finding good homes for our animals. Guess I learned to cook mostly from Mama, but show me something like *Helen Corbett's Cookbook* and I can spend days just reading it, and gettin' ideas, and fixin' dozens of great dishes. Of course I'm best at Southern and Tex-Mex, but when I wanna do real fancy foreign things like beef burgundy and chicken cacciatore, I couldn't do without my messed-up copy of *Joy of Cooking* that Mama once gave me for my birthday. And I wonder why I could never lose weight.

Anyway, my sweet daddy died of a heart attack when he was only forty-eight. Mama's up there at about 250 and has diabetes and hypoglycemia and obstructive sleep apnea. And my older sister Gladys, who's a year older than me and married with a fat husband and four chubby children . . . well, Gladys is only thirty-seven and has already had one knee replaced, and she's still about Mama's size. I've begged and begged Mama and Gladys both to bite the bullet the way I finally did, but they're both scared as chickens. Just terrified of the idea of having their stomachs banded—banded gastroplasty they call it. I told Mama she wouldn't be around many more years to bake biscuits and put up preserves if she didn't get over to the bariatric clinic, but then she gets on her high horse again and says things like, "It's not natural fooling around with your body like that, young lady, and you could end up paying a price worse than death." I do something like pat my tummy and hips and say, "But, Mama, look at me now. Just look at me and see how much healthier and happier I am." And she just makes that mean face the way she does when she disapproves of something and says, "Loretta, child, I liked you a lot better when you had more flesh and sometimes wonder who you really think you are."

Well, goddammit, if Mama and Gladys want to eat themselves into an early grave and spend the rest of their lives waddling around Houston like stuffed ducks, I'm out the door and can't keep worrying about them. Not after all the crap I've been through this past year and a half. Down from 280 to 162 and still have a good 30 pounds to go. It's been hell, though, I can tell you. Five-hour operation, gallbladder removed, a silicone ring cinched around my stomach so I have only a small pouch, hair falling out the first couple of months, thyroid problems, and now I'd probably upchuck if I ate more than an ounce or so of chicken Parmesan or fries or salami wrap or trail mix or lots of other things I've always loved. And this don't even count all the body contouring, and the expense, and the frustration of being around my wonderful cheese biscuits and chocolate-pecan balls and jelly treats the bank sometimes pays me good money to make for one of their fancy shindigs. What I do now is keep these little chocolaty candies called Nips with me at all times and suck on one if I have hunger pangs.

It's been no fun and takes lots of mental adjustment, that's for sure, but it does me good to remember what it was like before. Size 30 and Lane Bryant and Avenue. Gasping for breath when I picked up even a beagle at the shelter. Couldn't cross my legs to tie my shoes. Heart palpitations and sky-high cholesterol. Festered open sores inside my thighs. Saxophone balanced way up on my boobs when I played a gig at Ziggy's, and audiences calling me Bubbles. Even climbing the stairs at home on my hands and knees. And if I fell down, whoooa . . . ! One time, the small metal step stool in the kitchen just collapsed when I was fixin' to make some divinity fudge and reached up in the cabinet for some brown sugar. Had to lay there in the middle of the friggin' floor till Lyman got home and called the neighbors to help me up. Nobody can imagine the humiliation.

Worst, I guess, was the binge eating. Let me at a Dunkin' Donuts, say, and it was nothing for me to knock off maybe four or five with a couple of French vanilla coffees without blinking an eye. I was always crazy about any Chinese takeout since everything on those long menus is so tempting, but when the craving really hit, the folks at Panda Delight over on Richmond almost knew without asking to pack me up an order of wings, a couple of egg rolls, shrimp dumplings, pork fried rice, and the best General Tso's chicken this side of Hong Kong. When my friend at the shelter, Eileen Silvers, got married at Temple Beth Yeshurum, I had a field day over the roast turkey and lamb and rice and baked salmon and jelly cakes on the reception buffet, and when me and Lyman would go out to Pancho's Cantina for Mexican, nothing would do but to follow up margaritas and a bowl of chunky guacamole and a platter of beef fajitas with a full order of pork carnitas and a few green chile sausages. And don't even ask about the barbecue and links and jalapeño cheese bread and pecan pie at Tinhorn BBQ. Just the thought still makes me drool.

And sex? Oh, before I hit about 230 I could still go on top of Lyman pretty easy, but when I reached my peak . . . well, I don't mind saying that when I reached my peak my thighs were so goddamn big I couldn't even get a grip on the bed.

Guess I really couldn't blame the man for finally wanting to take a long walk.

Not that Lyman was ever any special catch, believe you me. Lyman's what you call an insecure girl's guy, not a wild woman's guy. Already balding with thin, frizzled hair, a stupid lizard tattooed up his left arm, geeky long boxers and shiny fake leather boots, and kinda bony and underdeveloped in the wrong places—if you know what I mean. Loves to play Grand Theft Auto and poker on his computer when he's not working at the muffler shop or riding his Hog. Dumb things like that. And the goat roper's so awkward on his feet he couldn't do-si-do around a chili pot without falling in.

But what in heaven's name was I supposed to do when Mama and Gladys kept saying that men weren't gonna be beating the bushes to my door, and that if I didn't grab Lyman and marry him while I had the chance the way she did Daddy and Gladys did Rufus, I'd just end up lonely and miserable the rest of my life. Of course, Lyman didn't fool me a minute, not one minute when he'd say, "Oh, Let, I like plenty of butter in my vinegar pie and lots of meat on my ribs, and, besides, it's what's inside that counts most." Yeah, sure. I mean, who doesn't know some guys hit on fat chicks because they're easy and available? And, boy, was I ever available.

So, yeah, I went ahead and married the jerk when he told me I had a great personality and was fun and all that malarkey. Wanna know Lyman's idea of fun? Dragging me and Mary Jane and Sam to Long John's Chili Parlor way out on Liberty for a bowl o' red and to listen to some crappy banjo quartet for hours on end. Or shootin' birds up at Sheldon Reservoir, which made me sick at my stomach. Or me riding behind him on his Hog along Buffalo Bayou while he and some of his trash friends with their gals tried to outscratch one another in the sand pits. Well, he changed his tune big-time when I got to be more than he could handle, and that brainless powder puff who worked down at Champagne Video sank her claws in him. Good riddance, I said at the time, and I remember also thanking my heavenly stars we'd decided to put off having any kids till we could afford something besides a mobile. Now, if I didn't have more manners . . . now, I'd love nothing more than to drive over to Sutt's Mufflers in my Ford Focus and just stand there in front of Lyman in my size 14 white ducks with my goddamn hands on my hips and say, "Wanna make some big-time, Bozo?"

2

SASSY SAL

I'd be lying through my teeth if I didn't admit that Lyman leaving me for that white trash Tiffany had something to do with my decision to have the gastric banding. But I'd also be lying if I said my one and only reason was to look pretty and sexy—especially after what I was always led to believe about myself in the past. I mean, Mama made it perfectly clear when I was a child that I was just fat and plain, and even after I started middle school and was making all As and Bs, she was still telling me I'd only make a fool of myself if I tried to be like everybody else and gussied up like other girls to attract the boys. "Sweetheart, you're happiest right here frying chicken and making gumbo with me, and I only want to keep you from being hurt," she'd say in that sugary tone she can have when she wants me to agree with her. Yeah, sure. No wonder the other kids made fun of my oversized tanks and half sizes from Sears and Walmart, and snickered behind my back, and I never had many dates.

Actually, when I think about it now, I realize I probably wouldn't have gotten through those times if it hadn't been for Daddy. I really loved my daddy, and I don't care what Mama said sometimes, he was a good man who called me Princess

and always made me feel special. Like when he'd take me out
to the rides at Texas Jubilee—just him and me—and hold me
tight on the Tilt-a-Wheel so I wouldn't be scared to death and
scream my lungs out. Or when he got me my first dog—
Cindy—to play with since I didn't have that many friends.
And later on when the music teacher said I had natural talent,
and he bought me my first sax to play in the school band. Not
that my main reasons for having the surgery included looking
like the princess Daddy always thought I was.

My main reasons were so I wouldn't die young, and so kids
at the strip mall and outside the movie theater would stop
mumbling "oink, oink," and I could shop somewhere besides
Big Country, and I wouldn't have to two-step with other girls
at Dixie Stampede, and I could maybe even ride the bull at
Ziggy's.

"Loretta," my good friend Sally at the shelter said when I
told her I'd made up my mind, "why put yourself through all
that hell? You know we all love you just the way you are,
honey, and the animals don't know any difference," and la-di-
da-di-da. Shit, Sally's up there herself way over 200 and doesn't
exactly have anybody banging her but that no-good Zach
who she sees maybe once every other week or so when he
needs somebody to light his firecracker. She stays on one diet
after another, and I can tell you she'd probably end up going
for the procedure in a split second if she qualified. One hundred pounds or more overweight: that's the rule at the clinic—
no exceptions, no excuses. What Sally wouldn't go for are all
the vitamins and mineral supplements you have to take afterwards. Or sticking to a tough exercise routine. Or having the
painful reconstruction to tighten up all the loose skin. It took
guts and all the money I could make working two jobs just to
pay the first MasterCard charges. And avoiding lots of Classic
Coke and suds and liquid foods like milk shakes and ice cream

that go down so much easier than solids—that's what takes real willpower and determination.

And much as I love Sally and consider her my best friend, I gotta say that willpower and determination are two things she don't have. Like the time she and Zach went with me and Lyman to Lucky Strike lanes to bowl and she's trying to stop smoking. Right off the bat Zach scores something like a strike on the first frame, then a turkey, then a couple of doubles and another strike. Lyman racks up a few strikes himself, and I do okay with a strike and some spares, but poor Sally's having a bad night and all she can score is one split after the next. Well, by about the fifth frame, I can see she's gettin' real frustrated and nervous as she readjusts the mitt on her hand, and the next thing I hear is "Zach, honey, gimme one of ya weeds."

"No, Sal!" I scream. "Please don't! That's not gonna help."

"Oh, one's not gonna hurt me," she says. "I'm really pissed off and gotta relax more."

So Zach lights a cigarette for her and she takes a few puffs, and, wouldn't you know it, on the next frame, with that damn butt between her teeth, she delivers one hell of a spin and slams a strike.

"Now you're bustin', gal," Lyman has to egg her on, and by the time we've bowled a few more frames, Sally's almost chain-smoking and racking up more spares than any of us.

What Sally does have that I don't have is lots of patience with people, which I guess comes from working checkout part-time at Country Foodarama the way she does and puttin' up with those crazies at the Assembly of God where she goes every single Sunday morning without fail. First, I never put up with much shit from Lyman, but Sally will let Zach string her out till kingdom come when it comes to catching a flick, or fixin' her Cavalier, or getting tickets for a Rockets game. This nice-looking couple from out in the Heights comes to the

SPCA not long ago looking for a small dog for their five-year-old, and when Sally shows them this frisky Jack Russell mix we'd been trying to place for months, the father and kid go crazy about the mutt but the wife keeps asking if he yaps that much all the time. On and on she whines about not wanting a yelping dog, and worries how barking might bother the neighbors, and wonders if the dog will ever calm down, and what have you. Hell, I would have just told the dame straight out that all Jack Russells are pretty noisy by nature when excited and maybe something like a poodle or cocker mix might be a better choice. But Sally sees a chance for a good home with a reliable family, and explains patiently the various ways any dog can be trained to behave, and oohs and aahs over the way the child and dog are so compatible, and before you know it, the mother seems to have forgotten all about barking and is cuddling the dog like a baby, and telling her husband to write out a donation. Lord, what I'd give to have Sally's patience. I remember when I was as fat as Sally and trying to lose all that weight, I was so anxious I couldn't get to the scales fast enough every morning. If that had been Sally, she would've probably been real calm about it all, but not me. When I got my mind set on most things, if it happens tomorrow, that's too late.

3

KNEE-HIGH TO A GRASSHOPPER

Crazy as it sounds, what's gotten me through my weight ordeal more than anything else is cooking—for myself, for friends, and church events, and SPCA fund-raising picnics, and birthdays, and Lord knows what else. Okay, so I can't actually eat like I did before the surgery without upchucking, and sometime my willpower's really put to the test. But believe you me, nothing can keep me out of the kitchen, and now I can be pretty satisfied with just the thrill of tasting all the dishes. I guess you could call cooking a passion with me, but the more I think about it, the more I realize it's also some kind of therapy. Always has been, I'd say.

And yeah, put out as I can be with Mama 'bout a lotta things, I gotta admit she gets all the credit for getting me interested in cooking when I was just knee-high to a grasshopper. Gladys never seemed to give a damn about it when we were kids, which I guess is why she and that family of hers nourish themselves today mainly on KFC and Whoppers and junk like that. But me, I couldn't keep my eyes off Mama when she'd fix a mess of short ribs, or cut out perfect rounds of buttermilk biscuit dough with a juice glass, or spread a thick, real shiny caramel icing over her 1-2-3-4 cakes. And I can remember like it was yesterday (must have been about 4 years old at the time) when she first let me help her bake cookies, especially the same jelly treats I still make today and could eat by the dozen if I didn't now have better control.

"Honey, start opening those jars on the counter," she said while she creamed butter and sugar with her Sunbeam electric hand mixer in the same wide, chipped bowl she used to make biscuit dough. Strawberry, peach, and mint—the flavors never varied for Mama's jelly treats, and just the idea of making these cookies with anything but jelly and jam she'd put up herself the year before would have been inconceivable to Mama.

Everything Mama did caught my eye, but I think what intrigued me most was when she separated eggs by rocking the cracked shells back and forth till the whites plopped into a bowl and then dropped the yolks in the batter. Next, she told me to cover the whites with plastic to use in scrambled eggs later on, and I just couldn't get over how sticky they were when some got on my fingers.

"Okay, precious," she said with a small amount of dough in her chubby hands, "help me roll clumps like this one into smooth balls and put 'em on the cookie sheet—not too close together, mind you." So I rolled and rolled the dough between the palms of my hands the way she was doing, and if the ball was too little or too big, she'd say, "Pay attention, young lady," and tell me they should be 'bout the size of marbles, and make me start over again. Soon the pan was full of balls the same size, and what Mama did then was take my index finger and push it down real gentle into the ball to make a dent for the jelly, and show me how to seal any cracks around the edges. The only problem was my fingers gradually became sticky again, and when I complained, Mama told me to hush up and just dip them in a little flour or water. And it really fascinated me how well that worked.

"Are we ready for the jelly yet?" I finally asked real impatiently.

"We certainly are not," she answered as she grabbed the cookie sheet with one hand and stuck it in the oven. "They gotta first bake about 10 minutes."

"Why, Mama?"

"Just because, child, that's why," she sorta huffed. "They gotta set up a little bit. Now stop asking me dumb questions."

Then the real fun began when she showed me how to fill the holes with jelly scraped from a small spoon with my fingers. First I used some of the strawberry, then the peach, and finally the pretty mint, and when I alternated the fillings to make the cookies more multicolored, Mama smiled and patted me softly on the shoulder and said, "I see we got a real artist in the kitchen." What she didn't like too much was when I licked the spoon every once in a while. "Child, you gonna rot every tooth in your head out if you keep that up, so stop this minute," she scolded kinda playfully.

Of course, Mama never asks, Mama dictates, and it was no different back then when she simply opened the oven door and told me to pick up the cookie sheet with two pot holders and slide it back onto the rack. Well, this scared me to death—that blast of heat from the oven, the fear of being burned, the sight of ugly red scars on Mama's hands and arms—but when I just stood there, she said, "Go on, sugar. If you're gonna bake cookies and biscuits with Mama, you gotta get used to the hot oven. Don't worry, Mama'll help you."

And she did help me, and after we took out the first batch of bubbling treats, I don't think I was ever frightened again of a hot oven. I noticed the way Mama watched the cookies like a hawk till they were just golden brown, no matter when the timer rang. I also learned to imitate her technique of nudging the cookies with gentle stabs of a spatula when we transferred them to a wire rack to cool. But I think what I remember most was the look on Mama's face when she simply stared at the beautiful treats like she was almost in a trance and mumbled, "Pretty, aren't they?" Mama was so proud of our jelly treats, and the way she put her arm around my shoulder, you'd never guess in a million years she could be so ornery. Soon as they cooled, we both ate a cookie, then another, then another, and still another, and I thought they were the best cookies I'd ever put in my mouth.

Biscuits were another matter, and nothing was (or is) more sacred to Mama than the hot buttermilk biscuits she served with everything from fried chicken to Brunswick stew to country ham with red-eye gravy.

"Time you learned to make biscuit, young lady," she sorta proclaimed one chilly fall morning as she stretched a red apron around her big stomach and handed me a smaller white one to tie around my waist. And to this day Mama still uses only the singular word "biscuit" whether she's referring to one or two or a dozen biscuits.

"Stick your hand in that sack of flour and grab me a couple of big handfuls," she directed me. Well, I thought that flour I dumped in the chipped, cream-colored biscuit bowl was the softest thing I'd ever felt in my life.

"One more handful, sweetheart," she then said after she'd studied the mound. "Your hands are a lot smaller than mine."

I did as she said, and when the amount of flour looked just right to Mama, she next sprinkled on some white powder she pinched from a purple can with her fingers, and another powder from a bright yellow box, and some salt from another box with a picture of a little girl carrying an umbrella, and then told me to stir everything with her wooden spoon. No measuring cups or spoons, no scales, nothing but our hands and fingers and a big wooden spoon.

"Honey, open that can of shortening," she said next as she

held out a large silver spoon, dug it four times into the can, and scraped the messy shortening off with a finger into the flour. She then took a few whacks at the flour with the metal pastry cutter, handed it to me, and said, "Here, Loretta, you cut in the shortening the way you just saw me do." I began hacking away at the pale gobs, but in no time Mama's howling, "No, no, no, angel" as she took my hand and guided the blade in more gentle strokes. "Don't crush those lumps so much, for heaven's sake. They're what make the biscuit flaky."

I noticed before Mama began pouring buttermilk in the bowl how she held the carton up, took a sniff and a few long guzzles, and declared, "Lord, that's good milk." Then she sprinkled a little flour on the counter and started stirring the dough fast as lightning, and when it looked and felt perfect to her, she gathered it into a big ball with her strong hands, plopped it on the counter, and said, "Okay, honey, pat that out gently with your fingers till I tell you to stop." So I began pushing at the dough anxiously with my hands, and within seconds Mama was telling me, "Not with your hands, precious, and not so rough. I said to just pat it out gently with your fingers. You gotta be easy with biscuit. If not, they'll be tough as whitleather." With which she coaxed my hands away and took over a few seconds as she patted away, then told me to try again.

When the slab of dough was about half its original thickness, she handed me her battered metal biscuit cutter, grabbed a small juice glass for herself from the cabinet, and said, "Now, let's cut 'em out nice and round and even and put 'em on the baking sheet—not too close together so the sides'll brown." To me, this was the fun part, but no sooner had I cut out my first biscuit than Mama had to correct me again. "Didn't I say nice and even? Just look at that biscuit. It's lopsided, and nobody wants to eat a lopsided biscuit. You can't twist the cutter, sweetheart. You gotta cut straight down if you want even biscuit." She cut a perfect one with her glass, and when I did the same with my cutter, she smiled and said, "That's the girl. And don't forget to leave plenty of room between the biscuit so the sides'll get nice and crusty."

Into the oven they went for twelve minutes, but before the timer rang, Mama peeped through the glass on the oven door, and handed me the pot holders, and ordered, "Take 'em out, they're done. Never can trust that damn oven, and if those biscuit stay in one minute longer, they'll be hard as rocks." How Mama could tell I couldn't figure out, but, sure enough, when I pulled the pan out, the biscuits were golden and puffy and crispy on the sides and pretty as can be.

Mama was baking hot biscuits mainly for us all to eat with something like her fresh vegetable soup at lunch, but, as usual, she could never wait to break one open, and smear lots of butter on the two halves, and hand me a half to taste, and soon pronounce the biscuit to be "perfect." The problem was that if it wasn't quite time for lunch, and the biscuits were particularly light and fluffy, and the butter tasted particularly rich and sweet, we never stopped with just one but might eat two or three before sticking the rest back in the oven to keep warm. I also gotta say it wasn't beyond Mama to even grab her jar of strawberry or peach preserves and spread a good spoonful of those on the biscuits, and yeah, I thought that was pretty sensational. I don't think it so much as dawned on Mama—not for a second—how fattening those biscuits were. If so, it didn't matter to her, and, of course, I never gave it a thought at that young age.

Whatever, to this day I've never tasted buttermilk biscuits that can equal Mama's, and to this day, goddammit, I gotta admit I still can't produce a batch that come out just as fluffy and beautiful as hers every single time she fixes 'em. Don't ask me why. I use the same brands of flour and baking powder and even buttermilk as she does. I've watched her over and over and follow religiously the same techniques she taught me as a child. And once I even had her watch me every step of the way to see what could be wrong. "You rush things," is about the only explanation she's ever come up with. Oh, I fix damn good biscuits. They just don't look and taste exactly like Mama's, and it makes me mad as a hornet.

4

BLOWBAGS

Sometimes I don't know why I go out of my way to be nice to my sister since she don't seem to really appreciate anything I do for her and Rufus and the children. Take the other day when I glazed a whole goddamn ham with molasses and brown sugar and mustard and dropped it off just so they'd have something to eat besides all that junk food they live on. Well, Gladys takes one look at the beautiful ham and, without so much as a nod of thanks, says, "Sis, I thought you knew the one thing these kids won't touch is ham—not even the potted stuff on crackers."

"That's news to me," I said, "but that don't mean you and Rufus can't enjoy it. That glaze is pretty amazing, if I say so myself."

"Hon, you know I'm trying to watch my weight," she commented next as she grabbed a knife on the counter, and hacked off a thick slice of the ham, and wolfed it down without saying yea or nay. She then let out a quick laugh. "And sometimes I think the only things my children really love are Double Whoppers with mayo and fries."

I don't waste my breath anymore telling Gladys for the millionth time that all four of those poor kids are already dan-

gerously overweight and just following in their parents' foot-
steps just the way me and her did Mama and Daddy—and
Rufus himself must now tip the scales at about 275. I mean, I
know if I dare criticize any of them, all Gladys will do is accuse
me of trying to be holier than thou, and tell me how healthy
the doctors says they all are, and repeat she's not about to put
Rufus on some cruel diet the way he works his tail off five
days a week hauling lumber out to big construction sites all
over town. You'd think after that awful operation she had to
go through to replace that knee, Gladys would have seen the
light by now, but even when we were kids, nobody could ever
tell Gladys anything, and she always did just as she pleased.

Not that me and Gladys were ever rivals or anything or
that Mama and Daddy treated us differently, though I do think
she'd get a little envious when me and Mama would spend lots
of time in the kitchen together, or when Daddy would take
me out to Texas Jubilee while Gladys was up the street watching horror movies on TV with her more grown-up friends.
Of course we were both fat as pigs, but, so help me God, I
don't think the weight ever fazed Gladys one iota, even when
we were older, and that eating anything and everything we
wanted was just another privilege she thought we both de-
served. Myself, yeah, I remember it really did embarrass me not
being able to wear anything but cheap tunics and shifts and
stretch leggings and to be called all those awful names by the
other kids, but what was I supposed to think or do at that age
when my own older sister was as convinced as Mama and
Daddy that we were all normal and nothing was ever going to
change?

Maybe nothing bothered Gladys since she's strong as an ox,
and could be tough as nails, and always knew exactly how to
handle herself and even look after me when trouble was brewing. Like the time in middle school when Bobby Wainwright
and Leo Schwartz and another guy scotch-taped a drawing of

a cow with huge utters on my locker and began mooing at me and called me horrible names when I went to get my math book for Mrs. Devereaux's class. Well, I could hardly keep myself from crying all through class, and afterwards at lunch in the cafeteria, I showed the humiliating picture to Gladys, and told her what had happened, and the next thing I know she's spotted Leo and marched up to his table with me right behind and told him to come outside a minute on the flagstone terrace so she could show him something.

"Leo, I see you and your buddies like to play games with Loretta here," Gladys says to him as she holds up the disgusting drawing, then begins to tear it into shreds.

Leo backs away against a ledge, and peels the wrapper off a piece of gum, and says, "Oh, shit, Gladys, we was just having a little fun."

I notice Prissy Killian and Marge Cunningham almost hidden at the other end of the terrace hovering over a cigarette, and they're watching us and giggling.

Gladys is a year older than Leo and about double his size, and she stands in front of him with her hands on her broad hips and says, "Don't put that gum in your mouth yet, bud."

"Why not?" he asks.

"'Cause you gotta eat something else first," she says as she holds up the handful of shredded paper.

"Whatcha talking 'bout?" he asks next, like he's either dumbfounded or kinda scared.

"You say you and your buddies like to have a little fun," she goes on, "so I think it's me and my sister's turn to have our own type of fun by watching you eat your funny picture."

Well, Leo's now got this real nervous look on his face, and pushes himself up from the ledge, and says, "Hey, I'm outta here." But no sooner has he budged than Gladys knocks him back with one stiff blow of her other hand, which almost makes him lose his balance.

I look around to see if anybody else but Prissy and Marge is watching, then tell Gladys, "Let's not get in any trouble, hon. Let's just forget about it."

"The hell we will," she almost explodes. "Our friend here thinks he's man enough to stick up ugly pictures and call somebody big names, so let's see if he's man enough to eat his words." She then holds out the paper. "Eat it, bud, and swallow it."

"You crazy or something, Gladys?" he mutters like a scared cat as he tries again to get up. "I'll report you."

She shoves him back to the ledge with a single thrust and says louder, "You do that, you jerk. You go report us to anybody you like, and while you're at it, tell 'em how many students saw that filthy drawing and heard what you and your buddies were calling my sister. Now, eat the paper or I'll cram it down your goddamn throat." Like I say, Gladys could be tough as nails when her dander was up.

I could still hear Prissy and Marge snickering as they sneaked puffs on their cigarette and watched as Leo took pieces of paper out of Gladys's fat hand, and stuck them in his mouth, and tried to chew while she repeated, "Swallow it, jerk." For a minute, I thought the guy was actually gonna start crying from the humiliation and felt sorta sorry for him, but all Gladys uttered when she finally stood back with her hands on her hips and watched him slink away was "Baaaaa!"

Okay, I guess that was pretty cruel of Gladys, but experiences like that did teach me I didn't have to put up with all the crap and that actually size could be to my advantage when having to deal with blowbags like Leo Schwartz and Bobby Wainwright. What's kinda funny is how, as time passed, Gladys seemed to tame down some while I became the one who could take the bull by the horns if anybody—including Mama—insulted me or her and tried to make us feel stupid or something. This didn't happen very often, but if it did, Gladys knew for damn sure I'd step up to the plate for her the way she did for me.

The truth is, Gladys was always more social than I ever was and, for some reason, had lots more friends and dates. Oh, I suppose any other sister would have been jealous, but how could I be jealous when my grades were so much better than Gladys's, and I won prizes for my sax playing in the band, and nobody but nobody could beat me at ping-pong tournaments or arm wrestling?

Of course everything changed for good when Gladys married Rufus and they started breeding like chickens. Now she no longer had the time or energy to go swimming out at Suttles Park, or play ladies pool on the team every Friday at Bigalo's Parlor, or drive over to LaMarque to watch drag racing, or do lots of the things we used to do together when she wasn't working a shift at Roy Rogers and me at Otto Glass and Aluminum. Then I met Lyman one night at Lucky Strike, and the problem there was that Lyman and Rufus couldn't have been more different and just didn't get on very good. Well, needless to say, with four kids to support and a mortgage to pay and Rufus on minimum wage at the lumberyard, it's about all the two can now do to make ends meet. No social life to speak of, no special church activities, no celebrations in restaurants, not even many ball games—I mean, sometimes I think the only things Gladys and Rufus do is fool around with those rotten kids and stuff themselves with chicken McNuggets and deli takeout and frozen pizzas round the clock.

Not that I'm one to talk, but I can boil an egg and do know the difference between real country sausage and a pig-on-the-stick. And unlike Gladys, I finally did take a big step to pull myself out of the gutter and improve my image and health.

"Oh, Miss Goody-Goody now thinks she deserves a goddamn medal," Gladys lambasted me during one of her foul moods not long ago in the car when I told her how much weight I'd lost.

"Honey, I don't think anything of the sort, and you're just being a bitch," I shot back at her.

"At least I still got a husband who gives a shit about me, not to mention a fine boy and three precious girls."

"Yeah, till he drops dead like Daddy from a massive heart attack, and you gotta have the other knee replaced, and . . . boy, sister, you can still be as hard-headed as you ever were."

"Let, why don't you worry 'bout yourself and stop sticking your nose in my business?"

"'Cause, honey, whether you believe it or not, I do worry 'bout you just the way I worry 'bout Mama."

"Whatta we gonna do about Mama?"

And with that sudden question, our little fight was over with—almost like the pointless arguments we had as young girls and then forgot about. I know Gladys is probably never gonna change her ways, but after all, she is still my sister and it's only natural for me to care about what happens to her. No matter that sometimes I could choke her to death.

5

CHEAP DATE

I gotta admit I hate working out at Body Tech almost as much as I miss eating something like a big wedge of grasshopper pie I made not long ago for the church charity bazaar. Yep, that's right: fixin' something like grasshopper pie while you're trying to knock off over a hundred pounds. Talk about self-punishment. Go figure. Don't know what I'd do without the Nips I carry everywhere to suck on and curb my appetite.

But it's all paying off in more ways than one. Eyes no longer puffy and really look hazel now. High cheekbones I never knew I had. My dark hair long and shiny since Roberta started styling it at Salon Magic and showed me how to wear it up sometimes with these designer clips. Much tighter skin on my arms, more tone and definition to my boobs and abs and thighs, and no more white splotches on my stomach. Yeah, incredible cosmetic changes, and don't think for a second all this wadn't connected to what happened with Vernon.

Just sauntered in the shelter one day looking for a dog, and the second I saw him and heard him talk, I whispered to Sally while he was flipping through our dog photos, "Boy, that's one who could put his shoes under my bed." I must have been about 185 at the time, but I remember I was wearing my shirt tucked in my jeans with a big turquoise belt buckle—something I'd never have dreamed of doing the year before. And I can tell you something else I never would have dreamed of: that this young, really well-built guy with gelled wavy brown hair and the whitest teeth I'd ever seen would give me the once-over that made me tingle all over and feel like the most glamorous woman on earth. I mean, by the time I'd finished asking him a few questions and helping him fill out the application we require of all adopters, it couldn't have been more obvious that the man was flirting with me—downright flirting. Have to admit I really didn't know how to handle myself.

Turns out the reason Vernon wanted a dog was because his young wife had been tragically struck dead by lightning at the nursery where she worked in east Houston. They hadn't been married but a couple of years, and didn't have chick nor child, and, plain and simple, he needed companionship while he was getting his life back together. At least that's what he told me, though I couldn't imagine a guy as nice and handsome and smart as Vernon having to look too long for a little human companionship. Wanna know just how smart Vernon is? He's with a company called Freedom Computers that installs and services computers—and I don't mean just in homes but in big corporations like Shell. Not bad, I say, for a kicker from Waco who's determined to make something of his life.

So after he looked at the pictures, I took him around the cages out back, and the second he spots this adorable young Lab mix somebody found abandoned over in River Oaks, he's like a kid; the dog licks his face and the two begin tussling right there on the concrete floor. We're always real careful about releasing our animals to the right owners, but since the bitch had had all her shots and I could tell right off that Vernon was a safe bet, I suggested he take her home for a couple of days to make absolutely sure the two were compatible.

Well, the very next day he calls to ask me a million questions about feeding and house training and bathing and what have you. Then he wants to know the name of a good vet. And the third time, he actually drops by the shelter to say he definitely wants the dog, and has already named her Daisy, and hands us a donation of fifty dollars. And get this: He also asks point-blank if he can express his thanks by inviting me to have lunch at 20 Carats over on Montrose. I almost faint but try to put on a good front.

"Loretta Crawford, I hope to hell you told him yes," Sally almost screamed, "and that you don't screw it up."

"Honey, I told him I should be thanking him for giving the dog a good home," I said.

"But you did say yes," she went on like he was Brad Pitt or somebody.

Well, of course I said yes, and the very next week we're sitting across from each other in a booth at the café and I'm a nervous wreck about what to order that will look normal. Tell him about my fat problem and surgery? Not on your life. Anyway, he orders short ribs with mashed sweets and fried okra and a Coors, which almost make me drool, but I just get a Waldorf salad and Diet Coke.

"Is that all you gonna eat?" he asks with this big frown on his face.

"Yeah," I say, "I go pretty easy at lunch so I don't get sleepy at work in the afternoon. And you know how us girls gotta watch ourselves."

"Married?" he then asks all of a sudden.

"Yeah, but now divorced," I say without any further explanation.

He wants to know if I like my part-time job at the SPCA, and asks how long I've been there, and what have you. I tell him how much I've always loved animals and about my two Lab mixes, Sugar and Spice, and how I also love to cook and would like to do some real catering. But what really makes us hit it off is when he tells me how much he loves country and blues music and I tell him I blow tenor sax most weekends in the dance band at Ziggy's over on Navigation to make a few extra bucks. Clint Black, John Lee Hooker, Vince Gill, Al King—he knows 'em all and can even run off a few lyrics.

"'Will the Circle Be Unbroken,'" he then tests me, humming.

"Nitty Gritty Dirt Band," I say as I pretend to finger my sax and hum along too. "Love 'em. Everything they do."

"Well, I'll be damned, gal," he says as he reaches over and smacks me real friendly-like on the arm, which I hope and pray doesn't look or feel too flabby to him. "I gotta get over there one night and hear you play."

Time comes for dessert, and he says 20 Carats's chocolate cheesecake is the best in Houston and that I have to order it. Of course I'd give my eyeteeth for a wedge but tell him what I really want is one scoop of cherry vanilla ice cream I saw on the blackboard up front.

"I love a cheap date," he jokes, and when the waitress brings his cheesecake, I notice he waits till she serves my ice cream before he takes a big bite and rolls his eyes like he's gone to heaven. Vernon's a gentleman like that.

"Here, little lady, take a taste with your spoon," he then says as he pushes the plate over. "You just gotta taste this cake."

This was one of those times I always knew would come and always dread, but I didn't want to act like a jerk, and am finally used to taking little tastes of things when I cook, so I cut off a smidgen with my spoon, and press it up on the roof of my mouth, and yeah, it was out-of-this-world delicious. Lord, I could have eaten that whole goddamn cheesecake, and make no bones about it, but didn't think anybody wanted to watch me vomit.

"I can tell you know good food," Vernon then says, which really upset me for a second till he went on to ask what I liked to cook most.

"Oh, mainly just honest Southern food. Spareribs, squash soufflé, smothered chicken, shrimp creole, persimmon pudding—things like that. And I'm not too bad at Tex-Mex either."

"Gal, you're right in my bull pen," he says with this big grin on his face. Vernon has a cute scar or something on his cheek, but his skin is smooth as a jalapeño. "Maybe you'll cook up something for me sometime—if I ain't being too pushy."

Since it's pretty obvious he's as crazy about food as I am, I just can't resist asking if he never gains weight eating like he does. He waits a second like he's surprised, then says, "Never gave it much thought. Just eat normal—anything I want. Don't you?"

Well, I could have told him a thing or two, believe you me, but instead just changed the subject and asked him about his wife.

"Oh, Mona was a great gal, and we had a good marriage and lots of plans. Losing her was a real shock. Lightning, like I said. Killed instantly on the job with no warning. A real healthy gal, and so unfair at her age. And these last few months—been kinda rough for me, ya know. What about your own marriage, if I can be so nosy?"

"Fair enough," I say. "Lyman's not a bad man, and I don't think I'm a bad woman. We really tried to make a go of it and had some good times the first year or so. But I guess our differences and financial problems and what have you got too much and, well, things just didn't work out the way we hoped."

Vernon sits staring at me with this really intense look in his eyes, then says, "Some things just ain't in the cards—like what happened to Mona and your marriage. But I can tell a little bit, it was Lyman's loss."

Him saying something that sweet really made me feel good, and it also made me want to reach over and rub the soft hair on his strong-looking arm.

"Hey," he then says as he snaps his fingers for the waitress and pulls this fifty-dollar bill off a roll held together with a big money clip with the head of a steer. "I promised to get you back to the shelter by two, and I'm a man of my word. Plus I gotta check on Daisy before getting back to this job over at Texas Life."

I thought that was so gracious and was reaching in my purse for my lipstick when Vernon says, "Hey" again. "You like Italian food?"

"Sure," I say.

"You know Amalfi Garden off Richmond?"

"I've heard about it, but hear it's high as a cat's back."

"Bull! Whatcha doing Friday night? Wanna ramble over there with me after I finish up? Great manicotti."

See there. Vernon's got style. And there's something else I like about him, and that's the way he don't mince words and just comes out with what's on his mind. Anyway, I found it pretty exciting him asking me out a second time, so even though I'd told Mary Jane I might drop over to taste her new Texas caviar recipe and watch a Comets game on TV, I said I'd love to go to Amalfi Garden.

6

HANKY-PANKY

I'm fixin' to do something about this stupid apartment I'm renting and find me a decent little house that's more in line with my new life. Of course the apartment's not as embarrassing as that tacky mobile Lyman and I had over off Memorial, but it's not a place where I can feel proud to have a few friends over, and it's sure not right for two large dogs and a cat. Moved in with Mama for a few months to save money and pay the bills while I was going through my banding ordeal, but that was a big mistake. Oh, I worry myself sick about Mama being in that old house all by herself, but, I mean, who wants to live like trash way out near Hobby in that low-class neighborhood, and spend an hour driving back and forth to work, and listen to Mama ranting on and on about how I'm starving myself to death? Just this morning at the gym it dawned on me that if I ever plan to do any serious catering, I've gotta have a bigger kitchen. No question about that.

And if I'm convinced of anything, I'm convinced I could be one of the best caterers in Houston if I play my cards right. I know that, and Billy Po Cahill has told me so a hundred times. Billy Po's the special events coordinator at Mutual Savings and Loan downtown, and that's not chicken scratch. He's also on the vestry at our Hawthorn Presbyterian Church, and it all began when Billy Po raved about a turkey and ham casserole and chocolate pecan pie I brought to a church benefit. Not that I myself have been exactly high on faith the last few years, but I do try to help out on benefits when I think the cause is right, and this time Billy Po was so impressed with my food he asked me if I'd be interested in fixin' some goodies for a snazzy bank reception he was setting up. Three hundred bucks for a shrimp creole, and a Lady Baltimore cake, and a few platters of cookies and pralines. Well, that was the most money I'd ever made at one time in my life. Then Billy Po hired me a second time for another promotion he was doing, and the next thing I know the phone's ringing, and this classy lady over in the Galleria who was at the gig is praising my crabmeat balls and lemon bars to the sky and wondering if I'd like to do some things for a private party she's giving. That was another three hundred big ones and got me thinking maybe I could make a go of this on a regular basis with the right contacts and the right setup at home and the right confidence in myself.

Of course there are a few hitches, and Billy Po Cahill hittin' on me is one of them. I guess I should've noticed that first day at the church the way he was looking me over months after I'd had the surgery—and he knew me before and after. But the truth is that at the time I was still pretty fat and didn't think there was a guy on earth who would give me a second glance. Besides, everybody knows that Billy Po is happily married to Sissy Cahill with two grown boys and has lots of respect at the bank, so who would have ever dreamed that this upstanding family man could have a shady side to his nature? I'd say Billy Po's around fifty, has a full head of thick hair graying just on the sides, and has puffy cheeks that always look pink. And even though he wears suits that cover up lots of sins, anybody can tell he's had his share of brisket and pecan pie. I gotta say fifty is a little old for my taste, but, then, who was I to be choosy the way I still looked and when here's this nice man offering to do me favors? Besides, Billy Po talks real well the way educated men do, and I like that.

What happened was after the second bank job, Billy Po just showed up in his white Cadillac Seville one afternoon at the apartment with two of my cookie platters and set Sugar and Spice to howling like mad dogs. Don't ask me how he found out where I lived, but him just dropping by like that really caught me off guard. Jeans and just a tank top with no bra. No clips in my hair or lipstick. Powdered sugar on my hands. Kind of a mess, like the apartment. But I didn't have much choice but to ask him in and offer him a glass of iced tea and some nutty fingers I'd just fixed for Gladys and the kids. Must say he couldn't have been more cordial and gracious on the sofa telling me how much better I looked, and how impressed everybody was with my catering, and how he planned to keep me in mind for some jobs in the future.

"Loretta, you got talent," he says, "and you could probably go to town if you know the right people and make the right moves."

"Oh, Billy Po, you're just puttin' me on," I say while I grab my lipstick.

"Not in the least," he says as he maneuvers over a little closer and gives my thigh a friendly pop. "You've turned into a good-looking lady, you know, and between your looks and great personality and special flair with food, you could make a name for yourself in this town."

"Why, gracious me, you really think so, Billy Po?"

He then moves over closer and squeezes my thigh and says, "Sure you could, and I could help you along if you play fair and square."

Well, I'm not exactly dumb, and even though I never had

many guys hitting on me before or after Lyman, I know when somebody's making a pass at a gal.

"Why, Billy Po, I'm not sure I know exactly what you mean," I say as I pull my open tank top up to cover my big boobs better.

"Oh, honey, I think you do, and bet anybody who's all woman the way you are likes to have a little fun once in a while. Don't mind saying I've had my eye on you for some time, and I mean that as a real compliment."

Well, you could have knocked me down with a feather, but frankly, I guess I'd been waiting a long time for a real man to say something like that to me.

"I don't know 'bout this, Billy Po," is all I could drum up in my state of mind, but before I know it, he's put his tea down and is flicking his fingers up and down my neck. Oh, I know I should have resisted at least a little, but I didn't.

"Can I tell you something, Loretta?" he then says while he's fingering me.

"You certainly can."

"I hope you know how much I respect you."

"Why, thank you, Billy Po," I say, "and the feeling's mutual."

"Now, do you trust me?"

"Sure I do, Billy Po."

"And can I trust you?"

"Of course you can."

"You know I have a reputation to uphold, and you have a new career that could take off any day now, and we gotta kind of protect each other and not get in any trouble if we're gonna be close friends and work together, don't you think?"

"Sure, Billy Po. Whatever you say."

He was now talking real nice and quiet in a kind of sexy voice, and the next thing I knew he'd moved his hand down and was rubbing his fat fingers on my breast, and breathing heavy, and making me tingle inside. I could smell his aftershave lotion and see some dandruff on his brown hair, which I thought he might have dyed a little. Don't get me wrong. Billy Po's certainly not my idea of Prince Charming, but at the time I was still pretty obsessed with my weight problem, and here's the first guy in ages paying me lots of attention and compliments, and I figured if he was good enough to help me along in a career I really had my mind set on, the least I could do was let him have a few kicks. Oh sure, I knew Billy Po was fixin' to take a little advantage of me, but I also knew he was taking a big risk behaving like he was—his family, the bank, the church, and all that. But, hey, like I say, I admit I got a wild streak in me, and always wanted to play around just like other gals, and what did I have to lose?

Anyway, I did let Billy Po pretty much have his way right there on the sofa, even with Sugar and Spice whining and barking and trying to nuzzle in, and before it was all over, I don't know who was panting and puffing more, Billy Po or the two dogs. Gotta say Billy Po's sure no amateur and has the equipment to back up his action. I also gotta say I gave him a four-alarm run for his money I bet he didn't soon forget. Funny, but I don't think it fazed Billy Po one iota that he was dealing with almost 200 pounds of Texan woman. In fact, while he was zipping back up and tying his tie and putting on his jacket and fixin' to leave, he said, "Loretta, I can tell you that cooking's not your only big asset." That's exactly what he said.

Okay, so we had a good fling, and yeah, this was all before I met Vernon, and I guess it's what my ego needed at the time. But I sure wouldn't say Billy Po was ever what I call a big deal in the romance department or that I was ever anything like his love slave who kowtowed to his every whim the way some of those idiot women do on *As the World Turns*. I guess we played around a couple of months, and it got to where I could almost expect to see that white Cadillac pull up on Monday afternoons when Billy Po said he always got his hair cut and his wife, Sissy, had her bridge club. Like I say, Billy Po's basically a pretty sweet guy who once even brought me a beautiful hanging pot of red geraniums for my little patio and always had a few treats for Sugar and Spice, and yeah, I'm the first to admit there was something kinda exciting about our sneaky affair. On the other hand, I think we both knew it was more a "you scratch my back and I'll scratch yours" kind of relationship, and I was never dumb enough to believe those shenanigans could lead anywhere except frustration and maybe . . . big trouble.

And the truth is that things began to come to a head the day we had this big household auction at the church to raise funds for a new electronic organ, and I had baked three coconut cakes for the occasion, and Sissy Cahill happened to also be working at the refreshment table and made a couple of snide remarks that made me real nervous.

"Billy Po tells me you been cooking up a storm," she said in this sugary tone of voice while she poured lemonade in cups, "and that you've even been whipping up some pretty fancy desserts for his bank promotions."

"Oh, heavens, no." I laughed as I arranged small nuggets of cake on paper plates. "Nothing really fancy. Just mainly old-fashioned cakes and lattice pies and plain cookies that Billy Po and everybody else loves to eat at those shindigs."

"You know, that's kinda funny," she continued in her hoity-toity manner, "'cause the one thing Billy Po's never had is a big sweet tooth—not even for my caramel brownies people rave about."

"You don't say," was all I could think to utter.

"Well, honey, I guess you must have a special touch, 'cause I heard Billy Po raving to Lance Buckley about your chocolate-pecan brownies."

I laughed again and said, "Oh, they're just my mama's plain old brownies, but now they're a real no-no for me—if you know what I mean."

Sissy's eyes gave my body a quick glance, then she said, "I did notice, honey, how you've dropped a few pounds. Congratulations."

"Thanks, but I've still got a long way to go," I said as I rushed to finish the plates, and felt my heart pounding, and pretended I needed to pass the cake among the crowd milling around the hall looking at all the lamps and crystal bowls and what have you.

Well, that's when I decided then and there that I could be playing with fire, and that I'd done too much to improve my physical self-esteem and maybe start a real catering business, and that I was gonna have serious words with Billy Po the next time he dropped by for me to light his firecracker.

"But I thought we were having fun and agreed to play fair and square," he said when I told him at my kitchen table I wasn't just a piece of meat, and I thought tongues were beginning to wag, and we both had our reputations and future to think about.

"What tongues?" he asked like he was a little shocked.

"Well, let's start with your own wife's."

"Whadda you mean? Sissy's got nothing to do with this."

I told him point-blank what comments she'd made at the auction, and when he heard this, he did get this real worried look on his puffy face for a minute.

"What else did Sissy say?" he mumbled as he ate another cheese stick and fingered the side of his hair.

"Oh, nothing really touchy or ugly," I said, "but I could tell she was wondering about lots of things."

"You sure you're not just imagining that?" he asked.

"Listen, honey, we do have fun, and you know how grateful I am for all your help," I went on. "But the truth is I'm trying to pull my life together, and this hanky-panky isn't getting you or me anywhere, and I think we gotta cool it before something happens we'll both regret. Don't you agree, Billy Po?"

Well, I was pretty proud of my gumption, but then I notice he's looking daggers at me, and, I swear, for a second I thought he was fixin' to reach over and smack me right in the face.

"So that's the way you want to play," he then said as he fiddled with his gold cuff links in the form of oil rigs.

"Billy Po, I'm trying to look out for us both and not risk any scandal, so, well . . . Billy Po, it's got to stop—that's all there is to it. I want us to be just good friends, honey, and, goddammit, if that means you can't use me for jobs any longer . . . well, honey, I hope you won't be that mean."

He then changed his expression and took my hand real easy. "Now, now, just hold your horses, little lady. You ought to know I'm not a mean man and just like to cut up now and then. So okay, I'll back off if that's what you want. Tell you what: why don't we let things simmer down a while, then just let nature take its course."

Yeah, I figured. Let nature take its course. Right to the sack whenever José wants his enchilada, and maybe right to the front page of the *Houston Chronicle*. Oh, I was real sweet to Billy Po before he left that day, and I'd be lying if I said we didn't have as much fun as ever, but when he left, I was pretty sure the guy knew exactly where he now stood with me. If I've learned nothing else lately, I've learned that sometime a girl just has to take control.

7

THE BOY FROM WACO

It's still too soon to know exactly how I feel about Vernon, but I can say that after our dinner at Amalfi Garden, I decided once again to put my foot down with Billy Po and concentrate on who matters to me most—jobs or no jobs. Will say I wasn't too thrilled about Vernon seeing where I lived, but he insisted on picking me up and arrived in his Cherokee decked out in a green cowhide jacket and string tie and hat and pair of snakeskin boots that had to set him back at least a couple of hundred. A real knockout. Myself, I let Roberta talk me into wearing my hair down for once to show off what she called the really nice sheen, and I must have spent an hour trying to decide whether I looked thinner and sexier in my new stovepipe jeans and eyelet denim shirt or in a fancy, low-cut blue dress with glitter beads I found at Macy's. Well, the way Vernon kept staring at my boobs all through dinner, I guess I was right to pick the dress, and the more red wine we drank, the more he worked me over with those dark eyes of his.

"You look like a really healthy gal," he kept saying, and all I was tempted to scream was, "Buster, you wouldn't be saying that if you'd seen me a year or so ago."

Of course, ordering food was the ordeal I expected it to be

even after sucking on a Nips, and when I picked a small tomato and mozzarella salad to start with, then a few shrimp grilled with garlic in olive oil, Vernon almost had a fit that I didn't order the fried calamari and manicotti the way he did. The truth is that I would have given my eyeteeth for the manicotti.

"Listen," I lied, "if you'd been making cheddar puffs and Texas caviar and snapper wraps all afternoon for a cocktail party job the way I have, you wouldn't have that much appetite either. Besides, you know, we girls have to watch our figures."

When I said that, Vernon looked at me again real hard, and cracked a big smile, and said, "Why don't you let me do all the watching?" which made me tingle inside and probably blush a little bit.

I'd be hard-pressed to remember what all we talked about, but I gotta say Vernon can talk about almost anything. Country music, computers, the Aeros' winning streak, barbecue, old cars, calf scrambles, Houston restaurants—everything you can think of. And, holy blazes, is the man drop-dead good-looking, especially when he gets kinda sad about something and runs his hand through his wavy hair. Which is why I had to keep my goddamn wits about me when he invites me back to his house and says he has a bottle of Wild Turkey we can crack open. Yeah, sure, I knew exactly what Vernon had on his mind, and I admit I was just aching to cut the buck with him. But this is one guy I really want to respect me, so what I did was tell him it was my turn to open up the shelter early the next morning, which was true, and say I needed a full night's sleep, and ask if I could have a rain check. What I sure didn't tell him was how worried to hell I was about the little bit of loose skin left on my thighs and abdomen, and that he might not like me as much with my clothes off as on. I mean, I still have to think about things like that.

Well, that question was answered on our date last Sunday night when we went to a movie starring Tom Hanks and ended up at Vernon's big ranch-style house over on Cameron. Actually, I'd fixed up the apartment nice and decided to invite him back to meet Sugar and Spice and eat some shrimp salad and ham biscuits so I wouldn't have to worry about ordering food in another restaurant, but Vernon had other ideas.

"Know what I'm really craving tonight?" he said on our way to the car before I could mention the salad. "A big fat juicy steak and some onion rings at Brick Oven. Whadda you think of that?"

Of course Vernon had no way of knowing how he was torturing me with those onion rings, and the last thing I wanted was to seem like a creep, so I just bit the bullet and said, "Sure, sport, but I think I'll leave the steak up to you this late at night and settle for maybe a piece of broiled fish myself."

"Doll, you're gonna grow fins if you eat any more seafood," he kidded as he grabbed me around the waist, and squeezed real hard, and made me wonder if I felt flabby to him. What I wanted to say is fins would be a hell of a lot better than the gobs of fat I once carried around, but no way could I risk grossing him out by telling him just how obese I was—not to mention showing him the hideous picture I carry around in my wallet to remind me.

So Vernon has his thick sirloin and onions and a beer, and me a redfish fillet and some spinach and a glass of Chardonnay. I take a tiny bite of his steak and eat one onion ring, and, Lord, did those taste good. Like always, we just love being together and getting to know each other better. He tells me about his uncle's farm machinery business up in Waco, and how he went to Baylor for a year to learn how to build and service computers, and about Bonnie and Clyde's shotguns in the Texas Ranger Museum where he worked in high school to make some extra money—really interesting things like that. I tell him about Daddy and simply say that my mama and I don't see eye to eye on lots of things.

"I think I know what you mean," he says with this strange look on his face, but before I can ask him to explain, he says, "I bet you had to fight off the guys in high school."

I just laughed and thought fast so he wouldn't even suspect that the only real date I ever had was fatso Gus Franklin who played trumpet in the band and got me drunk on tequila one night and made me lose my virginity in his daddy's pickup.

"Oh, no more than any other gal," I said with another laugh.

By now I was getting kind of nervous, so when Vernon rubbed his full stomach, and said he was taking me up on the rain check for a nightcap at his place, and peeled off a few bills from his wad of cash, I was more relieved than anything else.

Much as Vernon likes to play the big spender when we go out—and, Lord, does he love restaurants—I don't think he's rolling in clover. But, from the looks of his ranch house, I wouldn't say he's exactly scraping the bottom of the barrel either. Nice, big living room with gnarled pine floors. A hooked rug with the head of a buffalo in the middle. Maroon leather sofa and chairs. A shiny saddle fixed on a railing and lots of horns all over one wall. About what you'd expect of a boy from Waco, I guess.

Something else I also caught sight of was a framed picture of a woman on the wooden beam mantelpiece over the fireplace. "Mona?" I asked.

"Yeah," was all Vernon said.

Just a head shot, so I couldn't get much idea what the gal actually looked like. Pretty face, though. Short light hair, small eyes, real smooth skin. Only thing is she did look a little puffy to me.

"'Bout two fingers?" Vernon asks with a bottle of bourbon in one hand and a short glass in the other.

I hold up just my index finger and laugh, but when he keeps pouring I have to yell, "Whoooa, bud!"

Then he puts on a CD of country music—Toby Keith—and we play with Daisy for a while, and the next thing I know we're sort of tussling with each other and he's pulled me down on him on that leather sofa that smells so good and is kissing me to beat the band on my mouth and neck and chest and everywhere. Well, one thing led to another, and we end up in his king-size bed with a wrought-iron headboard in the shape of a big cactus, and all I gotta say is that nobody but nobody could ever say Vernon's not a wild woman's type of guy. For a minute I was scared to death he'd ask me about the scar underneath my navel where they did the surgery, but, to tell the truth, the man was so wrapped up in driving me crazy that I don't think he even noticed.

And, of course, it was really great cuddling up with Vernon afterwards in that weird cactus bed, and having him hold me close and rub me real gentle and romantic, and yeah, waking up in the wee hours with him on top again banging away like he just couldn't get enough of me. For a second, all I could think about was how I used to have to climb on Lyman when I was so fat and whether I now felt too flabby to Vernon, but Lord, the way he kept grabbing at my boobs and thighs and butt while he drove me crazy, you'd have thought I was somebody like Wynonna Judd or Jo Dee Messina.

Next thing I knew after all the carrying on I was hearing Vernon snore, and seeing the sun rise through the blinds, and feeling Daisy licking my face as she sat on the floor and whined like she wanted attention or to go out and pee. So I crawled out of bed without waking Vernon, and put Daisy out on her chain in the backyard, and closed the bathroom door quietly behind me to brush my teeth and take a shower. Then I slipped back into my jeans and violet pony tee, and went in the kitchen, and began rummaging in the cabinets and fridge with the idea of fixing Vernon a tasty, hot breakfast. Well, it didn't take long to see that Vernon's no slouch when it comes to keeping his kitchen well stocked. OJ, milk, butter, eggs, half a roll of country sausage, a cantaloupe, Kroger's whole-grain bread, a can of French Market chicory coffee, some blackberry preserves—just the right makings of a good Southern breakfast for just my kind of man. No matter that breakfast has always been my favorite meal and that this would be another major test of my willpower.

'Bout the time I'd started frying a big patty of sausage for him, I noticed a few red potatoes in a basket, peeled and cut one up, and tossed the cubes in the same large cast-iron skillet for hashed browns. At first I'd thought of doing soft-scrambled eggs for us both, but while I was beating four eggs with a little milk as quietly as possible, I remembered seeing a package of Jack cheese in the door of the fridge, as well as a couple of jalapeños on the windowsill, and suddenly decided to make my guy a spicy cheese omelette to really impress him.

"What in hell you doing, babe?" I then heard him yell from the bedroom.

"Just whipping up some breakfast chow to get your juices churning," I called back as he appeared in the doorway in his shorts with his wavy dark hair all over his forehead.

"Smells good, hon," he said as he meandered over blurry eyed, and hugged me around the waist, and peeped over my shoulder at the sausage and potatoes. "I'll be goddamned. You're really something, gal. Time for me to take a quick shower?"

"Hurry up," I said after I pecked him on the lips and hoped my whiskey breath wasn't as stale as his. "You're gonna be late for work, and I gotta stop by the house to feed the dogs, then to the gym and be at the shelter by nine."

Smelling the strong coffee and that sausage, and watching the potatoes as they turned crispy golden brown in the butter, made me hungrier than I'd been in months, and when the cheese began oozing out the sides of the puffy omelette, I really wondered for a minute how much longer I could keep torturing myself like this.

"Wow!" Vernon blurted when he saw the melon and omelette and sausage and hashed browns and buttered toast and small saucer of preserves. Then he looked across the table at my puny glass of juice and wedge of cantaloupe and piece of toast while I was pouring coffee into mugs and asked, "Where's yours, hon?"

I just laughed and lied, "Too early for me to eat like you cowboys. This is all I can manage till I finish at the gym."

"Goddammit, Let," he kinda moaned as he dove into all the food, and I begrudged every bite of sausage and omelette he took, "that's not enough to feed a biddy. And I don't know why you gotta go to that stupid gym."

I laughed again and changed the subject to a buff cocker at the shelter we were trying to place. Then, out of the blue, Vernon asked me when I was gonna let him meet my mama and sister. Oh, I knew that subject was bound to come up eventually, and I gotta admit I also feel a little guilty not telling them much about Vernon. Of course the truth is I'm downright embarrassed for him to see either one of them, which could open up a big can of worms. Plain and simple. I also made it damn clear to Sally and Mary Jane and the others at the shelter never to open their traps about my past looks when Vernon stops by, and Buzzy and the gang at Ziggy's all know anybody who dares call me Bubbles now is just asking for big-time trouble.

Sure, to appear normal I'm always casually making some quick remark about not having much appetite when you're cooking half the time to make money, but the funny thing about Vernon is sometimes I get the impression he doesn't give a goddamn about my extra pounds the way he eggs me on to taste all the fattening things on his plate. Oh, one day I'll get around to confessing my big secret to him since I believe in keeping things on the up-and-up with anybody I'm really crazy about. But I still just can't take a chance, not till I get down to about 130 or 135 and maybe a size 10 and all my skin's good and tight. Know what? I think when I'm ready to tell him . . . what I'm gonna do when I'm ready to tell him everything is say one night I wanna go to Tinhorn BBQ, then splurge for the first time and order just the small portion of brisket with coleslaw and beans, and tell Vernon how I used to knock off half a pound of barbecue, and rack of ribs, and SOS, and peach cobbler, and pitcher of beer with Lyman. Lord, for months I've been dreaming of eating barbecue again. Problem is, I wonder if I could keep it down.

8

WHOLE HOG

Of course I never think of barbecue that I don't remember the feast Mama threw at the house after my and Lyman's wedding at Hawthorn Presbyterian. Like I say, I wasn't exactly head over heels about marrying Lyman in the first place, and since Gladys and Rufus had only a very small civil ceremony after she discovered she was already pregnant, I sometimes thought one reason Mama talked me into my marriage was so she could really put on the dog herself entertaining and cooking for all her friends at Bingo Bonanza, and some relatives in Austin she hadn't seen in a coon's age, and lots of people I'd never even heard her mention before. We must have worked on that invitation list a whole week, and sometimes the fur could fly between me and Mama.

"Who is this Bunny Woodside?" I remember nagging at one point.

"Why, Bunny and Elmer Woodside ran the diner over on Henderson where me and your daddy used to eat breakfast every Sunday morning after church before you and Gladys were even born. Fine folks."

"And didn't you call Angie Jane Currie trash when she got nabbed snitching some crystal poodle at Rose Jewelers?"

"I certainly did not," she huffed. "And it so happens they dropped all the ridiculous charges and apologized to Angie Jane when she showed the cops exactly how that itsy bitsy poodle on the counter simply got caught in her big sleeve while she was looking at a very expensive ballpoint pen for Lucky's birthday. Angie Jane's a very respectable lady, and she was mortified by what happened. So there."

"Yeah, likely story," I snickered sarcastically.

"And speaking of trash, young lady," she said as she jabbed at a name with her pencil, "I think you could've picked a more respectable bridesmaid than this Sally McDonald down at that shelter."

"Now, why would you say something hateful like that, Mama? Sally's one of the sweetest friends I have, and Lyman's also crazy about her."

"All I know is what you've told me, and you said the girl don't even know who her daddy was and her mama mops toilets over in River Oaks."

"Mama, I never said anything of the sort about Sally's mama mopping any toilets, and don't know why you try to make everything sound so ugly. It so happens Mrs. McDonald's simply a professional housecleaner, and there's not one thing wrong with an honest job like that. She's not had an easy life, you know, and had to bring up Sally all by herself."

"Housecleaner," Mama muttered as she lit a cigarette. "We just call 'em maids."

"Well, I can tell you, Mama, Mrs. McDonald's certainly more respectable than your and Daddy's old buddy here, Jake Tyrell with those hideous tattoos all over his body."

Back then, Mama had graying hair that got real stringy when she'd forget to go to the beauty parlor, and let her be exasperated and she'd pull pieces of hair down over her forehead with her fingers, which made the hair look even messier than it already was.

"Listen, Miss Priss," she started as she puffed away and twisted her hair, "Jake was young and just didn't know any better when he was in Vietnam, and Phoebe Tyrell told me the only way he could get rid of those things later on was by having some dreadful laser surgery that left burns and scars."

"Well, it used to give me and Gladys the creeps seeing that awful dragon's head and snake tail peeping out from under his shirt when y'all would go bowling, and I used to wonder what others must think."

"Well, young lady, aren't you calling the kettle black considering that lizard the man you're gonna marry has running up his arm?"

"I hate it," I admitted frankly, "but at least Lyman doesn't have tattoos all over his body."

"You don't see any of that when Jake dresses up," Mama went on, "and as for what others think of him, I'll have you know that Myron Schumann told me Jake's one of the most liked and respected members at the Masonic Lodge." She stubbed out her weed, grabbed a handful of toasted pecans and pushed the bowl in front of me, then took a big slug of Coke. "You also seem to forget that Jake's company is the biggest distributor of tequila in the whole state of Texas, and that one time he helped me and your daddy out of a bad financial jam."

"What jam?" I asked.

Mama hesitated a moment like she was thinking or debating what to say, then continued, "Oh, that's right, you would've been too young to remember, but sometime I'll tell you all about it. And of course we're inviting Jake and Phoebe. They were both crazy about you when you were a child and always brought you and Gladys a present on your birthdays."

Just as long and involved were our discussions of what food would be served at the wedding reception for forty. Frankly, I would have been perfectly happy with just wine and booze and some nice canapés in the church hall since, after all, me and Lyman decided not to have a formal wedding, but as usual, Mama had her own ideas.

"What in hell are you talking about, girl?" she roared. "You don't get married every day, you know, and being as you refuse to wear a real wedding dress the way I did and let every-body else dress up, the least we can do is serve a nice buffet at the house. You just tell me, precious, what special you want me to fix and I'll fix it."

Okay, I gotta admit I couldn't have been more touched by Mama's care and concern in the matter, but what did kinda scare me was how she'd react when I told her what I'd really love to serve at my wedding reception.

"You know what me and Lyman were thinking about?" I said to her.

I could see the wheels turning in Mama's head as we sat at the kitchen table and nibbled on a tub of fresh pimento cheese and crackers while she looked off into space.

"Sweetheart, what if I did a few chicken pot pies, and maybe a big pot of Brunswick stew, and what about a real fancy stuffed country ham?" she suggested without paying the least attention to my question.

"Like I was saying, Mama," I went on, "what me and Lyman were thinking about, and what wouldn't be so much work . . . what we think everybody would really love is Pink Pig's pit-cooked barbecue and ribs. Whadda you think of that, Mama?"

She smeared pimento cheese on two more crackers and handed me one. "Anybody can serve that," she grumbled.

"I know, Mama, but everybody on God's green earth loves barbecue, and nobody caters it better than Pink Pig out on Memorial—the barbecue, the slaw, the dirty rice, the cobbler . . ."

"Wait just one minute, ma'am," Mama interrupted as I began to reel off some of the dishes they could handle for a crowd. "The only slaw and baked beans and rice ever served in my house are my own. If you and Lyman and the others have to have that barbecue, it's your wedding, but I'll fix everything else—including my ham hock collards and banana pudding. Why, the very idea: Texas barbecue without a mess of collards and big pan of banana pudding. Everybody loves my banana pudding. You can order the barbecue and whatever, but just leave everything else up to me. I may even get Tammy Lee Stroud to give me a hand."

"I'll help you, Mama," I said.

"You'll do nothing of the sort," she kinda snarled. "No bride fixes the food for her own wedding. That would be uncouth."

Well, I think Mama must have worked a whole week in the kitchen by herself or with Mrs. Stroud, and, in fact, I never did figure out exactly when she found time to get a permanent and how she went about making herself look so nice for the wedding in a lacy, floral muumuu that actually gave the impression she might have lost a few pounds. The ceremony itself was short and sweet just like I wanted, me and Lyman howled like kids when everybody threw shredded confetti and pelted us with rice on the way to the car, but nothing prepared us for the way Mama and Gladys and Lord know who else had decorated the house with colorful ribbons and balloons and Lone Star banners and for the array of dishes lined up on Mama's long dining room table that she'd covered with the Belgian linen tablecloth Granny had given her before she died from diabetes.

Of course, I myself had ordered the barbecue and links and ribs from the guys at Pink Pig—ten pounds of just the smoky brisket itself—and, of course, nothing would do but for Mama to serve them on her silver-plated platters somebody had given her when she and Daddy got married. But every single other dish on that huge table was Mama's handiwork. There were the collards she'd mentioned, but also her red cabbage cole-

slaw, and barbecued pintos, and big bowls of okra and tomatoes, and corn pudding, and potato salad made with potatoes
boiled in water spiced with Texas Pete, and baskets of jalapeño
cornbread, and not only two pans of her rich banana pudding
but also two sticky cherry cobblers. Must have been twenty
different items on that buffet—enough to feed double the
number of guests.

"Whadda you think, sugar?" Mama asked as me and
Lyman gawked at the incredible display, and he and Gladys
began picking at the barbecue with their fingers before other
people arrived.

I could tell how proud Mama was, and yeah, I was almost
speechless when I realized the time and work that had gone
into fixing all this food. For a second, I thought I might start
crying, but instead I just hugged her hard around the waist, and
pecked her on the cheek, and said, "It's so beautiful, Mama,"
and swore to myself never to argue with her again.

9

GOAT ROPERS

It was really nice of Mary Jane to give me and Sally both two tickets to last Saturday afternoon's Roller Derby at the Thunderdome. Mary Jane works with us at the shelter three days a week, but she's also a damn good cook and one of the Rhinestone Babes' best rollergirls. When she skates in a derby, she goes by the name of Cha Cha, and let me tell you there's not a better jammer on that team than Cha Cha Baxter. Of course Mary Jane couldn't be more trim and fit and full of pep, so no wonder her boyfriend Sam Radcliff thinks she hung the moon. And don't think it hasn't dawned on me that if I hadn't let myself go to pot all those years, I might make a pretty good rollergirl myself and maybe snag myself a man like Sam if Vernon doesn't work out. Sam's a great guy. Started his own landscaping business 'bout a year ago and has done pretty well so far, and I wouldn't be a bit surprised if Mary Jane called me one day and said he's popped the big question.

Anyway, Sally invited Zach to go with her, but when he came up with some song and dance about promising to cover for his buddy at Mickey's Smokeshop, it didn't take me a split second to say to her, "Well, Sal, you'll go with me and Vernon and Sam, and I don't wanna hear any argument." I mean, Sally really loves the derbies, and she don't have many friends, and believe me, I know the hell she's going through with the weight problem, so why should she miss out?

And the four of us did have a super time. Cha Cha was dressed in this frilly tutu and red fishnet stockings and a red, white, and blue helmet. During one bout, the crowd really went wild when she jammed this puta on the Angel Cowgirls team, and passed at least two opponents, and broke through the pack, and racked up three more points for the Babes. Then, after the big win, she and Sam joined everybody at Ziggy's to drink suds and hear me play in the band and ride the bull. I got them the best table in the joint—right at the dance platform—and when Venus Williams sang "Daddy's Gonna Keep His Eye on You" and I blew a little solo, the crowd clapped and whistled a lot and Vernon stared at me with the biggest grin on his face you could ever imagine.

Of course Vernon's good as gold, so when Cha Cha forced Sam up to two-step round and round the platform, I couldn't have been more happy to see Vernon grab Sally and pull her up too. And I gotta tell you, Sal might be a big girl, but, like so many fat women, she's light as a feather on her feet—light as a feather. Sam's not, which I guess is why Vernon and Mary Jane ended up dancing together so much while the other two just sat at the table drinking and smoking and listening to us play.

Now, I bet any other gal would have gotten real jealous seeing her boyfriend dancing over and over with somebody as good-looking and sexy as Mary Jane. But not me—no, siree. First, I know Mary Jane's as crazy about Sam as he is about her, and second, nobody on earth loves to dance and sing and just have fun like Vernon. Besides, Mary Jane's my good friend, and she'd never pull any backhanded stunts on me after all I've been through. What did burn me up was when some white trash in the crowd yelled, "Let's hear it, Bubbles" when I stood up again and was fixin' to blow the bridge on "Jesus, Take the

Wheel" for some line dancing. Was bound to happen, I guess, but I just ignored the jerk, and Vernon and Mary Jane were dancing and laughing so hard with everybody else that he couldn't have noticed a thing.

After we wrapped up the last set, Vernon and Sam said they wanted a Tex-Mex burger and fries and more beer before going into the bull room, and Sally and Mary Jane said that sounded good to them.

"Y'all count me out on the burgers," I said. "Blowing the sax really gets my adrenaline running, you know, and all I want now is some ice-cold suds."

Vernon pulled me round the waist and said, "Oh, come on, little girl, you gotta keep body and soul together. Shit, hon, how you gonna ride the bull without some meat on those bones?"

Everybody laughed out loud, but when Sally and Mary Jane glanced over at me, bless 'em, I could tell they understood and felt real sorry for me.

By the time we got to the bull room, some dude holding his hat in the air was already bucking away and people were yelling, "Turn it up! Turn it up!" So they did turn the machine up and he got thrown in no time and landed smack on his big hat. Next, we saw a bunch of shit-kickers on a bench push a pretty hefty gal holding a bottle of beer toward the platform and bellow, "Go for it, Maud! Go for it, sweetheart! Show 'em your stuff!" When one guy pushed a little too hard, she jumped up and saddled him around the waist with her knees and dumped half the bottle over his head. Then everybody on the bench started clucking like chickens, so she finally marched out and swung herself up on the bull and raised her hand for the machine to start bucking. Well, there for a few seconds that gal was as good and tough as any goddamn cowboy riding that bull, and the crowd really went crazy. But then they jacked it up a few notches, and her big boobs were really flopping up and down in her white tee, and soon she was sailing through the air screaming like a mad billy goat.

Sam went and got some more beers, and I gotta say we were all feeling our oats by the time a few more ropers shelled out the five bucks and took their turns on the bull. Of course, since she's in such good shape and used to stiff competition, it didn't take much to coax Mary Jane to try her luck. Down in no time. Then Sam landed on his ass. Next, Vernon jumped up on the bull and didn't last five seconds and we're all laughing our fool heads off.

He then grabbed me hard and pushed and shouted, "Your turn now, baby doll."

I squirmed and finally dropped to my knees and yelled, "Not on your life, cowboy. If you think I'm gonna get up there and crack my ribs . . ."

"Oh, don't pitch a conniption, babe," he joked out loud while he rubbed his sore arm. "What about you, Sal? Go, girl!"

Well, I couldn't believe my eyes when Sally gets up from the bench, and stuffs her sequined shirt in her jeans over all that fat, and throws her hands in the air laughing like a hyena, and sort of waddles across the platform while some people clap and howl "Yeah, big mama! Buck it, mama!" I mean, the last thing I wanted was to watch poor Sally make a real fool of herself, but lemme tell you: Sal grabs that saddle horn, and bounces like a real buckaroo with her blond ponytail flopping up and down, and even when they turn up the juice she lasts a good ten seconds till she finally tumbles and lands on her flabby rear end. The crowd really went wild, and when Vernon rushed out to help her up, she was still hooting and poking her fist in the air like some giant who'd just brought down a grizzly or something. "Whoooa, girl!" I yelled when I started hugging her.

"Okay, doll, how 'bout it? You ready yet?" Vernon kept bugging me. "Here's five big ones that say you can sock us all."

What I wanted to scream was, "Buster, here I got a god-damn ring looped round my gut, and no gallbladder, and a thyroid condition, and you're telling me to get up on that bull." Instead, I just shoved him away real playfully and said, "Okay, okay, I'm chicken. I admit it. So just forget about it, okay?" And he did. Vernon's like that when he knows I mean business.

I guess we would've stayed at Ziggy's till midnight if Mary Jane hadn't said she'd had it and I said it was my turn to go by the shelter to check on some sick animals and the water bowls and what have you. Of course, Sally offered to help me, but she'd done it the night before, and that's a job, and I knew she had to get up early to attend her Assembly of God prayer service out in Jacinto City. So I said, "That's ridiculous, Sal. Vernon can just run me by the shelter, and drop you off while I get things done, then pick me back up on the way home."

Well, after I finished up at the shelter, I waited and waited and popped two Nips in my mouth since I really felt hungry. Then I wondered why he hadn't called me on his cell and began to worry myself sick he might have had a wreck or been stopped for drunk driving or something. But when he finally showed up, he was mad as a hornet and explained he had to take a construction detour off Katy Freeway and said his cell's on the blink. Then, on the way back to his place, I was scared as the dickens we were going to total the Cherokee the way he kept rubbing and squeezing my thigh while he was driving, and all I could really think about was flexing my leg as hard as I could so it wouldn't feel flabby to him. When we get home, he says he is hungry as a horse and that I must be starved since I hadn't eaten a thing all night. So he takes a meat loaf he'd gotten at Central Market outta the fridge, and pulls off a big piece with his fingers, and pops a can of Shiner Bock. What I do is cut off a small slice with a knife and eat it, but I gotta say nothing ever looked so good to me and I could've eaten that

entire greasy meat loaf if I hadn't known what the consequences would be.

"Tastes good," I say, "but that's a little heavy this time of
night, don't you think?"

"Doll, you gotta eat," he says while he wolfs down another
chunk and washes it down with another slug of beer. "At this
rate, you're gonna waste away to nothing one day."

I guess that's the closest I'd come to telling Vernon the
damn truth about my fat problem, but I kept my wits about
me 'cause I still wadn't ready to do or say one thing to screw
things up. Things were just going too well, and I realized I was
getting really crazy about Vernon—crazier than I ever thought
I could be about anybody. In fact, I was all ready to jump in
bed with him and be wild the way he likes, but after he'd finished his meat loaf and beer, he just pulled off his shirt and
jeans and flipped the TV on and was dead to the world by the
time I'd brushed my teeth and gargled with this green stuff
he has.

10

BLUEBIRD

Who needs guys like Billy Po Cahill if they can't behave themselves? Word of mouth spreads fast in this town, and just in the past month I've had two calls and an e-mail about catering. Small jobs, yeah, but one was from a director of that posh Menil Collection over in the Museum District who needs canapés for fifty at some cocktail reception next Thursday. "What can you provide for five hundred dollars?" asked this Miss Block in a real classy voice. "We'd like it to be nice, but we are on a budget, you know, and understand you're quite reasonable."

Well, five hundred dollars sounded like five thousand to me, so I began thinking fast about my time and costs and what have you and then mentioned celery stuffed with pimento cheese, and maybe sausage-stuffed mushrooms, and some small ham biscuits, and my special pecan tassies. A cinch, and I figured I could still make a little profit.

"Oh, that does sound lovely," Miss Block said. "Do you require an advance against expenses?"

I gotta say that caught me off guard, but since I certainly don't have any spare cash to throw around, I tried to sound real professional and said, "If that's convenient with you, ma'am." That's exactly the way I phrased it.

As they say, when it rains it pours. First, I hit my lowest ever on the scales at Body Tech—158. Next comes the three catering jobs. Then some part-time work at Bluebird Bar & Grill over on Shepherd. What happened was Mary Jane told me about this rollergirl who'd been bartending at Bluebird till her husband got transferred to some job down in Galveston, and how the owner was looking for a nice-looking temp to fill in three weeknights. Respectable-enough crowd, she said, and pretty good food to boot. Burgers, tacos, sausage-on-the-stick, Frito pie—things like that. Just five hours a night. And really big bar tips in addition to minimum wage. Well, it's for sure I can use the money to pay off those last bills for the surgery and get my catering off the ground, and Vernon's been tied up more and more late at night with a couple of big commercial jobs. So, I figured, why not? At first I thought Vernon might raise hell about me slinging drinks at a bar, but to tell the truth, he thought it was a good way to make a little extra cash for the future. Of course I had no idea what he meant by "the future," but it sounded good.

In any case, the minute Lester saw me and we talked, he offered me the job. Took me a couple of nights to learn how to pour short the way Lester showed me, and get things like gimlets and margaritas just right, and coordinate with the table waitresses, and ring up everything on the computer. But now I've pretty much got the hang of things. Even have lots of fun sometimes talking with customers, even though I'm not allowed to drink even a beer on the job. And I gotta say this type of job can do wonders for a girl's ego—not to mention my pocketbook. Take this one guy who often shows up in a nice jacket at 9:15 on the dot and drinks Absolut with a splash. Rudy's his name. Single, maybe a few years older than me, works at Folger's Buick down the street in the next block, and not at all bad looking with lots of straight sandy hair and a pretty solid physique. Well, he's always making these come-ons, like, "What's there to do in this lousy town when this place closes?" Or, when I ask if he wants a sweetener, "Better keep your distance after I've had about three of those babies." Makes me feel real good getting that sort of attention now, but, mind you, I never forget Vernon's my man and I'm not looking anyplace else—not on your life. So I just play along with guys like Rudy when they try to hit on me, and most of them do respect me, and it's nothing for them to tip me five, maybe ten big ones when they're tanked.

I've told Vernon and my friends to drop by any time they don't have anything better to do, and they have. Just last Tuesday night Mary Jane and Sally came in after working late at the shelter. Of course poor Sally's on another one of her stupid diets so she wasn't drinking anything except club soda with a wedge of lime. But Mary Jane . . . sometimes I think Mary Jane could swizzle a whole keg of beer without gaining a single pound. Then who should show up a little after ten but Vernon, who plopped down at the bar, and said he'd almost been electrocuted installing a big computer at Mobil, and told me to fix him a double Cutty and water. Well, things got pretty crazy on the floor, so while I was pouring one drink after the next for the waitresses, I noticed Mary Jane talking to this Rudy, and Vernon and Sally yapping like there's no tomorrow. What I wanted to do was warn Mary Jane that Rudy's always on the make, but then I figured if Cha Cha Baxter can't take care of herself by now, she deserves what she gets.

"Whoooa!" is what I heard next, and when I snapped my head around Vernon was already trying to help Sally get up off the floor. I mean, the stool had just collapsed under her, and there she was with her shift halfway up her flabby thighs sprawled out on the filthy floor laughing while others at the bar jumped up to help or just gawked. Rudy also came rushing over, but Vernon's strong as an ox, so he just laughed too, and heaved her up like a sack of potatoes and offered her his stool. Happened in less than a minute. Well, all I could think about was that time I fell in the kitchen when I was so goddamn fat and how embarrassed and humiliated she must feel. "Are you okay, Sal?" Mary Jane and I both asked over and over. "Sure, she's okay," Vernon said. Both of them kept laughing, but I could imagine what he must be thinking about this tub of lard making such a fool of herself. "Tell you what, Let," Sally then said. "Why don't you fix me a strong J.D. on the rocks?" So much for the diet, I thought.

After things calmed down a little, Rudy pointed to Mary Jane's beer for a refill, but she shook her hand no to me and jumped up and told everybody she has an early day tomorrow. So much for Cha Cha taking care of herself, I said to myself. Of course, Rudy looked like he'd been slapped in the face, and I have to admit I sort of knew what Vernon felt like when he threw his drink back, and said he was really beat, and swaggered out not long after Mary Jane with no more than a friendly pop on Sally's arm and a "Call you tomorrow, doll" to me. Don't get me wrong. Vernon works hard at those big jobs. I know that. And it's not like we've ever made a habit of fooling around much on weeknights. Besides, I got gym every morning at seven. But "Call you tomorrow, doll." Sally looked as surprised as I was when she got up to leave too, but I just rolled my eyes and said I'd see her at the shelter. Then Rudy thumped his empty glass and I poured him another Absolut.

"Hey, toots, can a guy still order a hamburger around here?" he then asked as he patted his flat stomach and looked around.

"'Fraid not, bub," I answered, and began dumping ice in the sink. "Kitchen closed at eleven, and I'm outta here myself in about fifteen minutes."

"Shit," he grumbled, and it was pretty obvious he was feeling his oats. "We had to do inventory tonight at the dealer, and I ain't had a bite since lunch."

"You and me both," I said without thinking.

"You ain't had no dinner either?" he went on.

I laughed and said, "Who's got time to eat when you cowboys gotta be kept tanked till midnight."

He pulled a twenty and ten out of his jacket pocket, tossed them on the bar, and told me to keep the change. Then he said, "Hey, Loretta, I got an idea. You know Scooter's over on Sunset?"

"Passed by it a million times," I answered as I pulled pouring spouts from the bottles and covered my garnishes with plastic wrap.

"They got the best chili dogs and cheese fries in Texas, and open all night. What say you let me treat you to a dog when you finish up here?"

"Thanks, Rudy, but it's late, and I got gym and another job to work in the morning, and . . . you ain't exactly gone thirsty tonight, you know."

He gave me this real serious look and said, "Naw, naw, naw, babe, no heavy stuff, if that's what's worrying you. I ain't plastered, and I ain't talking about no heavy stuff. Just a friendly dog and some fries and a cold beer. I mean, come on, we're both hungry and gotta eat something, and, girl, you ain't lived till you've had Scooter's chili dog. Whadda you say?"

I don't know what came over me, but, without thinking again, I asked, "What's so damn special about it?"

"Everything," he exclaimed in his husky voice. "Longest and fattest all-beef dog you ever saw, sourdough bun with jalapeño mayo, confetti slaw and ranch relish, lots of red onions, and the best goddamn homemade chili over the top— Scooter himself told me and my buddy Karl all about it one night when we went over after work and got to rappin'. Never ate a hot dog like it."

Well, I could just imagine what that dog must taste like, and the more I thought about what Rudy had described, the more I began to salivate and feel like I was starving to death. Normally, I would have just gone home and had a salad or nibbled on something I'd prepared for a job while watching Paula Deen or an Emeril rerun on TV. But, goddammit, all I'd had since noon were a few pickled shrimp in the fridge and two or three cheese straws, and the sound of that chili dog was driving me crazy, and the most important lesson I've learned during my weight ordeal is never, ever totally deny myself at least a taste of something I crave.

I figured Rudy was nice enough and could be trusted not to pull any stunts, so yeah, I finally told him I'd drop by Scooter's with him to sample that dog but swore to myself I wouldn't get near any cheese fries. I also told him I'd just follow him in my car since I couldn't stay too long and it would save time. Well, I gotta say the dive ain't gonna win no decorating awards—scarred linoleum floor, plain wooden tables with rolls of paper towels for napkins, pictures of prize steers on the walls, things like that—but pretty good country music playing, and regular guys and cowgirls having a good time, and . . . Lord, I could smell chili and meat cooking the second we pushed the front door open.

"Two chili dogs and cheese fries and ice-cold Copperhead Reds," Rudy told the waitress without even glancing at a blackboard menu on the wall or asking me anything.

I reached up and grabbed her arm and said, "Just one cheese fry for the gent here, honey—none for me."

"But you gotta have some fries, little lady," Rudy tried to coax me.

"Too much for me this time of night," I insisted without mentioning the weight issue. "I'll taste a couple of yours."

"Gram Parsons," Rudy then muttered as he pointed in the air to the music playing.

"Yeah, 'Return of the Grievous Angel,'" I said when the waitress plopped the two beer mugs on the table. "I play that."

"Whadda you mean?"

"I blow sax."

"You play saxophone?"

"Yeah, some weekends over at Ziggy's. You know Ziggy's on Navigation?"

"Knock me down," he said, taking a slug of beer, then pushing his blond hair off his forehead.

I let out a quick laugh and said, "And I also cook—a little catering in my spare time."

He looked really surprised. "I'll be goddamned. Bartender, horn player, big-time cook. What else you do, girl?"

I laughed again and said, "Oh, I got lots of secrets. Now, what about you, bub? How long you been with Folger's?"

"Just a couple of months. Before that it was Harrelson Ford over in Pasadena, and before that lots of years at Storms Chevy–Cadillac in South Houston. Been selling cars my whole life—ever since high school."

I sipped my beer, and gazed at his watery blue eyes, and asked, "Is it true you're all crooks?"

For a second, he got another serious look on his face, then broke into a big smile and pretended he was gonna punch me with his fist. "Between you and me, smart-ass, yeah."

"Mind if I ask you another question?" I then said.

"Guess you also wanna know if all us car salesmen wear clunky jewelry," he joked, holding up his silver turquoise ring. "Birthday present from my former wife."

Gotta say this remark caught me by surprise. "You been married?"

Before he could answer, the waitress brought the food, and I should've known I was in for trouble the second I saw and smelled that incredible chili dog, which was so big and had so much hot chili covering the top and running down the sides onto the plate that it had to be eaten with knife and fork.

"Wow!" I yelped as I cut off an end, and spooned a little extra chili over the bite, and rolled my eyes after I'd tasted it.

"Told you so." Rudy smiled. "Here, now, you gotta also have a cheese fry."

"Just one," I said, popping it also in my mouth and noticing how crisp the potato stick was even with all the hot, oozy cheddar cheese.

"Best in Houston," Rudy proclaimed in his cocky way.

"So, you said you were married," I picked up as I cut off another bite of the dog and washed it down with suds.

"If you wanna call it that," he said kinda sad in his boozy, low voice.

"Sorry. Just didn't get along?"

He looked like he was thinking about the question, then said, "Pretty well, in fact, but we really wanted to have kids, you know, and Mother Nature had other ideas, and . . . why am I telling you all this, Loretta?"

I took what I promised myself would be my last bite, and couldn't resist just one more fry, and said, "So she had medical problems?"

He waited again, and slugged his beer, and finally said like he was a little embarrassed, "Not her, hon, but me. Found out after we were married. Yeah, I was the one who was dealt a rotten hand, and . . . well, in the long run Dottie just couldn't deal with it."

"Oh," was all I could mutter, and I was now so wrapped up in what he was telling, and feeling so sorry for him, that I wasn't even aware of finishing off that whole goddamn hot dog till all I saw was some chili left on the plate.

"Can't really blame her, I guess," he added as he ate a few more fries and kept his head down.

What I did then was reach over and touch his arm, and I was on the verge of telling him things like that didn't matter to some gals when, all of a sudden and almost like I'd been hit by lightning, I felt the urge to burp, then could taste that wonderful meat and onions and chili right at the top of my chest, and knew instantly what was about to happen. Oh sure, I'd learned about foods that could trigger an accident more than others, and I'd paid the consequences of overeating more than once at home. But this was the first time I'd been so careless in public and was just thankful a door with a cowgirl on the front was only a few feet away.

"Nature's calling," I managed to say calmly without gasping as I stood up fast. "Excuse me a minute."

Rudy stood up also like a gentleman, and I just held my breath and prayed there was nobody else in the bathroom. Well, within seconds I was heaving to beat the band as most of that great food disappeared down the toilet and I was cursing myself for being so stupid. It was all over as fast as it began, and once I'd gargled with some water and checked my hair in the mirror, I returned very casually to the table, and took a few sips of beer, then told Rudy I really had to call it a night. What's funny is that by the time I got home, I was hungry again, so what I did after playing with Sugar and Spice a little was grind up some sharp cheddar, and mix it with chopped pimentos and Worcestershire and a squeeze of lemon juice and mayo, and fix me half a pimento cheese sandwich to eat while watching that stupid *Iron Chef.*

11

A Duck Peeping at Thunder

Like I say, when it rains, it pours, and these last few days there's also been plenty of thunder and lightning. Rufus called Monday at the crack of dawn yelling about him and Gladys having to rush Mama to emergency at TMC after another attack of hypoglycemia and telling me to get right over there. Monday's the day we spay and neuter dogs at SPCA, but my mama's certainly more important than the dogs, so I didn't waste a second tracking Sally down on her cell and telling her I had an emergency on my hands.

By the time I got to the Medical Center, they had Mama stabilized with glucose dripping from an IV, and she was already raising hell with Gladys about getting out of there and going back home even though she was pale as milk. Now, Mama might be fat as they come, but normally her color couldn't be more rosy and healthy looking. In fact, when Mama's well and taking good care of herself, her skin and complexion are almost like that of a woman half her age. Not a line or wrinkle in her face, no dark circles under her eyes, high cheekbones, and after she's been to the beauty parlor to have her thick silver hair washed and set, she's actually a very pretty lady from the shoulders up—especially when she's wearing rouge and her coral beads and a pair of earbobs for church or one of her bingo games. Me and Gladys both inherited Mama's big hazel eyes, and now that I've lost so much weight, I can tell I must have also inherited her prominent cheekbones. Not so with Gladys, who got not only her sorta flat facial features from Daddy but also his reddish hair that looks more kinky and washed out the older she gets. Gladys could probably improve her appearance a lot if she paid more attention to her hair and makeup and, of course, tubby body, but as usual, nobody can tell Gladys anything and Rufus don't seem to give a damn what she looks like so long as she takes care of those kids and puts plenty of pizza and beer on the table.

"I don't think Mama's been taking her tablets," Gladys whispered to me at the bed as I studied Mama's face.

"Have you been taking your tablets, Mama?" I asked.

"I declare, you two, there's not one thing wrong with me, and all I had was a little dizzy spell," was all she said.

"Mama, have you been taking your tablets?" I asked again real sweet while I held her hand.

"What tablets?"

"Oh, Mama, you know what tablets," Gladys said. "Your glucose tablets. You know you're supposed to take one every morning when you spray for the diabetes."

"I hate all those things," she said. "It's not natural, and the Good Lord didn't intend for us to poison our bodies with things like that. I just wanna get outta here, and get my hair fixed, and have some decent food."

"Mama, they'd like to move you to a room and keep you overnight to make sure you're okay," Gladys said.

"Like hell they will!" Mama shouted. "Who's gonna pay for all this? And you know what the food's like in these places."

"Mama, we're not gonna argue with you, and that's that,"

Gladys went on. "If you'd take your tablets the way the doctor told you to . . ."

I noticed Mama was now starting to get a little more color in her face when she stared up at both of us and said, "That's right, you two. Just leave your own mother here by myself to rot and put up with all this crap and let them poison me and starve me to death."

About this time, a doctor showed up with a clipboard in his hand and began feeling Mama's pulse. "This was a close call," he said, "and the next time your mother might not be so lucky. The next time, you know, she could go into a diabetic coma. We see it all the time, especially with patients as heavy as she is."

"I've tried to get her and my sister here both to do something about the weight," I commented while he was poking his stethoscope all over Mama.

"Please, Let, can we keep me out of this?" Gladys said. "This is no time or place for your lecturing."

"I've had banded gastroplasty," I kinda whispered to the doctor, but he didn't seem very interested.

"All I'm saying to you ladies is that your mother may not be around much longer unless she takes her medication and loses some of this weight."

"Hear that, Gladys?" I said. "Did you hear what the doctor said? Why don't you listen to the doctor, honey?"

"I told you, sis, just to please shut up. This is about Mama, not me or you or anybody else."

"I've warned them both, Doctor," I then said. "I've begged and pleaded with them both to reduce the way I did, but it's like talking to a brick wall. Maybe they'll listen to you."

Well, he didn't say a word, and about this time Mama starts crying, and telling the doctor that me and my sister only care about ourselves, and saying awful things like she'd probably just be better off dead.

Then Gladys has the nerve to say, "Hope you're satisfied, sis. Here Mama's sick as a dog and all you can do is criticize and lecture and get her all upset."

"It's just because I care and worry my head off about you both, honey," I say. "Can't you understand that, Gladys?"

"Please, sweetheart," Mama suddenly says real nice to me. "Please, Loretta, won't you and your sister stop bickering and just get me out of this hellhole?"

The doctor is now scribbling something on the chart and looking at his watch. Very cold man, I thought.

"I really want to keep your mother overnight for observation in case there're complications," he says real serious.

Of course, Mama throws a few more fits and accuses me and Gladys of wanting to torture her, but when I say I'll bring her some mac 'n cheese and stay with her overnight to keep her company, she finally calms down and lets them wheel her up to a semiprivate room with some old man on a breathing machine that drives me and Mama both crazy.

Next afternoon I drove Mama home, and fixed her some pimento cheese and guacamole, and got her settled, then got the surprise of my life when I went back to the apartment to change for Bluebird and eat some leftover tomato and olive aspic and who should be sitting on his Hog out front wearing a baseball cap and drinking a Dr Pepper and talking on his cell but . . . Lyman.

"Hi, Let," was all he said as he snapped the phone shut.

First time I'd seen him in over a year, and if I hadn't known the jerk had called Mama a couple of times, he might as well have been dead. I did notice that he'd cut off his ponytail, and lost some more hair on top, and put on a little weight.

"Well, look what the cat drug in," I said. "What in hell are you doing here, Lyman?"

"You look real fine, Let," he said in his squeaky voice and looking like a duck peeping at thunder.

I stood with both hands on my hips, and looked at that stupid lizard tattoo on his arm, and said, "You really got your nerve, bub, after all these months coming over here out of the blue, and the last thing I need is compliments from you. Whadda you want?"

"Just to see you, Let," he sort of mumbled, "and tell you I made a big mistake."

"Yeah," I said as I stuck the key in the door and heard Sugar and Spice howling. "We all make big mistakes, and my big mistake was gettin' mixed up with you."

He follows me in like he owns the place, but I don't say anything and just check my e-mail and wonder more what he must be thinking about my new look.

"I only wanna talk, hon," he says, and I notice he's really giving me the once-over and glancing at everything in the apartment. "Can't we just talk?"

"Sure, bub, talk all you want to, but you better make it snappy 'cause I gotta be at work in a little while."

"Your mama told me about all you've been through, and goddamn, Let, I gotta take my hat off to you."

"No thanks to you, Lyman," I say. "No thanks at all to you."

"You're right, Let. I was a real bastard. I admit it. But I've changed, hon. I've really changed my ways."

I head back to the bedroom to get out of my floral dress and into a peach denim shirt and jeans, and Lyman follows right behind like we're still married and he lives there. I think about asking if I can have a little privacy, but, hell, I'm so used to Lyman that I change my mind and ask instead, "What happened, bub, did Miss Champagne Video tell you to get lost or something?"

I can see he's watching me real careful as I undress down to my panties and bra, and, to tell the truth, I think I wanted him to get his eyes full and eat his heart out.

"Oh, Let, Tiffany was never any big deal, and we never had fun the way you and I did. You gotta believe me, hon."

"Yeah," I say, and don't pay him any attention. Then I start to put on lipstick and fix my hair and what have you before going out to the kitchen and getting the aspic out of the fridge and taking a few bites at the counter.

"How can you eat that stuff?" he asks while making these disgusting sounds at the back of his throat.

"Lyman, I don't think that's any of your goddamn concern."

"Oh, don't be like that, Let," he says. "I'm just trying to be nice, and tell you how sorry I am about the way I acted, and say I wish we could get along the way we used to."

"So, bub, you think you could handle Miss Former Fatso now. Is that what you're saying? Now that this gal ain't got so much meat on her ribs she's good enough for you. Right?"

He tries to put his arm around my waist, but I push him away and spill some aspic on the floor and yell, "Cool it, Lyman! Just cool it, buster!"

"Okay, hon, okay," he says as he bends down and picks up the mess with his fingers. "Don't go crazy on me."

"Listen, Lyman, I'm fixin' to go to work, and don't have time to stand here fooling with you, and just wish you'd get the hell out of here and go install a muffler or something. Understand?"

"Sure, Let, sure thing. I get the message," he sort of whimpers. "But can I ask you something?"

"Would it do any good if I said no?"

"I can't blame you for still being pissed off, hon, but I was just wondering . . . if I kinda dress up the way I used to when we went to Chiquita's for the beef enchiladas and Frito pie— remember that?—would you go out with me somewhere to eat one night so maybe we could start to patch things up?"

Okay, I gotta admit that, for a minute, I began to feel a little sorry for the guy—just the really sweet way he asked that question, I suppose. Lyman's not a mean man, you know, and he did sound pretty lonely. And yeah, Chiquita's did bring back some nice memories, and yeah, I did love those enchiladas and that pie.

"Well, first of all, Lyman, I can't eat like that anymore," I say real calmly. "My new stomach won't take it. And second, I better tell you, bub, I've been seeing somebody the last few months—somebody kinda special."

"Oh," is all he says as he chews on one of his stubby nails, then pushes a few strands of scraggly hair back over his ear.

"I gotta new stomach and a new life, you know, and I'm also trying to hold down three jobs to pay for everything."

"I can help you out a little bit, Let, if you need it," he says. "And we can always just go to the Lone Star if you have to be on some diet. They got everything there."

"Thanks, but I don't need any help, and I'm not on any goddamn diet. I just can't keep down lots of any food with this pouch for a stomach I now have—simple as that."

"Will you at least think about it, Let?" he then asks as I almost push him out the door. "Will you at least think about letting me take you to the Lone Star one night—just for old time's sake?"

"Call me sometime, bub, and maybe we'll see," I say mainly just to get him out of the apartment.

Well, I don't know why it mattered to me, but the more I thought about Lyman coming on to me now that I'd lost so much weight and his wanting to romance me again like nothing had ever happened between us, the madder I got while working at Bluebird. I mean, I may have changed lots on the outside, but, I asked myself, is that all men really care about—women as no more than pieces of meat? Don't what's inside count a hoot? Lyman, Billy Po, Rudy, Sally's Zach, and Mary Jane's Sam, even Vernon—don't any of these guys realize lots of us gals have more to offer than just a good romp in the sack when somebody's firecracker needs lighting? Goddammit, I sure do, and when I stop sometimes to face matters head-on, I can't help but wonder why I can't be treated more like . . . a human being who's got the same needs and hopes and pride as any buck on earth. Oh, I know . . . boy, do I know there's not much attractive about a walking tub of lard, but I also know there's nothing exactly wonderful about jerks who have to have stupid tattoos, or two-time their wives and families, or eat meat loaf with their fingers, or shoot birds, or . . .

Like I say, I don't know why I let things like this get to me sometimes, but when I got home from work, I was still riled up enough after seeing Lyman that all I could do was watch *Top Chef* on Bravo for a while, then go in the kitchen and start a batch of pecan-cheese wafers I promised Sally I'd fix for Eileen Silvers's surprise birthday party over at the shelter. What I figured was I'd just grate the cheese, and mix the dough till I got sleepy, and have it ready in the fridge to make wafers the next morning. Then, while I kept thinking about what all Lyman had said, I found myself rolling one ball almost instinctively, then another one, then another one till, before I knew it, I'd preheated the oven, and the baking sheet was full of small balls, and I was pressing a pecan half into the center of each.

While the wafers baked, I watched Lidia on TV making a squash risotto, but since she didn't seem to be doing anything but stirring rice and adding chicken stock on and on, my mind drifted back to Lyman and Billy Po and Vernon and how I wished they'd all treat me with more respect. Then, hard as it was to admit, it suddenly dawned on me that maybe, after all, I wasn't being very fair to any of these guys and was maybe as much at fault as they were. I mean, it does take two to tango, and I ain't exactly been a wilting violet when it comes to playing bedroom games, and what can any wild woman expect from a man when she don't make herself more of a . . . challenge? Well, now I got real confused trying to figure all this out, but before I could give it much more thought, there was this fabulous smell of cheese in the air, and the timer went off in the kitchen, and I had to go see if my wafers had just the right texture and the pecans on top weren't overbrowning. They looked perfect. I waited a couple of minutes and popped one in my mouth, and if I hadn't had more willpower, I could easily have eaten a half-dozen more.

12

GUMBO

This week I bought my first gun and am now waiting for my permit to arrive. Automatic double action Beretta 92 just small enough to fit in the glove compartment or my bag. And the reason I bought the gun is because not long ago another gal who plays fiddle in the band at Ziggy's got raped in the parking lot on her way to her car. Some drunk roper who really worked her over good and got away scot-free. Vernon took off work to go with me to the Hyatt Gun Shop, and after I attended a lecture on firearms, and passed a written test, and was taught how to blow hell out of paper targets, all I had left to do was fill out an application for a permit.

"Watch out, Annie Oakley," Vernon kidded as he grabbed me around the waist on the way back to the car. "Shit, gal, you're a real natural and just need a little practice, so I ain't gonna worry anymore about you protecting your sweet self."

To tell the truth, Vernon's always looking out for me like that, in fact, and just this past weekend he showed me something on the computer I didn't know about and even helped me peel shrimp and shuck oysters for a seafood gumbo I had to fix for a small sit-down wedding luncheon for eight at a socialite's home over near Rice. Billy Po, bless his naughty heart, recommended me to this lady, and who was I to say no when she didn't blink an eye at seven hundred dollars for a pot of seafood gumbo and a few dozen corn sticks and congealed sunshine salad and a hummingbird cake? Of course, Vernon says I'm working too hard and ought to give up either the shelter or the Bluebird gig, but the way I figure it, if I can keep holding down the three jobs, I might save enough bucks to move somewhere with a bigger kitchen and even hire somebody to help me with the catering.

"Doll, I can already tell it's wearing you down," he said while we sat on the kitchen stools deveining the shrimp. "And the way you go to that stupid gym every morning, and eat like a bird . . ."

"Oh, Vern, working out calms my nerves, and I've told you a dozen times how doing all this cooking sometimes turns me off just the sight of food," were the only quick comments I could make as I tossed another shrimp in the bowl and laughed.

"But you gotta keep your energy up for me," he joked with a smile on his face, which made me feel even more jittery.

I laughed again, leaned over and pecked him on the cheek, and said, "You telling me, bub, I can't cut the mustard or something?"

Then he cracked an even bigger smile and said, "Babe, you ain't heard me complaining, have you?"

The truth is that, fat as I still feel sometimes, Vernon and I couldn't get along better in the sack, and I don't think he's ever had any reason to doubt he's got a live chicken on his hands. It's also true that the scales read 156 this past week—down 2 more pounds—though I wish I could get to 150 faster and that the loose skin on my butt and thighs would tighten up more. Anyway, like he said, and like I told Sally, he ain't complaining about anything, and, boy, does Vernon know how to satisfy a girl when he's in the right mood. Yeah, I've noticed he's best when he's had lots to drink, but Lyman was always like that too, and one day I heard Mary Jane telling Sally there's a cooling-off period for most guys when they're banging the same gal over and over. Might be true, but I gotta say there's more than one way to skin a cat, and believe you me, when Vernon's not exactly on fire, I've learned other ways to fan the flames that really drive him and me both crazy.

Take that same session with the gumbo. Had a Randy Travis CD playing, and we finish all the prep work, and I start the roux in my big iron pot while Vernon holds me around the waist and watches. Then, suddenly, I have to go tinkle real bad, so I hand him the wooden spoon and tell him to stir the flour and bacon grease without stopping one single second so the roux won't burn. Well, I wasn't gone more than a minute, and when I get back he's popping the cap on a Big Red, and the roux is scorched to hell, and I have to throw it out and start all over again.

"All I did, hon, was grab a beer in the fridge," he almost cries like a scared child.

I just shake my head and laugh and say, "That's all it takes, you dope, to ruin a roux. When I said stir constantly, I meant goddamn *constantly!*"

"Shit, Let, I'm sorry. I'm really sorry, hon."

"Oh, forget it, bub. Everybody burns a roux at one time or another. Just calm down and hand me some more bacon. It's not the end of the world."

When I see that worried look on his face, I let him fry the bacon to make him feel better, then I start over with the grease and flour and stir till the roux is a really beautiful light brown while Travis sings "Diggin' Up Bones."

"Smells great," Vernon says as he watches like a hawk and squeezes me again.

"Make yourself useful and hand me those vegetables one by one," I tell him, and by the time all the stuff is added and the mixture is ready to simmer for a couple of hours, I get this tingling all over and turn around to plant a big one smack on his lips, which taste like beer.

"I'm really sorry I let that burn," he says again.

"Oh, Vern, let's just forget about the roux and relax awhile," I say as I kinda grind against him right there in front of the stove.

Like I say, sometimes Vernon has to be in the right mood to play around, and when I realize how upset he is about messing up the roux and notice he's not being wild the way he can be, I take the bull by the horns, and pull him into the living room 'bout the time Travis breaks into "Look Heart, No Hands" again, and sit down in front of him, and undo the longhorn buckle on his jeans, and start to fool around, and all I can say is in a minute or so Vernon is chomping at the bit to get down to serious games—right there on my green plaid affinity sofa.

What's really nice is how considerate and loving Vernon can be after one of our romps—not like that geeky Lyman who just always got his kicks, then went to play one of his computer games, or fiddle around outside with his second-hand Hog, or something else stupid. I mean, I might be a pretty frisky woman, but after all, I do have feelings and like to be treated with affection and respect as much as the next gal. Here's a good example of how sweet Vernon can be. When we had finished making love on the sofa and got dressed, and I'd come back from stirring the gumbo, he wraps his arms around me again, and just holds me real tight, and says, "Sometimes, doll, I don't think I can get enough of you." Then he starts hinting at lots of other things.

"You know, I was just thinking how much easier it might be for you to do some of your cooking in my big kitchen."

"Are you serious, hon?" I asked while he sort of stroked my tummy under my blouse, which made me keep wanting to flex my stomach muscles.

"Sure, why not?" he said. "There's sure a hell of a lot more room over at the house, and you could bring some of your fancy pots and pans, and, best of all, I'd get to taste all that good stuff you fix."

"Aha!" I yelled. "Free meals is all you want!"

"Don't be nuts. And you could teach me a thing or two about cooking, and I could even help out on your jobs in my spare time—just like partners—and you'd relax more."

"Oh, stop worrying about me, bub," I said. "I'm healthy as an ox with energy to burn."

Then he got this kinda sad look on his face and started rubbing my arm real slow. "I also figure, Let, it might be good having you around the house more with me and Daisy. Know what I mean?"

That caught me off guard, then after a minute, I said, "Not really, Vern."

"Oh, you do know what I mean, Let," he went on. "Shit, I ain't no cottontail, but ever since Mona died . . . Don't you sometimes get lonesome too, here all by yourself with only the dogs to keep you company?"

I reached up and pushed his hair off his forehead and said, "Vernon Parrish, I can't imagine you ever being lonesome or unhappy a minute in your life."

Well, he sat real still, and stared off into space, then said, "That's 'cause you never had a daddy who lived inside a bottle of Old Crow, and told you you were good-for-nothing dumb, and used you for a whipping board when things didn't go right in the house."

I pulled myself up from his lap and looked him in the eyes. "Whatta you talking about?"

"Yeah, could get pretty bad," he went on in this real low voice. "Night after night when I was a kid. Sometimes I even had to run lock myself in my room if I said the wrong thing at supper and Daddy was soused and on his high horse. Where do you think I got this scar on my cheek?"

"You gotta be kiddin', Vern," I said in real shock.

"Yep, that's the way it was even up into middle school. Daddy could be a real bastard—especially when he'd get laid off at the lumber mill and then hit the bottle big-time."

"But what about your mama? Didn't she try to help?"

Vernon just laughed. "Mama try to help? You gotta understand that Daddy could do no wrong in Mama's eyes. Either that or she was scared to death of him as much as I was and would just start bawling and slug another shot of whiskey herself. But I always loved my mama—I really did. Problem was she just couldn't cross Daddy."

"But why didn't you tell somebody?"

"'Cause I was scared shitless, that's why. Finally did, though, one night when I forgot to empty the garbage, and Daddy took it out on my hide with a curtain rod till my arms were bleeding, and I ran as hard as I could to one of our neighbors down the street."

"So what'd they do?"

"A big stink. Cops, school principal, stuff in the Waco paper, and they told Daddy he'd be behind bars if he so much as laid hands on me again. After that, I pretty much kept my distance from Mama and Daddy best I could—though I really missed my mama. Good woman who did the best she could for me. My uncle Garth's the one who got me interested in computers and paid for me to go to Baylor for a year, but when I finished my training there, I was out of Waco for good—once and for all."

"Good God, Vern," I said as I gave him a big hug. "Why didn't you tell me this before?"

"What for? I just wanna forget it, and pretty much did after I sowed my oats in Houston, and landed this good job, and met Mona."

"So what about your parents today?"

"Haven't seen or talked to them in maybe fifteen years, but I know they're still at the same house in Waco, though Uncle Garth says poor Mama goes to AA and Daddy had a bad stroke and is in a wheelchair. Serves him right as far as I'm concerned."

"Oh, hon, you really shouldn't talk like that," I sort of mumbled. "I mean, he's your daddy, after all."

"Sure, you can say that, doll, 'cause you probably had a normal childhood like most people and didn't have to put up with any crap like that."

Yeah, I thought to myself, I had a real normal childhood I could tell him all about—chapter and verse. Best a youngster could wish for. Like Mama always saying it was the Lord's will for me to look like a mound of biscuit dough. And having to wear nothing but loose tanks and tent dresses from Sears and Kmart since other places didn't make junior jeans and skirts and blouses big enough to cover my fat. And listening to bullies calling me Miss Piggy, and Loretta Lard, and Moose behind my back. And not riding a bike like everybody else. And boys never asking me to two-step at the Valentine's Day Mad-Heart Dance in the gym. And finding a bottle of Slim-Fast at my place in the cafeteria. Yeah, growing up was a real picnic for me. But at least I had a sweet daddy who was nothing like this monster Vernon was describing.

Like what happened with Daddy at my high school graduation, something I'll never forget as long as I live. 'Bout the only thing I remember about the outdoor ceremony itself was the sweltering heat, and the way I was sweating in that heavy gown when I waddled up the steps to the platform to get my diploma, and how relieved I was to get in the air-conditioned gym afterwards for the refreshments and dancing. Not that I had a date like most of my classmates, or that I could expect to two-step with anybody except other wallflowers who always huddled together near the food and drinks at any school social like this. Oh, I hate to guess all the cruel remarks the other kids made when two fatties like me and Mary Jo Sykes got on the dance floor and twirled around to the Dixie Chicks belting over the loud speakers. And yeah, come to think of it, I'm sure some of the parents and teachers up in the bleachers must've felt a little sorry and embarrassed for any of us gals forced to dance with each other if we wanted to dance at all.

In any case, what I'll never forget in the clearest detail is that Madge Simpson, who was right up there herself in the plus-size department, was telling me and Josey O'Brian a dirty joke while we were eating some devil's food cake, and Clint Black—I remember exactly it was Clint Black—was singing when, all of a sudden, I heard over my shoulder, "Has my princess saved at least one dance for her old man?" It was Daddy in his good-looking gambler's jacket and longhorn string tie, and he was holding both arms open just waiting for me to get out of that heavy gown so we could two-step with everybody else reeling around the floor.

Now, I still can't say why so many fat people are such good dancers, but if anybody ever doubted it, all they had to do was see me and my daddy in action on that floor just the way we sometimes did at home when he'd had a few beers and was feeling good. Double turns, lots of twirls, fancy side steps—Daddy could do 'em all naturally, and lead me like a real pro, and when we did a few forward slides, we could've almost been dancing competition like on TV. Then we did some triple two-steps, and when we did those, I noticed a lot of other dancers starting to stand back and watch us, and before I knew it, some of my friends were actually clapping and egging us on. Of course by now sweat was just pouring out of every pore on Daddy's puffy red face, and I could feel my aqua tank clinging to my clammy skin, but we just kept on dancing to one song after the next, and the more we did our thing, the more people hooted and cheered and yelled, "Go, Loretta! Go, girl!"

Well, huffin' and puffin', Daddy finally pulled me close to him, and hugged me real tight, and said, "Princess, I guess we showed them kickers a thing or two 'bout two-steppin'." Why, even Mama and Gladys and some of the other parents and teachers up in the bleachers were applauding, and, to tell the truth, I don't think I ever felt so proud and respected in my whole life.

13

BEARS AND BATS

Yesterday afternoon, I got a real stern lecture from Dr. Ellis about not losing any more weight and how drinking lots of carbonated diet colas could stretch my stomach pouch. He also warned me to go easy on the beer and booze or I might get hooked on alcohol the way I was hooked on food, so I guess at least it's a good thing Lester don't allow no drinking on the job at Bluebird.

"Loretta," Dr. Ellis said, "your recovery and progress have been remarkable, but I really don't want to see you reduce much more—not if you intend to stay healthy and avoid additional medical problems and skin contouring."

For a minute, I thought I was going to panic. "But I gotta reach 130, Dr. Ellis. That's my target."

"Why?" he asked while he tapped his fingers on the desk. "I can tell by the figures that you've begun to plateau, which means your body's telling you to stop. Don't push it, young lady. You've come too far."

"But sometimes I still feel so fat, Dr. Ellis, and sometimes I worry my boyfriend thinks I'm too fat."

"You're not, Loretta. That's all in your head—just the image you have of yourself."

I felt like I wanted to cry, and asked, "But what if I start gaining again, Doctor?"

"You probably won't, not unless you revert to bad habits and stretch the pouch. And that's something you'll have to watch carefully the rest of your life. By now, Loretta, you know the rules."

"And I shouldn't drink alcohol?"

"I didn't say that, Loretta. I only said that some patients with your condition can convert the compulsion to overeat into alcohol dependency. Plus, alcohol is loaded with calories." That's exactly the way he put it—in just those words.

"And all the exercise?" I asked next.

"That's important. I know you don't like it, but remember that your body is still changing, and common sense should tell you that exercise can only help tighten up muscles and skin and keep weight off."

Well, to tell the truth, I thought Dr. Ellis was pretty uppity this time, and I gotta say I was real upset when I left the office. Oh, I'm sure he knows what he's talking about, and has my best interests at heart, and all that stuff, and yeah, I do respect the man since he's seen me through a lot. But I don't understand why he has to try to scare hell out of me. And I don't think he has any concept of how important Vernon is to me now. And, believe you me, I gotta think long and hard about giving up my goal of 130. I know what I'm doing. I'm not dumb.

In any case, I didn't have much time to dwell on it since it was Friday and Vernon and I had planned to meet Mary Jane and Sam and another couple at Waugh Bridge to watch the bats fly out before we showed up for my gig at Ziggy's. Rosemary's one of the gals I work out with at Body Tech, and she's got a new boyfriend from Shreveport named Bear Dillard who'd never heard of our bat colony under the bridge and wanted to witness one of the nightly spectacles we Houstonians have seen more times than we can count. Personally, I find the filthy creatures pretty gross—thousands and thousands of Mexican free-tailed bats leaving their crevices in the bridge, and screeching, and whirling through the air in search of insects and Lord knows what else to eat. But most others, Vernon included, find it all fascinating, so who was I to be a killjoy if Rosemary's date wanted to see the goddamn bats.

Rosemary works at CVS over on Montrose and used to be even fatter than I was—over 300, she says. Went for a full gastric bypass at some clinic up in Dallas about the same time I had my surgery, so we got lots of war stories to share when we jog and lift weights together. Only thing is she ended up with strictures in her esophagus, and bowel blockages, and lots of other complications afterward, and because she has to be more careful, she's still a pretty big girl at about 180. Of course, like me, Rosemary also loves to cook, so what I suspect is she sneaks more tastes of this and that than she lets on.

"Any problem with your guy?" I asked her just the other day.

"Are you kiddin'," she said without blinking an eye. "Wait'll you see Bear. Real name's Barney, but everybody calls him Bear, and shit, honey, Bear could pass for a baby elephant, so I guess I now look like Madonna to him."

Of course I explained again my touchy secret from Vernon and made her promise never to let the cat out of the bag, but I gotta say she wasn't exaggerating about Bear Dillard—who lives up to his nickname lock, stock, and barrel. There he stood with Rosemary against a rail of the bat colony observation deck with a can of beer talking to Mary Jane and Sam when we arrived. Maybe a solid 250 pounds, wearing a red trucker hat, a ponytail and lots of bushy dark hair on his arms and creeping up the back of his thick neck, bulging bug eyes, puffy cheeks, the deepest voice I ever heard, and a hand that felt like a giant claw when I shook it. Frankly, I couldn't imagine what Rosemary saw in the guy.

"So, this is the little lady who's been trying to become the next Miss Texas" were the first words to come out of his big mouth.

I almost froze with Vernon standing right there, but he seemed too busy shaking the man's hand to think much about the remark. Rosemary glared at Bear and had this really mad look on her face, but I still could have murdered her.

"Rosey tells me you in computers," Bear then said to Vernon after taking another slug of beer.

"Yeah," Vernon said. "What you up to, sport?"

"Industrials. Worth Industrials. Drill strings, tungsten bits, mud pumps—shit, we manufacture 'bout everything they need on them oil rigs over in Frio and Atascosa counties."

"Yeah?" was all Vernon said, and it was pretty obvious he didn't have any idea what Bear was talking about.

"Hey, where're my manners?" Bear said as he unzipped the lid on a plastic cooler of beer near his feet. He then let out this loud laugh. "We don't go nowhere without our suds. You guys want a pop?"

Mary Jane and Sam wiggled their cans to show they were okay for the moment, but what Vernon did was pull a pint of whiskey out of his jacket pocket, say "We gotta have more for-tification than that against those flying varmints," and hand me the bottle to take a big sip.

Across the platform, another couple stood with two kids, but we didn't pay them much mind.

"Man, this is friggin' wild—bats!" Bear kind of bellowed like he was already smashed. "Rosey tells me the bastards fly up from this bridge every night of the year, and I couldn't believe my ears."

"Every night about now at sunset—except when the

temps drop down below about 50," Sam told him. "Then they stay home."

"Everybody in Houston calls it the emergence, and they scare hell out of me," Mary Jane piped in just as she pulled down on her tight tank top with a devil logo, then reached for another beer.

"Oh, hon, you know they're pretty harmless and won't get in your hair or anything spooky like that," I said.

"Son of a bitch," Bear muttered. "Aren't the little bastards supposed to carry rabies and shit like that?"

"Yeah," Vernon said, "but everybody knows not to touch a grounded bat. They'll bite, then you could be in a fix."

"And everybody knows . . ." I started to say, when we heard Rosemary scream.

"Look! Y'all look! Here they come! Listen to 'em squeak. Look! They're gettin' ready."

"Well, I'll be goddamned," Bear yelled as more and more bats dropped out of the crevices of the bridge and swooshed up in the air and headed for the bayou in the direction of downtown. "Go to it, you little suckers!"

"Hush up, Bear," Rosemary said as she tugged on his arm. "They don't like lotta noise, and if they get disoriented, they go crazy."

Bear just let out another loud whoop, then swung his arm back and hurled a beer can at a big cluster of bats, which made them fly every which way and caused the man across the way with the kids to shout, "Hey, you folks, cut the crap."

"Man, you lost your mind?" Vernon sort of snapped at Bear just as Mary Jane screamed and dropped her beer and pulled her jersey up over her head like she was terrified.

"Okay, bud, okay," Bear said. "Sorry. Sorry, you guys. Just having a little bit of fun."

"Calm down, honey," I said to Mary Jane. "You know they're not gonna get in your hair. Tell her so, Sam."

Sam laughed and hugged her real tight and said, "Come on, doll, they're scared of you as much as you are of them. Everybody knows that."

"I hate 'em," Mary Jane says.

By now, the sun was almost set and we could see this huge, dark cloud of bats flying away toward town and hear their squeaky sounds. Vernon takes another gulp of whiskey and hands me the bottle. All Bear does is stand there with his arm around Rosemary, and stare up at the sky with his big head kinda weaving, and say, "Son of a bitch" over and over. Funny, but all I could wonder was whether she felt fat to him.

14

TRASH

I figured Bear was trash the minute I saw him. What I didn't
know was just how bad he was till we got to Ziggy's and I left
the five of them at the bar to go up and play the first set. Of
course we'd all had a little bit to drink at the bat bridge and on
our way to the club, but what I didn't know till Rosemary told
me later on was that Bear also sniffed some coke in the truck
and was already pretty ploughed by the time everybody started
ordering margaritas. Vernon don't have much patience with
drugs, and I don't either. Besides, I've heard a few scary stories
about bariatric patients turning to drugs, and I want no part of
that scene.

In any case, still weren't that many customers at Ziggy's
that early at night since the bull room's closed on Fridays, but
Buzzy told us in the band he expected a big dancing crowd by
eight and for us to beef up the country and go easy on R & B
till the tables began to fill and Venus came on. Buzzy's the club
manager. He's also a husky full-blooded Comanche from up in
Lubbock, and believe you me, Buzzy's all professional and
doesn't take any crap from anybody. He's even laid the law
down that nobody in the band is allowed to dance with customers even if we're not playing a set. Nobody's ever asked

him exactly why, but I'm sure Buzzy's got his reasons. Buzzy respects me and has seen me through a lot, and I'm crazy about him.

So we start off with "Finger on the Trigger," then I do some solo in "Nobody's Fool" with backup from Tricksy on keyboard and Bobby on double bass, and Matt really shows his stuff on acoustic guitar in "Wicked Ways." First set goes really well with lots of applause and not many people in the crowd screaming "Bubbles," but when we take a break and I join my gang at the bar for a beer, right off the bat I hear Bear bad-mouthing Joey the bartender about the margaritas. Voice already shaky and slurred, and he's puffing on a cigarillo.

"And what's that orange juice shit you keep puttin' in?" he's asking real loud like he's some world authority on margaritas.

"Just a touch," Joey says as he pushes his cowboy hat off his forehead in the sexy way he does and rings something up on the computer. "Helps the color and sweetens 'em up a little."

"Don't need no sweetening, pal. Triple Sec's sweet enough. Any kicker knows that."

"We think the juice rounds out the liqueur, and nobody complains," Joey says.

". . . rounds out the liqueur," Bear mimics him in a high pitch, then turns toward Rosemary and Sam on his right. "Well, just listen to that. Cowboy here says the friggin' OJ rounds out the liqueur. Rounds out the liqueur, mind you."

"Cool it down, bud," Joey warns him like he means it. "This ain't no honky-tonk, and you're gettin' out of line."

'Bout this time, Mary Jane gets up and excuses herself to go to the little girls' room. Bear now has both elbows on the bar and is sort of weaving to and fro, and blowing smoke at Joey, and pointing to his drink.

"Listen, cowboy, goddamn margarita's got four things: Tequila, lime juice, Triple Sec, salt, and no friggin' orange juice, and when me and my friends are paying eight big ones a pop, we expect a real margarita without all the shit. Tell him, computer boy."

I'm now standing behind Vernon squeezing his shoulders, and when he hears Bear make that remark, he leans down and says, "Just let it go, sport. No need for a commotion."

Then Rosemary, who's sitting on Bear's left, pulls on his arm, and has this embarrassed look on her face, and says, "Sweetie, maybe you've had a little too much to drink."

Bear pulls down the bill of his cap and acts like he didn't hear her and says, "Who says I'm causing a commotion? I ain't causing no commotion. Just wanna know why this here poke has to fuck up a good margarita with OJ."

"Okay, Bear," I finally say—and I'm pretty mad. "I gotta work in this goddamn place, so would you please cut the shit and just drop it and let Joey do his job?"

Bear snaps his head around at me, and I can tell how glassy and watery his big bug eyes are and see his head sort of reeling. I also notice Joey waving his hand in the air and looking in the direction of the bull room.

"So, the next Miss Texas with the new bod wants me to drop it," Bear blurts out in his deep voice even though Rosemary keeps yanking on his arm and repeating, "Hush up, for God's sake, honey." He then picks up his drink, and pours it in the ashtray till it overflows on the bar, and says to me, "There, little lady, is that dropping it enough? That's what I think of the margaritas in this joint."

For a minute I think Vernon is going to get off his stool and slug the guy, but then I see Buzzy come up behind Bear and hear him say, "You folks gotta problem here? These your friends, Loretta?"

"Yeah, we gotta problem, a big problem," Bear says before I can answer. "This cowboy behind the bar's fuckin' up the margaritas with fuckin' orange juice."

Buzzy notices the mess Joey's sponging up on the bar and

says, "Sorry, bud, you don't like our margaritas, but if you're gonna talk and behave like that, I'm gonna have to ask you to leave."

"And who the fuck are you, wise ass?" Bear grunts as Rosemary gets up and moves to the side and looks like she's gonna cry.

"Manager, and we run a respectable club here."

Bear takes a puff on his stogy and blows smoke directly in Buzzy's face, which is all it takes for Buzzy to grab the cigarillo, stomp it out on the floor, and say, "Okay, friend, you're drunk and way out of line, so why don't you get out—pronto?"

By this time, the couple next to Rosemary knows trouble is brewing and they begin to slide off their stools, but before them and Rosemary can get out of the way, Bear staggers up and shoves Buzzy hard with both hands and bellows, "Nobody throws me out of no motherfuckin' bar." Then, when Sam tries to hold Bear back, Bear shoves him too, and knocks him to the floor, and causes people at tables to begin staring. Next, Joey jumps over the bar, and Vernon's helping Sam up, and before I know it there's this big brawl with Bear slinging fists and everybody trying to restrain him. Now, Bear's big as an ox and strong as a bull. But he was also smashed out of his gourd, and Buzzy's no minor weight himself, so for one split second when the guys have the lug's arms, Buzzy draws back and slugs him one in the face and knocks him almost out cold on the floor.

"Get him outta here, and don't ever bring him back," Buzzy tells Sam and Vernon. So they grab Bear under his hairy arms and sort of drag him out by the exit door to the parking lot. Then Buzzy says to me, "Sweetheart, you better pick your friends more carefully and not give the place a bad name," which really upset me.

Of course by this time people are really gawking and mumbling things, but Buzzy fixes his string tie, and waves his hands in the air, and yells, "Excitement's over, folks. Drink up and let's get dancing." Then Mary Jane meanders back from the bathroom, and sees Rosemary crying, and asks, "What's wrong? Where're the guys?" just like nothing happened.

"We hope putting Bear to sleep out in the truck," I say.

"What'd I miss?" Mary Jane asks.

"Oh, Loretta, I'm just mortified," Rosemary sobs into a paper napkin. "Can't imagine what got into Bear."

I put my arm around her shoulder and said, "Little too much to drink, for one thing, but we all have our bad nights, don't we? Forget it, hon."

"Come on, doll, let's get rolling again," Buzzy tells me. "Venus is up, and the crowd's ready for you to show your stuff."

I finish off my brew and am just tucking my sequined pony tee in my jeans when I hear some blowbag close by holler, "Yeah, go to it, Bubbles baby!" So what I did was walk directly over to the table, and put my hands on my hips, and stare at the guy real hard, and say, "Listen, buster, Bubbles don't play here anymore, and it so happens my name is Loretta. Get it?" I also thanked my heavenly stars that Vernon wasn't back to hear the crack, though, even if he did, I doubt he'd have caught on.

"Gotta request for 'Sky Is Crying,'" I heard Venus telling everybody while I snapped on my sax chord and wet the reed real good with my tongue. Venus is black as the ace of spades, and thin as a razor blade, and has this gutsy smoker's voice that makes an audience melt, and when I saw she was wearing this bright, short, low-cut silver dress that barely covered her big boobs and showed off her curvy ass, I knew the crowd would go wild. Me and Venus and Tricksy sometimes go next door to the diner after we've wrapped up a gig and don't have any guys waiting for us, and what really beats me is the way Venus can knock off two or three jelly doughnuts and a root beer shake and never gain one goddamn pound. Know what she says?

"Child, the trick is to smoke a pack of Camel Lights a day, and besides that, what I put on at the table with my friends I take off in the sack with my man." Yeah, sure.

Anyway, when Venus did her vocals and we played some light swing, I noticed Vernon and Rosemary at first just sat at the bar and talked and watched while Mary Jane made poor Sam two-step all over the dance floor. Of course I figured Rosemary must have been pretty down in the dumps over Bear's acting up, so, to tell the truth, I guess it was a good thing she had somebody as nice and understanding as Vernon to listen to her problems. After all, like I say, Rosemary's still a pretty chubby gal despite the eating regimen she's now forced to follow and all the exercise we do, so it's not like she's gonna have many guys much better than Bear Dillard exactly begging her to dance. Also on my mind was whether she might slip up with the margaritas and spill any beans to Vernon about why we go to the gym so much.

Lord knows, I never worry about friends like Rosemary being a threat when it comes to Vernon, but I gotta admit I couldn't help but feel a little envious when the two of them finally got up and began slow dancing, and then Mary Jane grabbed Vernon when Venus broke into "Buy Myself a Chance," and then they switched partners with another couple on the floor for the next swing dance. Oh, I know I can't expect Vernon to just twiddle his thumbs while I'm working and everybody else is kicking up their heels and having fun, but, yeah, when you're as crazy about a guy as I am about Vernon, it's only natural to get this achy feeling in the pit of your stomach when you have to watch him wrapped up in some other gal's arms. Of course I love to dance, but even if Buzzy allowed us to when we take a break from a set, I really couldn't be rude to my friends by spending the whole time dancing with Vernon. Maybe it's all just because I never had reason to be jealous over a guy before Vernon came along.

15

ANIMAL COPS

Thought I'd seen everything there is to see when it comes to animal cruelty: starved, half-dead horses with nothing but heads and rib cages, cats with no teeth or a missing eye from infections left untreated, roosters shaved and clipped to help them fight, dogs with embedded chain collars or chemical burns over half their bodies, stab wounds, claws grown back into paws—routine stuff we deal with every day at the shelter. But what me and Sally were exposed to this past Saturday now has to top the list of atrocities and still makes me sick.

All started with an anonymous call reporting some guys dressed in militia outfits down at a farmhouse near the Space Center shooting dogs for target practice. Most cases we can handle as uniformed animal cops in our SPCA squad cars, and we do get some good basic training in kickboxing if we ever need to protect ourselves. But when something that sounds this grotesque and dangerous comes in, we don't take chances and call armed Houston law enforcement for backup since we're never armed with weapons.

What we found was not so much a house as a dilapidated shack hidden in some woods with a dirt yard and no shrubbery and two pickups parked out front, and when me and Sally got out of the car, we could hear a ball game on TV blaring through a window and some yelping voices. Backup stayed in their unmarked car behind ours the way we're trained to position ourselves in this type of investigation, and when I banged on the door, a middle-aged guy with a bushy beard wearing camouflage fatigues opened it and looked surprised. He had a can of beer in one hand, and I could hear a gal inside screaming, "Who's out there, Jake?"

"Sir, we're from the Houston SPCA and would like to talk to you about a complaint we received," I said very officially.

"Houston what?" he asked.

"The Houston SPCA—Society for the Prevention of Cruelty to Animals."

He stared at me real hard and said, "Yeah, so whatcha up to?"

"Like I said, we got a report about some dogs being mistreated, and we're here to investigate. Could we come in?"

"We ain't got no dogs, lady, so you must got the wrong address."

"Sir, can we just step inside and talk with you a minute and look around?" Sally asked in her patient way.

"Jake, who in hell ya talkin' to?" the woman inside yelled again, and when I looked over the man's shoulder, I could see what looked like an assault weapon hanging by its strap on a nail on a far wall.

"Listen, lady, we don't know nothing about no dogs, and we don't want no trouble," he said.

About this time, another guy dressed in the same kind of outfit came up behind the other man and said, "What's up, Jake?"

"These people here about some dogs, and I told 'em we don't know nothing 'bout no dogs."

"Listen, sir," Sally said, "it's our job to check out any abuse allegations, so if you would just allow us to look around, perhaps we could get to the bottom of this."

"You got a warrant?" the other man asked.

"No," I said, "but we can get one in a snap if you refuse to cooperate."

"Then get off our property till ya do," Jake sort of growled as a gal about my age wearing a stained yellow tee and with pimples on her forehead suddenly appeared and said, "What's going on around here, honey?"

"Just let me handle this, Peppy," he said.

I noticed her gawking at the insignias on the arms of our jackets, and she looked a little scared.

"Are these women cops or something, Jake?" she then asked in a shaky voice, and I figured she must be the guy's wife.

"Naw, they're from some animal pound asking about dogs, and I'm telling 'em we don't know nothing 'bout no dogs."

"Are you in trouble, Jake?"

"Just shut up, Peppy, and let me handle this," he said in a mean way.

"I warned you and Willie." She then almost started to cry. "Ya can't say I didn't warn you and Willie about playing around."

"I told ya, Peppy, to keep ya damn trap closed," he yelled at her. "We don't know about any goddamn dogs, and we ain't done nothing illegal, so just keep ya trap shut."

We're all trained at the shelter to take no chances if we feel the least bit threatened on an investigation. Not that me and Sally are not both big and strong enough to kickbox and defend ourselves if things get out of hand—especially Sally, who's still well over 200 pounds and knows exactly how to grab a lug from behind, and put her wrist up against his Adam's apple, and choke off his oxygen supply. Yeah, there are some advantages to being a fat animal cop, but we don't look for trouble, so when it became pretty obvious we could have a serious problem with these people, I pushed the button on the remote beeper in my jacket, which brought the two uniformed police officers in the other car over in a jiffy.

"Show 'em the warrant," I told Ernie, who held out the folder for them to see and said, "I suggest you folks cooperate with these reps and step aside."

The woman was now running her fingers through her frizzy black hair, and said, "Are we being arrested, Jake?"

"You got no right to barge in here like this," the man called Willie shouted as we pushed our way through the door and began inspecting the three rooms littered with beer cans and food containers and dirty dishes and clothes.

"What are you doing with these guns?" Ernie then asked the men when he noticed two assault weapons hanging on the wall.

"Huntin'," Jake said. "Snipes, prairie chickens, rabbits. Nothing wrong with that, is there? We got licenses."

"My buddy here told you we ain't got no dogs in this house," Willie said to me and Sally after we'd inspected the rooms.

"We're gonna look around outside," I then told Ernie and Frank. "You fellas mind keeping an eye on things in here?"

"Goddammit, lady, we told ya we don't own no dogs or any other animals 'round here," Jake shouted again while Peppy just sat in a torn armchair sort of sobbing with her head in her hands like she was scared to death.

Well, for a few minutes we thought he might have been telling the truth when we found no dogs or pens or other evidence around the outside. But then Sally noticed a ditch about twenty-five feet away from the shack and some kind of steel rod stuck in the ground, and when we walked up to the edge and looked down, what we saw were two bloody dead dogs with darts in their bodies and riddled with bullet wounds. Both of the poor creatures still had collars and ropes around their necks that cut deep in the flesh, and it was pretty obvious they'd been tied to the rod to run around wildly while they were being darted and shot at. The most sickening sight was one dog with an eye hanging from its socket.

"Holy shit," was all I could mumble, and I thought Sally was going to throw up.

"You and Frank better get out here and get a look at this," I said to Ernie on the beeper phone. "Bring the two bastards with you, and be sure to keep 'em away from those rifles on the wall."

"Son of a bitch," Ernie said calmly when I pointed down in the ditch. "You boys care to explain this."

"Man, they ain't nobody's dogs," Jake kind of grunted. "Just a couple of skinny strays roaming around that needed to be put outta their misery."

"And make for some good target practice and fun with metal darts and rifles, right?" Sally said in a really angry voice.

"Jake, I said you and Willie shouldn't've brought 'em back here," the woman sobbed while pulling on his arm.

"Just shut up ya goddamn mouth, Pep," he bellowed at her. "There ain't no law in the state of Texas against shooting dogs roaming around like wild coyotes and causin' trouble."

"Buster, that's where you're dead wrong," I almost exploded, "and especially when the dogs have collars and have been tied up before being shot. Don't it matter a hoot to you that the dogs most likely have owners?"

Sally just glared at the two men with more hate in her eyes than I'd ever seen, and for once lost her cool. "You jerks are sick—really sick—and we'll do everything we can to see you two bastards prosecuted for this."

"Oh, come on, lady, it's just two lousy dogs," Willie chimed in. "Guys over at the Center and everywhere else do it all the time."

"Lousy dogs!" I then yelled, though I really was trying to stay in control the way we're trained to do under pressure like this. "Whatta you mean, lousy dogs? Only scum like you could torture helpless animals like this, and it so happens you've committed a crime—a bad crime."

"Okay, let's everybody calm down," Ernie said as he un-hooked a pair of handcuffs from his belt and looked at the two men. "You boys got some explaining to do, and we're gonna have to take you both into custody and see what a judge has to say about this."

"I warned you and Willie," the woman began screaming again, and I noticed Frank kept a hand on his holster while Ernie cuffed the two creeps and pointed in the direction of the squad car. "You can't say I didn't warn ya, Jake."

Me and Sally got back in our car and filled out a report Ernie and Frank had to sign. Then I told this Peppy we'd have to confiscate the two guns and for her to stay put in case we had to question her later on. And then came the worst part when we had to bag the two dead dogs and put them in the trunk as evidence.

"Beats all," Sally muttered in disgust as she lit up a cigarette in the car, and blew smoke out the widow, and said she might call in sick on her shift later on at Country Foodarama. "Makes you wanna puke, and makes you wanna quit this kind of work, don't it?"

"A fine and maybe a month probation—that's probably all the bastards'll get," I said.

"And now we gotta try to track down the owners. Really makes you wanna puke."

"Know what scares me most?" I said. "There's nothing I'd love to do more than take that new gun of mine and blow both their goddamn heads off—point-blank. No questions, no trial, no judge—just shoot 'em execution-style."

Of course I didn't shoot nobody, and instead tried to forget the horror me and Sally had witnessed by flipping on the Food Network when I got home and giving Sugar and Spice a few extra treats and lots of attention. Rachael Ray was in the middle of making small lemon bars, which reminded me almost immediately of a new recipe for lemon drop cookies I'd been wanting to try and maybe serve at an upcoming children's birthday party I had scheduled.

Like I say, cooking can be like therapy for me when I'm real upset, and no sooner had I grabbed a bag of lemon drop candy in the cabinet, wrapped the nuggets in a towel, and begun beating them to bits with a hammer than I calmed down and concentrated on making the batter just right. Butter, sugar, grated lemon rind, heavy cream, an egg, flour, baking powder and salt, the crushed candy—the ingredients couldn't have been simpler. What I wondered about was whether the candy would melt during the baking, and I got my answer after the cookies had been in the oven about twelve minutes, and I finally bit into a cooled one, and noticed a slight crunch that was one of the most wonderful sensations I'd ever experienced. Yeah, the cookies were out of this world, and I knew kids would love 'em, but since I personally like most of my cookies to be kinda chewy, I did decide then and there that the next time I baked a batch, I'd test the texture after only ten minutes of baking—or till just the edges of the cookies browned. I also decided these cookies could give Miss Rachael Ray's lemon bars a good run for their money, and that they should have me on that program doing something a little different. I mean, anybody can make ordinary lemon bars. My only real problem was the yield on that recipe was three dozen cookies and, I swear, I could have eaten a dozen without blinking an eye.

16

BIG HAIR GLAMOUR

I really should have two good reasons to celebrate today. First, the scales said I've lost 4 more pounds this past month, which is a small miracle 'cause of all the beer I've been swigging lately and the food I had to taste for that child's birthday party I catered last week at a really cool Mexican house over in Pasadena. Second, it's my own thirty-seventh birthday, hard as that is for me to believe. Sally and Mary Jane sent funny cards, and Vernon and Billy Po and about everybody else except Mama and Gladys say I don't look a day over thirty. Yeah, I know they're mostly puttin' on to make me feel good, and Billy Po would say I looked like Paris Hilton if he thought there was any chance for more fun and games, which there's not. But to tell the truth, when I streak my new short hair a little bit, and put on lip gloss, and wear something like my felt poodle skirt and lace-up denim vest and the hornback lizard boots I got over at City Buckaroo on Navigation, I gotta say I can look pretty damn glamorous. Or so I thought till the humiliating incident with Vernon at the Riviera two nights ago.

Of course Vernon wouldn't have even known I was having a birthday if Sally hadn't told him when he dropped by the shelter the other day to pick up some heartworm pills for

Daisy. So happened I'd been called out on a rescue case and couldn't have been more surprised when I got back and saw Vernon sitting there at the front desk just chatting with Sally decked out in her turquoise muumuu and looking at the computer screen.

"Well, look what the cat dragged in," I remember saying real sassy-like. "Nobody told me we'd ordered a new computer installed by Houston's number one expert."

Sally laughed, then Vernon said, "Naw, nothing that unimportant. Heartworm pills. Didn't know a thing about heartworm pills till Hank mentioned it on the job this morning."

"Oh, you dope, everybody knows about heartworm pills for dogs," I said as I stood behind him and squeezed his shoulders. "I could have brought you a goddamn package, for heaven's sake."

He looked up at me with this big grin and said, "Then I wouldn't have heard about the big secret."

For a second, I felt my heart thump, then, when I saw Sally smiling, it dawned on me he was referring to my birthday.

"Loud mouth," I kidded Sally.

"What's the big deal?" he asked.

"I hate birthdays, that's what," I said.

"Oh, honey, I was telling Vernon that you don't look a day over thirty," Sally said, "and he agrees."

I still wondered why Vernon hadn't simply called me about the pills on my cell instead of blowing his lunch break to come by the shelter, but I didn't give it much more thought when I walked him out to his truck and he grabbed me around the waist and said, "I think this calls for something special, gal. Sorry I gotta work Thursday night, but if you can get Suzy to sub for you at Bluebird tomorrow, I was just thinking: How would you like to doll up and celebrate a little early at the Riviera?"

Well, a feather could have knocked me down. "You don't

mean that highfalutin Riviera over in Tanglewood where all the big hairs go?"

"I do."

"Yipes, honey, I don't know. Isn't that a little rich for our blood?"

"Nope," he said. "My money's as clean as Mr. Hunt's and all the rest of them gusher big shots. And when my gal has a birthday, she deserves the royal treatment."

Like I said, nobody ever better accuse Vernon Parrish of not having style. I mean, it's no news that the Riviera is the best and snazziest and most expensive restaurant in Houston. Dressy River Oaks people, glamorous big hairs, valet parking, continental cuisine—I've always read about it in the society section of the paper, and seen pictures, and heard ladies at Salon Magic and catering functions talking. But never in a million years did I dream I was good enough to be invited to actually eat there—and by a beau I'm so crazy about, no less.

Well, I don't think I've ever been that excited in my life, but what's more important is I decided then and there I was gonna order exactly what I wanted to eat for once, and bite the bullet, and finally tell Vernon all about my weight and the surgery and Mama and Gladys and just pray it didn't gross him out. No more secrets. No more lying. No more bull. Just the awful truth. I also figured I might even show him my fat picture if he didn't look too disgusted. I mean, I'm not dumb, and the way things were going, he was bound to find out about my past one way or the other, and, like they say, I knew I was on borrowed time.

Clothes are now real important to me, and I'm learning more and more about different designers and styles and fabrics and what have you. So I put on my best Macy's floral halter dress with a plunging V-front and my tassled midcalf boots. Vernon looked like a real prince in his bronze microsuede blazer and chambray shirt with pearl buttons and his snake boots, and when we pulled up in front in his Cherokee right at seven, I felt like the Queen of England when the boy opened my door for me and said, "Good evening, madam," and handed Vernon the valet ticket. Then another boy in a black and white uniform pushed the big wooden restaurant door open, and standing there in this marble vestibule behind a tall desk was a much older man with a tiny mustache wearing a tuxedo. He reminded me of some famous actor or another I'd seen in an old movie. But that's when the problem started.

"And what name, sir?" he asked Vernon in what sounded like some foreign accent as he looked down at a book, then at me kinda snootily.

"Parrish—with two *r*'s. Vernon Parrish."

"Ah yes, Mr. Parrish. Reservation for two at seven. Smoking."

"Naw, nonsmoking," Vernon corrected him. "We don't smoke. I told them that on the phone when they asked."

The man sort of frowned. "Here it says smoking, sir, and we're quite careful about that."

"I told 'em nonsmoking," Vernon repeated.

"I see," the man kinda mumbled. "We'll try to handle that, but there's also another matter I must bring up. You see, Mr. Parrish, we have a jacket and tie dress code at this restaurant."

Vernon looked real surprised. "Nobody told me anything about a tie when I called."

"Yes, that's always been our policy at the Riviera, sir. Jacket and tie. But if you'd like to step over to the cloak room, we do keep a few neckties for customers like yourself."

Vernon didn't say anything at first, but, boy, I could tell he was getting his dander up.

"I don't wanna wear nobody else's tie," he said.

"I'm sorry, sir, but it is our house policy, and I hope you understand."

Vernon crossed his arms over his chest the way he does

when his dander's up, and stared at the man a long time, then said, "Listen, mister, you oughta tell people about this when they make a reservation. Now, I ain't gonna cause a ruckus or anything, and I'll put on your tie, but I wanna tell you that if it wasn't this pretty little lady's birthday, I'd tell you exactly what you could do with your goddamn tie."

"I understand, Mr. Parrish, and I do apologize for the mis-understanding and inconvenience," the man said just as he no-ticed an older couple come through the door and rushed over to sort of bow and shake hands and say something real quiet to them. The other man was wearing a dark suit with a puffy red handkerchief in his jacket pocket, and the woman had on a very expensive-looking navy dress, and was wearing pearls and a big ring that was probably a diamond, and looked like she'd just stepped out of the beauty parlor. Kind of people who go to the Houston Symphony and the opera and things like that, I figured. For a minute, I could have sworn they were staring at me and Vernon like we were creeps or something, which made me real nervous. Then they were led directly into the dining room and seated at one of the first booths, and I noticed the woman looking around and kind of clicking her fingers in every direction like she knew everybody in the restaurant and was waving.

I gotta say the striped necktie made Vernon look like a jerk, and after I caught a glimpse of some of the other people in the dining room dressed like real squares, I started to won-der if my outfit wasn't maybe too risqué.

"Would you two like to have a drink till your table is ready?" the man with the moustache then asked as he pointed to a small area in one corner of the vestibule with a bar and two cocktail tables.

"How long will that be?" Vernon asked in his frank way.

"Oh, I really couldn't say, sir, but we'll do our best. We're very busy this evening."

"Doesn't a reservation mean anything around here?" Vernon kept on.

"Yes, indeed, sir, but with this little mix-up about the smoking table, I regret I'll have to ask you and madam to wait till I can work you into the nonsmoking section."

That's exactly the way he talked—"indeed," and "I regret," and "madam," and huffy stuff like that—and I don't mind saying it made me feel out of place. Anyway, me and Vernon do like we're told and go sit at the bar since the little tables were taken up by couples who sounded smashed and were either waiting like us or had already finished dinner and were having more drinks and a good time. I order a bourbon and splash and Vernon gets his favorite Cutty on the rocks, and we're talking about maybe going with Mary Jane and Sam to an Astros game on Saturday when I suddenly think I overhear the middle-aged woman with big bluish hair at one table kinda snicker and whisper, "Buffalo Bill and Annie Oakley out on the town" to the real skinny woman next to her wearing a fancy brown chiffon dress and a huge, shiny gold bracelet. Both of them are obviously in their cups, and when I cock my eye, I notice the thin one glancing at my legs and boots or both.

". . . doesn't miss many meals." She thinks she's whispering, though I can make out every word of that crack.

Vernon soon orders another round and just keeps talking about whether maybe we should call Sally about the game on Saturday, and the stupid necktie policy, and how we're not gonna wait all night to be seated, but I'm still trying to catch what all the two women are saying while their husbands go on about sports cars real loud.

". . . JC Penney special, I'd say. Full-figure department." Miss Chiffon now snickers very distinctly like she's totally unaware of how her voice is carrying.

"More like Kmart, my dear." The other one giggles as she

glances in our direction again and sips her drink real prissy-like.

"Where's that guy?" Vernon asks as he watches more people being led into the dining room.

". . . downhill—way downhill. And next it'll be the Mexicans," I hear Miss Big Hair say next.

Now I really did feel embarrassed and mad and would have loved nothing more than to march over to that table and slap those two women to kingdom come. But then the man with the moustache saw Vernon waving, and I heard Vernon say, "Hey, bud, we been here half an hour, and who're all those people going in before us?"

"Those guests have reservations, sir."

"So do we, and I wanna know what in hell is going on around here."

"I thought I explained, sir, about the smoking table mix-up."

Vernon stood up, and I noticed all four at the cocktail table now turned and stared. "Yeah, bud, you explained, and we've tried to cooperate, but all I know is nobody's coming out of that dining room and you keep taking new people in there before us. So what's up?"

"They're all nonsmoking, sir, and have reservations. I'm doing my best."

"Okay, so we'll eat in the smoking section if that's all you got," Vernon said. "We're tired of waiting."

The man had his hands behind his back and his feet were shuffling back and forth. "Oh, I'm sorry, sir, but when your smoking table opened up, and a gentleman informed me he would like to enjoy an after-dinner cigar with his coffee, I seated the couple at your table."

"So why can't we have the nonsmoking table he was supposed to have?" Vernon asked.

"Because that was a four-top, and I need that extra seating on a busy night like this."

"A what?"

"A four-top, sir. The table seats four persons, and you're only two."

Vernon stood there for a second like he was confused without uttering a word, then said, "Listen, mister, all I know is we had a reservation that you screwed up, and I put on your goddamn tie, and we've been patient, and it's now pretty obvious we're being given the old runaround in no uncertain terms."

"I beg your pardon, sir."

"The old runaround. You know, bud, the song and dance routine."

"I'm sorry, sir."

I then tugged on Vernon's sleeve and said, "Vern, let's just leave. It's not worth this mess."

"The hell we are. I wanna talk to the owner or manager of this joint."

"Please keep your voice down, sir," the man said, and I noticed everybody at both tables were now gawking at us. "It so happens I am the manager."

"Oh, you are," Vernon said. "Well, all I gotta say is this is one hell of a way to run a restaurant."

I pulled on his arm again, and got down off my stool, and said, "Vern, it's not worth it, and I wanna leave. Please, hon, let's just get outta here."

Vernon stood dead still again, then slapped his hand on the bar, and began undoing his tie, and said to the man, "Hope you're satisfied, bud. You've ruined this lady's birthday, and obviously don't want our business, so we're outta here. Get it?"

He then turned to the young bartender and asked, "Whadda I owe you, sport?"

"Sir," the manager interrupted in a wobbly voice, "I do apologize for the problem, and the drinks are on the house."

Vernon then reached in his pocket, and pulled out his wad, and peeled off two twenty-dollar bills, and tossed them on the bar, and said, "Listen, mister, nobody pays for my drinks—especially in this hotsy-totsy joint."

"Come on, honey, let's go," I said again as I saw the couples at the tables whispering to one another.

I still don't know what came over me all of a sudden, or how I worked up the nerve, but just as Vernon grabbed my arm and we began to head out, I stopped in my tracks at the table with Miss Chiffon and Miss Big Hair, and leaned down, and looked them both square in the face, and said, "Not Penney or Kmart, ladies, but Walmart—on sale." And I would have given a thousand bucks for their expressions.

"What was that all about?" Vernon asked while we were waiting for the Cherokee with his arm around my waist.

"Just one bitch putting two other bitches in their place," I said, which made Vernon howl, then say, "Phony sodbustin' bastards."

I was real proud of Vernon when he gave the valet boy a dollar tip. I mean, believe you me, I know what it feels like to be stiffed at Bluebird when a customer's not happy with the table service or food and takes it out on me, so we sure couldn't blame the valet guy for the lousy treatment we got in the restaurant. Besides, my daddy always taught me better.

"Sorry about all that, Let," Vernon says when we pull out of the lot and he reaches into the glove compartment for his pint of Scotch. "I wanted you to have a nice birthday dinner. The bastards."

I nuzzle up close to him as he takes a quick slug and puts the bottle back, then rub his arm real easy and say, "Oh, honey, I don't need all that put-on to have a good time with you. You oughta know that by now."

"So where do we go?" he asks in a kinda sad voice that made me feel he was more disappointed than I was. "We gotta eat."

"It don't have to be big-time, Vern. No bull. But I have sorta lost my appetite."

He now puts his free arm around my shoulder, and before I can straighten up, he pulls me close, and grabs a chunk of flesh on my side, and says, "Doll, if you don't do something about your goddamn appetite, you're soon gonna be just skin and bones. Nobody'd ever guess you cook part-time for a living."

Skin and bones. Me, skin and bones. Whatta joke! I don't know what to think, so just laugh it off and say, "That'll be the day. Stop worrying about me, Vern."

"Bayou!" he then blurts out like he's suddenly thought of something. "Bayou over on Westheimer. My buddy says they got tablecloths and a piano bar and a little dance floor and the best snapper soup and fried rabbit him and his wife ever put in their mouths. Shit, why didn't I think about that before?"

I don't know how Vernon learned about all these restaurants, but in almost no time we're perched at a romantic table with little candles at this restaurant where everybody's dressed as nice as we are, and the waiter really respects us, and I couldn't feel more . . . well, special. As usual, Vernon studies the menu like it's going to be his last meal, and, sure enough, there's snapper soup and fried rabbit, and that's exactly what he says he'd be ordering—along with sides of dirty rice and stewed okra and tomatoes and some red wine. I see fresh clam fritters with remoulade sauce and a pork, mushroom, and hominy casserole that almost makes me drool, so no matter what I told Vernon, I'm hungry as a horse now, and it's my goddamn birthday, and even if I have to pick at the food, I'm gonna eat what I want for once, and then finally spill the beans about my past, and if I have to pay the price on the scales tomorrow, so what?

Well, the fritters were out of this world, and so was the casserole, but I'm not stupid and really did try to watch how much I ate of each one. Funny, everything went great for a while, and we even got up after the appetizers and danced close to the romantic piano music. Then, just as I was taking another bite of pork and working up the nerve to do my big confession and even make a joke of it, I began to burp and got that familiar sensation like . . . like I'd eaten an elephant. Yeah, I knew exactly what was happening and what I had to do, so without making a big to-do, I told Vernon real calmly I had to go tinkle, and went in the little girls' room like I'd done at Scooter's with Rudy, and vomited my guts out in the toilet while another lady stood in front of the mirror fixing her makeup. Of course it was humiliating, and she asked if I was okay, but what really bothered me most was what I might look like when I got back to the table.

"How 'bout some blueberry cobbler?" was all Vernon said when I sat back down and tried to pull myself back together.

"Lord have mercy, no," I said real playfully after I drank a big slug of water to get that awful taste out of my mouth and slipped a Nips out of my pocketbook to suck on. "You saw what all I ate, and I'm stuffed."

Vernon then reached in his side pocket, and took out a small blue box with a white ribbon, and handed it to me. "Then what about a little surprise for the birthday girl?"

"But this says Tiffany!" I almost screamed, and wondered if it could be what I hoped. "You can't afford Tiffany, you crazy kicker, you."

"Sure, I can. Just open it."

I shook it first and heard some jangling, and inside was not what I was dreaming about but four little silver measuring spoons on a ring.

"Oh, Vern, they're beautiful," I exclaimed with lots of enthusiasm.

"Sterling," he said like he was real proud.

"Why, I've never even heard of sterling silver measuring spoons," I went on. "First sterling anything I've ever had, in fact. Thank you, hon. You're an angel."

"Only the best for Houston's number one cook and caterer."

I laughed and said, "Not yet, bub."

Then he got up, and leaned over the table, and pecked me on the lips, and said, "Happy birthday, doll."

All this just when I was fixin' to tell him really why I'd gone in the bathroom and get that awful secret about my weight out in the open once and for all. Instead, I thanked him over and over for the spoons, then watched him finish off his cobbler while we talked a little more about me using his kitchen and spending more time at the house.

Ends up I didn't have to worry much about my breath after all since I was a little surprised in the parking lot when Vernon announced he had to be on the job at the crack of dawn, and he was dropping me off at my place, and we'd have to wait till the weekend for more fun and games. Just like that. Oh, I can never figure what all's on Vernon's mind or really how he's gonna act smashed or sober, but, to tell the truth, that's one thing that makes him so damn exciting to me. Still, I gotta say I was sorta disappointed when all I got at the front door was a big hug and kiss on the cheek, and the only thing I could imagine was that maybe Vernon was finally getting a little put off by my extra pounds.

17

HUMMINGBIRD CAKE

I was lying to Vernon when I said I hate birthdays. What I hate is getting older, but as for actual birthdays, I've loved 'em ever since the times when Mama would throw parties for me or Gladys, and decorate the porch with millions of colorful balloons and ribbon streamers, and ask a couple of our friends' mothers to bring a small homemade cake or pie or batch of cookies. Then Mama herself would bake a real big beautiful cake with candles, and she'd also have at least three different flavors of ice cream and make her special punch with ginger ale and orange juice. Gladys loved Mama's red devil cake with chocolate icing, but what I always begged her to fix for my birthdays was her rich hummingbird cake with pineapple and bananas and pecans and a real sweet cream cheese icing. Daddy adored that cake too, and I can still hear him telling me before he'd go to work to be sure and cut him a thick slice and wrap it in plastic and put it in the fridge for him.

To this day, I don't know how the cake got its crazy name, and when I finally asked Mama not long ago if she knew, all she did was twist her mouth and frown the way she does when she's exasperated, and tell me not to ask dumb questions, then say, "Maybe it's because hummingbirds love red sugar water and the nectar in flowers and anything else sweet. But I can tell you one thing, and that's that I'm not about to put a cake outside to see if hummingbirds'll peck at it." Lots of times, Mama can be real funny without realizing it, and when she came up with that comment about hummingbirds pecking at her hummingbird cake, I laughed so hard I almost choked to death.

In any case, since I took the day off at the shelter and Mama's really no longer able to tackle a big birthday cake, I decided this morning to tell her I'd just make myself a hummingbird cake with the fancy, new silver measuring spoons Vernon gave me and take it over for the small family birthday party she was determined to have for me and that frankly I could have done without. I mean, first of all, I was in no mood for those rotten spoiled kids of Gladys's. Second, I knew good and well Mama would invite her sister, my aunt Polly, who's been in AA at least ten years and talks about nothing but how the Mexicans are taking over the entire city of Houston. And then there'd be my three cousins I see exactly twice a year, at Christmas and on my birthday. Mary Beth's okay, I guess, though she's gotten more and more hoity-toity ever since she married this filthy-rich guy who controls half the real estate in the Galleria. Daddy's niece, Sara Lee, who's a born-again Christian at the same arm-waving Assembly of God where Sally goes, drives me nuts when she starts harping on the Rapture and other crap like that, and as for Bippie, Aunt Polly's youngest, it's not discussed, of course, but everybody in the family knows she's a lesbian who's been mixed up for years with some gal who works out at the Beer Can House.

Nothing is simpler to make than a hummingbird cake so long as you pay attention to what you're doing, which is why I ended up having to make two cakes and literally put the first one down the disposal. What happened was I'd just begun to beat the ingredients for the cake layers when I was distracted by that fat Mario Batali on TV stuffing a pork loin with prunes. Now, if I've learned nothing else about beating cake and cookie batters, I've learned if you overbeat after adding eggs, nothing will rise just right when it's baked. And there I was, my eyes glued on Batali as he arranged these plump prunes and some sage leaves along this slit loin and tied everything up with string while, all the time, I was just beating away. Then it suddenly dawned on me how careless and stupid I'd been, but since the mixture looked okay, I went ahead and added the crushed pineapple and mashed bananas and chopped nuts and vanilla, and divided the batter between three cake pans, and stuck them in the oven, and just hoped the layers would be puffy and golden. Well, they looked like hell— real droopy, kinda dry and cracked on the edges, not at all springy on top when I pressed them with my fingers—so what else could I do but cuss myself out, and dump the cakes down the disposal, and start again.

Lucky I had some more bananas and pineapple, and of course I always have plenty of pecans, but no sooner had I greased and floured the cake pans again than Sugar and Spice started howling and I see Billy Po's Cadillac out front. As usual, he's dressed in one of his expensive suits, and I'm just thinking what to say if he's got any wild ideas up his sleeve when I notice he's carrying a fairly large package with a big green ribbon in his arms.

"Why, Billy Po, what in heaven's name are you doing roaming around on a Thursday?" I call out as I wipe my hands on my apron and button my blouse all the way up.

"Happy birthday, young lady!" he says in his cultivated tone when he reaches the door and hands me the present. "I hope you don't think I'd let this special day pass by without bringing a little *cadeau* to Houston's number one chef."

"A what?" I ask.

"A gift. A birthday present."

"Oh, Billy Po," I exclaim. "Are you crazy? And look at me.

I'm cooking, and just ruined a whole goddamn cake, and am a mess. My mama's giving me a party this afternoon, but I'm baking the birthday cake myself."

"You look just fine," he says as he pecks me on the cheek and wishes me happy birthday again.

Holding the heavy present in my hands, I give him a stern look and say, "Now, Billy Po . . ." but before I can finish the sentence he laughs and says, "No, no, no, Loretta. I'm not playing big bad wolf, and no strings attached, and actually I'm on my way to interview a jazz combo we might engage for a bank event. Okay, open your present."

"Oh, Billy Po, you really shouldn't have," I sorta stammer as I put the gift on my table, and begin tearing off the heavy cream-colored paper, and notice WILLIAMS-SONOMA stamped on the box. Then, when I open it up, there's this shiny, absolutely beautiful, big copper pot like the ones French chefs use and that I know cost a small fortune.

"My God, Billy Po," I really shriek as I rub my fingers all over the smooth surface and lift the pot up and down by the handle. "Have you gone stark raving mad—Williams-Sonoma?"

He just stood there with a wide smile on his face and his thumbs hooked in the pockets of his vest and said, "You deserve it, little lady—especially now that you're big-time."

I wasn't sure what to do next, but finally leaned over, and kissed him on the cheek, and noticed the same aftershave lotion, and said, "Billy Po, this is the most wonderful present anybody's ever given me."

All he did was squeeze my arm real gentle and mumble, "Better watch it, miss, or you might bite off more than you can chew."

I just snickered and said, "Behave yourself, Billy Po. I gotta get this cake made so the icing will set by this afternoon. Got time for a glass of iced tea?"

He looked at his flashy watch, and when he said he had a few minutes, I told him to come in the kitchen while I prepped the three pans. Then, after I'd poured him a glass of tea, I peeled three more bananas, and pulled another apron out of the drawer, and said, "Here, bub, why don't you make yourself useful and mash these bananas for me?"

"Loretta, you know I don't cook," he protested playfully as I tied the apron around his chubby waist and pointed to the bowl and fork on the counter.

"Oh, hush up, honey. Any child can mash up a couple of bananas."

And he was just like a kid in the kitchen for the first time, so after he'd mashed the bananas and while I was measuring flour and sugar and baking soda and cinnamon and salt in another bowl, I told him to start chopping a big handful of pecans on the chopping board. Well, in no time nuts were flying everywhere as he clumsily hacked away with my chef's knife.

"No, no, no, honey," I said calmly as I grabbed the back of his hand and showed him how to hold the tip of the knife stationary on the board with one hand while chopping up and down with the other.

"I'll be damned," he uttered in fascination when he noticed how the nuts no longer scattered. "You know every trick in the book, don't you?"

I tapped out the excess flour in my pans, added the eggs and oil to my dry mixture in the bowl, handed him the wooden spoon, and said, "Here, why don't you stir this all up just till the dry ingredients are moistened. I'll make a cook out of you yet."

He hesitated a few seconds kinda like a child would, began stirring slowly, then, when he got his confidence up, started going to town on the batter.

"Whoa, bub!" I hooted and grabbed his hand again. "Slow

down, and bring the spoon up and over, and don't overmix. That's how I screwed up the first cake. All you want is to moisten that flour."

"Hey, this is kind of fun," he muttered without even noticing the flour on the right sleeve of his jacket.

"Sure it is. See there, Billy Po, you can cook after all. Now, add those bananas and pineapple and nuts while I measure the vanilla."

"Well, I'll be damned," he said again as he next stirred the composed batter and studied it like he was seeing the moon for the first time.

I gotta say it did my heart good teaching Billy Po to do something I know lots about, but when it came to dividing the thick batter evenly between the three pans and smoothing the tops with a rubber spatula, I took over.

With the cakes in the oven, me and him sat out on the small patio and drank tea, and I'd be lying if I said I didn't notice the way he'd glance up and down at my boobs underneath the apron and my legs from time to time while I told him about some recent catering jobs and he mentioned an upcoming cocktail reception at the bank he'd like me to handle. Then, after he'd looked at his watch again, he smiled, and whisked flour off his sleeve with his fingers, and said, "Sounds like you're pulling your life together the way you were hoping to do."

"I am, Billy Po," I said. "I been real happy lately."

He fidgeted a little in his chair, then bluntly asked, "Does that also mean maybe you've met some prince on a white horse?"

I laughed nervously, and felt myself blush, and answered, "Yeah, I have met somebody kinda special, Billy Po. A real nice single fella—almost nice as you are."

He let out this little chuckle, reached over and took my arm again, and said, "Young lady, flattery will get you everywhere, but don't worry, I have a pretty good idea now where we stand with each other."

I looked at him sincere and said, "Thank you, Billy Po. You're a real gentleman—one of the nicest guys I've ever known."

"Loretta," he went on, "you're a special, good-looking gal with a lot to offer the right man—especially since you took off that extra weight—and if I were ten years younger and foot-loose and fancy free . . ."

"I need to lose some more, but that's sweet, Billy Po, so sweet of you to say that, and I know we're gonna stay great friends no matter what happens."

"We will as long as you keep cooking up a storm the way you do—that's for sure. People who taste your food are always asking me about you, and, well . . ." He laughed again. "You know, I always feel like I'm the one who discovered you."

I can't exactly explain it, but suddenly he seemed to have a sad expression on his face, so, without thinking much, I said, "Billy Po, do you mind if I ask you a real personal question?"

"Sure," he answered. "Since when did we stop trusting and leveling with one another?"

"Well, what I was wondering, Billy Po . . . what I want to ask is whether you consider yourself a happy man. I mean, I know how successful and respected you are everywhere, but you are married with a family, and my guess is I haven't been your only intimate playmate, and . . . well, Billy Po, I was just curious why a man like you has to kick up his heels and take chances the way you do."

He swirled the tea in his glass, then looked back over at me with a smile, and said, "You really don't pull any punches, do you, young lady?"

"Oh, sorry, hon," I apologized, "I didn't mean to be too nosy and offend you."

He laughed as he pulled his vest down over his paunch,

then patted Spice on the head. "You don't offend me, Loretta. Not at all. And I guess you have the right to ask that question since you were such a good sport about my shenanigans. Well, the truth is I love Sissy and my boys more than anybody on earth, and I think I've been a pretty good husband and father. Problem is, sometimes a man like me still has needs that can no longer be totally satisfied at home—something you should remember when you get along in years and try to preserve your own marriage and family at any cost. Oh, I'm not too proud of my behavior, and, as you know, I'm pretty careful when I step out of line like I did with you. But, to answer your question, no, I really can't say I'm an unhappy man." He fidgeted again. "Tell you what can upset me, though."

"What?" I asked as Spice now nudged me for a pat.

"That an attractive, talented girl like you might not realize how much I truly enjoy and respect her beyond all the hanky-panky—which is one reason I brought you the birthday present."

"Thank you, Billy Po" was all I could think to utter.

He looked like he was ready to keep talking, but before he could say anything else, I heard the timer ring in the kitchen, and jumped up to see how the cakes had turned out, and told him I'd now show him how to ice a big birthday cake.

"I really gotta get going," he said as he glanced again at his watch and flicked more flour off his sleeve.

"Oh, come on, Billy Po," I nagged. "Just ten or fifteen more minutes. You gotta taste my cream cheese icing and see what my birthday cake's gonna look like."

So he followed me back into the kitchen, and I took the cakes out, and they were perfect.

"Here," I then said as I grabbed another big handful of pecans from the bag, "chop these nuts just the way you did the others while these cakes cool and I whip up the icing. We're gonna sprinkle 'em all over the top of the cake."

In no time, I'd beaten cream cheese and butter and confectioners' sugar and more vanilla with my electric hand mixer till the icing was real light and fluffy, and when the cakes were cooled a little, I handed Billy Po a serrated knife, showed him how to level the tops, and we both tasted the rich leftover pieces of cake.

"Boy, that's delicious," he exclaimed as he nibbled real slow and his eyes got big.

"Know what I love?" I said. "All those different textures. The smooth bananas, the stringy pineapple, and crunchy pecans. Nothing like it."

Next, we took big tastes of the silky icing with our fingers, then began spreading it with knives between the cake layers and all over the sides and top while sometimes licking the knives.

"Pretty, isn't it?" I said when we stood back and admired the frosted cake, and what I think Billy Po really loved doing was scattering the chopped nuts all over the top. "Honey, you're on the road to a whole new career," I then joked.

"I don't suppose we could cut a small slice?" he asked next with his eyes still fixed on the cake.

"Not on your life, bub! That cake's for my birthday party, and Mama would kill me if we touched it." What I didn't tell him was that I could have eaten half the whole goddamn cake myself if I didn't know what would happen.

I did peck him on the cheek again at the door and thanked him over and over for the beautiful pot as he climbed into his shiny Cadillac, and yeah, I gotta say I have a real soft spot in my heart for Billy Po after that visit and know we'll be good friends for a long time to come.

18

JESUS, TAKE THE WHEEL

Venus gets lots of requests at Ziggy's, but the country song they now wanna hear her sing over and over is "Jesus, Take the Wheel." Tells about this gal who's driving with her baby to visit her mama and daddy, and she's way low on gas and faith, and when her car goes into a dangerous spin on the wet expressway, she begs Jesus to help her out and give her another chance to put things right, and a miracle happens. Well, I gotta say that lately I've been in a pretty bad spin myself and sometimes wish Jesus or somebody would take my wheel and turn it in the right direction.

All began one night when Lester let me leave Bluebird a little early and I decided to swing by Sally's house to drop off some chicken manure in my trunk. Sally swears nothing makes tomato plants grow like chicken manure, so when I went to Green Thumb for azaleas, I'm always watching out for Sally and decided to get her a big bucket full. Usually, I would've just waited till I went back to work at the shelter on Thursday, but if you've ever smelled chicken shit . . . well, I wasn't about to drive around with that stuff stinking up every inch of my Focus. Oh, I was pretty sure she'd already turned in but figured

I'd simply make the detour over to Shepherd and leave the bucket next to the carport.

Did sorta surprise me to see the light still on in the living room, but what really knocked me for a loop was when I no ticed what looked like Vernon's Cherokee parked behind Sally's Cavalier in the driveway. Same red color, same license plate, same dent in the back left fender, same everything. For a few minutes I just sat staring at his car, and feeling my heart thump, and wondering what in hell could be going on. Then I marched up and banged on the door and yelled, "Sal, you there?" Well, I waited and waited till she finally shows up in her flowery caftan with her hair a mess and stands at the door real nervous-like and says in a whiny voice, "Let, what in heaven's name you doing over here this time of night?"

"Brought you some chicken shit for the tomatoes," I say, "but I think I'm the one who should be asking you what in hell Vernon's car's doing here."

I pull the door open, and she keeps running her fingers through her straggly sandy hair, and I can smell booze on her breath.

"That is Vernon's car, isn't it?" I ask, and when she just stands there gawking at me, I say, "What's wrong, Sal? Cat got ya tongue or something?"

"Vernon just stopped by earlier on after work for a drink," she says in a real shaky voice.

"You don't say. Just a friendly late-night visit. When did you two get so chummy?"

"Let, it's not what you think," she then sorta mumbles.

"Naw, of course not. Just two old friends having a night-cap, right? And where is Buster Boy?"

"Let, you don't understand."

"Naw, honey, I don't understand, so why don't you explain what in hell's going on around here."

And about this time Vernon stumbles through the bedroom door with his plaid shirt half tucked in his jeans, and a boot in one hand, and combing his hair with the other, and says, "Hi, doll. What's up?"

I can tell by his voice he's really bombed, and by now Sally's puffy face is rosy and she's starting to cry.

"I think I oughta be asking that," I say to him as he sticks his comb in his shirt pocket and weaves back and forth.

"It ain't what all you think, doll," he then says with his head down. "I gotta get home. See you gals later."

"Not so fast, buckaroo," I say, but before I can grab his arm he's out the door in a flash and scratching the Cherokee back out the drive.

I stood and stared at Sally while she sobbed on and on and said to myself this couldn't be happening. I mean . . . Vernon and fat Sally McDonald? My guy and my best friend? Don't know whether I was mad as hell or just dumbfounded or really . . . crushed.

"How long's this been goin' on, Sal?" I asked.

"It just happened, Let, and I don't know how. I swear I don't."

"Sister, you betta come up with a better explanation than that," I said. "And dry those tears up. You ain't fooling nobody."

She kept on crying and said, "You really don't understand, Let."

"Oh, I understand alright. I'm not dumb. These the kind of morals they teach you over at that Assembly of God?"

"Let, I'm telling you, you really don't understand."

"Understand what? I'm not blind as a bat, you know."

"I guess Vernon drinks too much, and maybe I do too, sometimes, and nobody was more shocked than I was. . . ."

"Cut the crap, Sal. It takes two to tango, you know."

"I know it does, Let, but one thing just leads to the next and . . ."

"So this ain't the first time, you're saying, and you telling me Vernon just gets drunk and starts hittin' on you—on you, Sal?"

She wiped her eyes with her sleeve and said, "You still don't understand, Let."

"Understand what, goddammit? Whatta you trying to say, woman?"

"That Vernon likes big girls," she said. "He likes really big girls, Let. Like me, and like his wife, Mona, and even like his own mama. That's what he's told me over and over, and he even showed me a picture of Mona."

Well, I just stood there without saying a word—shocked to the quick. Then I said, "You expect me to believe that hogwash, Sal? You expect me to believe my guy sweet-talks you, then hits on you 'cause you're fat?"

"Let, I wouldn't lie to you about something like that," she sobbed on. "Vernon's crazy about you, Let—he's told me so a million times. But he's also said . . . what he's also said, Let, is you're starting to look like a scarecrow and he's scared to say anything to you about it."

"A scarecrow?"

"That's what he says, Let."

"And I guess you blabbed my big secret to him," I said. "I guess you had to open up and spill the beans, didn't you?"

"Not a word. You gotta believe me, Let. I've never said one word about your weight problem or the operation or anything. Not a single word. You're my best friend, Let, and . . . I just don't know how all this could've happened and how I could've been such a jerk."

So I told Sally I'm disgusted, and she's no friend of mine, and something's fishy, and I'm heading straight over to Vernon's and have this out right then and there. Which is exactly what I did. Boy, I was mad as a hornet by then, and when Vernon yelled he wasn't going to open the door till I calmed down, I yelled back that if he didn't, I'd take my gun outta the glove compartment and blow the lock to kingdom come.

Well, he was even more boozed up than I thought, and when I noticed he had another drink in his hand, I drew back and swatted the glass so hard it sailed through the air and splashed all over the saddle hanging on the railing.

"What the hell did you do that for?" he bellows.

"'Cause you got plenty of explaining to do, buster," I blurt even louder.

"Oh, Let, for God's sake, you're making a mountain out of a molehill."

"A scarecrow, huh," I say.

"Whadda you talking about?"

"Fat Sally says you been calling me a scarecrow."

He goes and plops down in the maroon chair and puts his head in his hands like he's wondering what to say.

"I don't know what she's talking about."

What I did then without blinking was reach in my bag for my wallet, and pull out the photo of me when I looked so gross, and hold it up close for him to see, and yell, "Scarecrow, huh. Does this look like a scarecrow to you?" I thought I'd be shaking, but I wasn't.

He grabs the picture, and looks at it real hard, and says, "Who's this?"

I take a deep breath and say, "Who in hell you think it is? You blind? It's me, Bozo, that's who. All 280 pounds of me."

His glassy eyes get bigger and bigger as he keeps staring, and he says, "You gotta be kiddin'."

"Don't be a jerk, Vern. Why would I kid about something like this?"

"When?"

"A couple of years ago when everybody called me Bubbles, that's when. 280 pounds of solid fat."

He doesn't take his eyes off the picture and just says, "Man!"

Now I really glare at him and say, "So that's what turns you on. Sally was right. Fat's what really turns you on."

"Why didn't you ever tell me, doll?" he then asks in his wobbly voice.

"'Cause I thought it would disgust you the way it does most normal guys, that's why."

"Son of a bitch," he mumbles. "So that's why you ain't ever got no appetite. You been on some diet."

"Wrong, bub. Diet's got nothing to do with it. So happens I had surgery, and for your information, I got a goddamn silicone band tied around my stomach that makes me puke if I overeat. Get it, or do I have to draw you a diagram?"

"I'll just be damned," he almost whispers as he keeps gawking at the photograph like maybe he's in some trance. And then I notice . . . I can't help but notice the bulge in his crotch that he wasn't even trying to cover up.

For a minute, I thought I'd start crying, but then I just snatch the picture back and say, "You got problems, Vern."

"Fuckin' son of a bitch," he says as he sits there now studying every inch of my body and rubbing his crotch like a madman. "Should've told me, hon. Nothing wrong with anybody being a little heavy."

"So, after all the hell I've been through, after everything I've had to give up to look like a normal woman, I don't really turn you on anymore 'cause I'm not fat enough. Right? You gotta now get your kicks with some piggy like Sally. Right?"

"Sally don't mean much to me, Let," he says while he now runs his fingers through his hair. "I just got a little drunk, and . . ."

"Oh, Vern, don't pee on my boots and tell me it's raining," I say. "And you got so little respect for me you gotta hit on my best friend since she's so . . . available. Boy, do I know all about that, lemme tell you. I know all about it."

"It ain't like that, babe," he kinda grunts. "You and I get along the way I don't get along with nobody else."

"Yeah, like a good friend, or maybe a sister, or somebody to keep you company and feed Daisy, but no longer like a firecracker 'cause I ain't fat enough for you. Right?"

"Oh, doll, don't be like that. A man likes a healthy gal, ya know. My mama was always real healthy, and that's one thing I always loved about Mona: She was healthy looking as my mama."

I still couldn't believe what I was hearing, and finally say, "Yeah, both real healthy-looking women. And you never mentioned this to me."

"Aw, doll, I just don't see why you trying to be a bag of bones—that's all."

"A bag of bones, huh."

"Oh, you know what I mean, Let."

"Wanna know what you make me feel like, Vern?" I then say. "A freak. You almost make me feel more like a freak than when I was so fat. Well, bub, I felt like a freak my whole life, and I'm no longer a freak, and nobody's gonna make me feel like a freak ever again. Get it?"

He then reaches out to grab me, but I push him away, and look hard at him, and say, "Vernon, you're just perverted. You're the real freak. You got problems, Buster. Bad problems." Then, when I felt myself shaking, I stuck my wallet back in my bag and screamed, "I'm outta here, bub."

I thought Vernon might try to follow me, but when he didn't, I gunned the car out the driveway with Randy Travis singing "Honky Tonk Moon" on the radio. I don't remember exactly what all was going through my mind, but I know I was still shivering like a leaf and stopped a few blocks from Vernon's house, and put my head down on the steering wheel, and

cried out loud like I was going to die. Now, I'm not a big cry-
baby, but what in hell was I supposed to do when it really
dawned on me that everything I'd done to improve my looks
had been a joke and that I'd been made a ridiculous fool of not
only by the guy I was so crazy about but also by my best
friend. I kept telling myself this just couldn't be happening, but
by the time I'd stepped on the gas again and pulled out onto
Montrose, I must've woke up from the nightmare 'cause I'd
stopped crying and was only wondering what to do next.

And that's when I spotted the sign PIZZA VILLAGE all lit up
ahead on the right and, almost without thinking, slammed on
the breaks and turned in the small parking lot. By now, all I felt
was kinda numb the way I used to feel when I'd hear Mama
and Daddy having one of their arguments or when kids on the
sidewalk outside Bayou Cinema would squeal "Oink, oink" at
me. I don't think I was even feeling sorry for myself—just
numb and maybe mad as hell. Normally, since I'd had no dinner, I would have simply gone home and fixed myself the usual
salad or low-cal pasta or bowl of leftover gumbo or whatever,
but now I had a craving for pizza like never before, and I told
myself that, goddammit, if I wanted pizza while figuring out
what to do about Vernon and Sally, I was gonna eat all the
pizza my heart desired no matter what time of night it was.

So I march into this pizzaria, and smell hot cheese and basil
and oregano and garlic and onions and maybe pepperoni in
the air, and notice some youngsters and loud cowboys eating
pizzas and drinking beer at wooden tables, and start studying
all the scrumptious pies in the display case in front of the big
oven. There's one with sausage and mushrooms and three
cheeses, and one with bacon and charred peppers and black
olives and shrimp, and another with tiny meatballs and broccoli and whole garlic cloves, and one called the Super Deluxe,
with everything but the kitchen stove.

"What'll it be, sister?" asks the real gruff older man with

thick eyebrows and long sideburns behind the case as he taps his fingers on the top counter.

My eyes keep going from one pizza to the next, and the more I look at them the hungrier I get, and I can't quite make up my mind, but finally tell him, "The Deluxe."

"How many slices?" he sorta grunts.

"The whole pie," I say. "To go. And no need to reheat it."

Now, I might've still been pretty upset and mad over everything that had happened, but I'm not so dumb I didn't realize how stupid it was for me to get that whole pizza I knew I couldn't possibly finish. The truth is, I simply didn't give a damn, and for once in a long, long time, I was gonna do something that would really make me happy, and just stretch my luck to the limit, and to hell with the consequences. What's funny is that, driving home, I kept thinking I'd break down again and really start feeling sorry for myself, but then I'd get another wonderful whiff of that pizza that seemed to be all over the car and my thoughts would shift to how delicious every single bite was gonna be.

Like I sometimes do, I'd forgotten to cut the TV off when I went to work, so when I got home, who should be on the food channel but Emeril, and what should he be showing everybody how to make but pizzas with a million toppings— dough and all. I couldn't believe it! Well, much as I think Emeril's the best of the lot on that network, I gotta say not even he can convince me that pizza made at home holds a candle to the real McCoy baked in those special brick ovens at pizza parlors—just like genuine pit-cooked brisket barbecue. And I've made my share of pizzas—large and small, simple and fancy—for parties and receptions and even for friends. Anyway, after I let Sugar and Spice out to pee, I didn't waste a second sticking my deluxe pizza in the oven, box and all, and I didn't waste a second cracking open a bottle of Big Red to help calm my nerves.

All I can say is the bubbling pizza tasted as spectacular as it looked, and I didn't even fool with fixin' a salad to go with it. Since Sugar and Spice were begging and whining, I picked off a few pieces of sausage and pepperoni and tossed them to the dogs while I kept watching Emeril roll out and stretch some dough and trying not to think about Vernon and Sally and the way they'd deceived me. What I really wanted to do was scream at Emeril that his dough was too thick and more like the Chicago style than the crisp classic Neopolitan one I was eating. But, instead, I finished munching on the slice, and looked at the meatballs and pieces of bacon and golden mushrooms and shiny olives and onions nestled in all the melted cheese on the next slice, and started nibbling on that one. By now, Emeril was chopping herbs while he sautéed onions and garlic in olive oil, and when I wasn't concentrating on him, my thoughts shifted again to Vernon and Sally, and the humiliating stunt they'd pulled on me, and how I'd really like to take my gun and blow both their brains out. Then I wondered why in hell Emeril would sog up his pizza with so much tomato sauce, and Sugar was driving me crazy begging for more meat, and before I realized it, I was sinking my teeth into a third slice loaded mainly with red peppers and sausage that had a wonderful fennel taste and telling myself how much better this pizza was than the one Emeril was fixin'.

Then my damn cell rang just as Emeril was scattering fingerfuls of cheese over the sauce, and bellowing that stupid "Bam!" over and over, and I knew it had to be Vernon or Sally calling this late with some song and dance. For a second, I thought about answering it and doing the riot act, but decided the damage had been done and all this would do was upset me even more. So I ignored the call, and went back to the fridge for another beer, and was just popping the cap when . . . whoa, I let out a big burp, and all hell began to break loose in my gullet, and I didn't think I was gonna make it to the commode before spewing half that delicious pizza to kingdom come while Sugar and Spice howled and howled.

So much for my stomach pouch maybe having expanded a little, I said to myself as I went back into the living room and lay down on the sofa and wondered just who in this world I was trying to punish. Then Sugar nuzzled me with his wet snout, which made me hug him real tight and start crying my eyes out again.

19

SUGAR DADDY

Mary Jane just called to tell me the judge slapped a six-month stay in the slammer on those two bastards who shot the dogs, plus a $5,000 fine apiece. I'd have made it six years and $50,000, but at least those judges are starting to show we mean business when it comes to animal cruelty, so I guess I have to say the penalties did my heart good. Now, if only there was a stiff penalty for breaking somebody's heart the way Vernon did mine, I'd have even more faith in the system. Yeah, he broke my heart bad, and sure, I gotta admit I miss the bastard, and the good times we had, and the sex. But you can bet I'm dealing with it okay, I guess, 'cause Lord knows I'm not exactly a stranger to hurt and humiliation, and a gal starts to develop a pretty tough hide over things like this. I'm not a fool.

What I am determined to do is use my common sense, and not think about Vernon, and just move on with my life. After that big blowup at his house, I was crazy enough to actually think about having my stomach noose removed and returning to my old fat self just to make him happy. Well, it didn't take me five minutes to realize how stupid and really insane that would be. I mean, first of all, no man's gonna tell me how I have to look to light his firecracker, not after all the hell I've been through to improve myself. And second, I'm still young, and if I stay on the right track, there's no reason on God's green earth why I can't find another guy who's more . . . normal. Sure, I had my heart set on Vernon, and even once thought he might pop the big question, and still get a tingle when he calls sometimes and begs me to meet him at so-and-so restaurant since I'm the only person he can talk to. No, thanks. I'm not ready to play mother or big sister or best friend like insecure gals do. My guy's gotta know I'm a woman making up for lost time, and I don't make no bones about it.

And Sally? I had to think long and hard about Sally and finally decided to just take pity on her like Daddy would have told me to do. After all, I'm not a mean person who's out to get vengeance on someone who's going through what I went through with the weight, and the more I thought about it, the more I realized poor Sally was mainly a victim of Vernon's sick perversion. Oh, I'll never trust her again, that's for sure, and I've switched my hours at the shelter so we don't have to work close together. But I know Sally could never get very far with someone like Vernon, much less tie the knot, and, like Mary Jane and Rosemary said, she could really fall off the deep end if she thought her friends hated her for pulling one stupid stunt.

Mama's another matter, and only because I had to open my big mouth and finally tell her all about me and Vernon when I went over to the house to check on her and she noticed I wasn't myself.

"Serves you right, young lady," were the first words she uttered. "I told you you were barking up the wrong tree fooling around with the body God gave you."

"Mama, I'm not gonna argue with you about that, so please just lay off."

She sat there in the glider on the porch drinking the iced tea I'd made her and smoking one of her Merits. "And there's something else, Loretta. Don't you think it was pretty sneaky and ugly carrying on with this new buck for so long and never once introducing him to your own mother and sister? What you got to say to that, young lady?"

Of course I couldn't hurt Mama by telling her the truth about how embarrassed I was to let Vernon see either one of them, so I simply said, "I guess I was afraid you wouldn't approve of him, Mama. That's why."

"Well, from what you've told me, he sounds like real trash," she then says after taking a big puff and picking at a scab on her flabby elbow.

"Vernon is not trash, Mama, I can tell you that," I said calmly as I took a Nips out of my bag and unwrapped it. "He may have his faults, but Vernon's not trash. I don't go out with trash."

"Then maybe some kind of sex maniac—like your good friend Sally, who, by the way, has never given me the time of day."

"Mama, you don't have the right to call him names like that—somebody you never even met. I think Vernon mainly has a small drinking problem, and . . ."

"Aha, now we're talking turkey," she said with that vicious tone of hers. "Yep, they always use alcohol as an excuse. Happened to your uncle Bobby when they caught him with that filly behind the circus tent over in Galena Park, and the time Wendel Potter at the bingo parlor had his way with Ruth Ann Werner, and, yes, ma'am, that was always your own daddy's excuse when he'd go on the prowl and end up having to eat crow."

I pressed my hands down hard on the banister where I was perched, and really glared at her, and exploded, "What in hell are you implying by that nasty remark, Mama?"

She flipped her butt in the yard, then started twirling the ice in the glass with her finger, and said, "I wadn't blind, sugar. Yep, I could always tell when Buck would come home late from the tire company all tanked up that he'd been out carousing with some chicken. Oh, you and Gladys were too young to realize what was going on, but I sure did."

"Stop it, Mama! I ain't gonna sit here and listen to garbage like that about Daddy," I yelled at her.

"Like I say, maybe you two didn't realize what was happening, but believe you me, honey, I did, and let him know in no uncertain terms. Guess he thought I was blind as a bat, but I had your daddy's number a long time."

"You're just making that up, Mama, and you know it." I let her have it again full blast. "Why in hell do you have to be so mean? Daddy was the sweetest man alive, and he loved you as much as he did us."

"Yeah, honey, if you wanna believe that." She lit another cigarette, and I could see her hand was shaking a little. "Oh, grow up, Loretta," she then sort of growled, "and learn to face the facts about some things at your age—like why Lyman walked out on you, and why this Vernon who you apparently think hung the moon decided to look for greener pastures. Men!"

"I'll tell you exactly why Lyman walked out, Mama. He left because I was so fat . . . because I was gross—that's why, and you know it. And who could blame him, Mama. Who could really blame any man for not wanting to be married to a blimp?"

"And that floozy over at the video shop had nothing to do with it, did she?"

"You know, Mama, I don't have to sit here and listen to this crap. First, you ridicule me for losing all the hideous weight, and now you have the nerve to bad-mouth Lyman and my boyfriend and even Daddy with no idea what you're talking about. Well, for your information, Lyman's been to visit me and couldn't get over the way I look now . . . couldn't get over it. Whadda you think of that?"

She took another big drag, and handed me her glass, and said, "Honey, would you be a real sweetheart and run get me a little more ice? Then I'm gonna tell you something I should've told you a long time ago."

So I did like she asked, and got her ice, and sat back on the banister since Mama takes up almost the whole glider, and said, "Whatcha talking about now?"

She kept picking at her scab, and said, "Something you need to know that might open your eyes about your daddy—that's what, angel."

"I told you, Mama, I'm not gonna sit here and listen to you rake Daddy over the coals. Understand? I loved Daddy, and he loved me, and I don't know what I would've done without him."

Then she reached in the pocket of her muumuu, and pulled out her comb, and began running it through her kinky gray hair she'd just washed. "You don't remember the name Sandy Alexander, do you?" she asked.

"No."

"No, of course you wouldn't. You two were just kids. Well, Sandy Alexander was this hefty young hussy who stamped bills at the accounts desk at Lone Star Tire and Alignment."

"What's this gotta do with Daddy?"

"Just hold your horses, young lady. What this has to do with your daddy is your daddy took a shine to this trash the way only he could do and in the state of Texas could've ended up behind bars for molestation—that's what."

I just stared at her and said, "I don't believe that, Mama. Why do you make up nasty stories like that?"

She kept swinging on the glider like she was telling somebody how to put up peach preserves and said, "Why would I make up something that disgusting?"

"Because I think you hated Daddy for not paying you the attention he paid us girls and were always bad-mouthing him—that's what I think. You forget we used to hear those awful arguments and the way you'd scream at him."

"Uh-huh," she said. "So you think I'm just fabricating all this about Sandy Alexander. Well, child, it so happens there's probably a young man or lady roaming somewhere around Texas at this very minute who you could call . . . how can I put this? . . . Who you could call your half brother or sister. Whadda you think of that?"

If Mama had thrown her iced tea glass in my face, I wouldn't have been as shocked as I was by that filthy remark.

"Do you know what you're saying, Mama? How could you be so hateful about your own husband and my daddy?"

" 'Cause it's true, young lady, and it's high time you learned that Buck Crawford was not the knight on a white horse you cut him out to be. Why, he didn't even bother to deny the scandal."

"You're just making that vile story up about Daddy," I almost cried. "If it was true, we would've heard about it by now."

She sat gliding and twirling her ice cubes again and said, "Oh, honey, we hushed it all up to protect you girls, and keep the cops away, and so Buck wouldn't lose his job. It almost killed me, of course, but we hushed it up alright, and we paid . . . lemme tell you, Buck paid through the nose for that little fling with young Sandy Alexander."

"Paid who?" I asked.

"Paid the little slut and her parents, that's who," she blurted. "Almost every dime we had for her to keep her mouth shut about the baby's real father and get outta town. Why do you think we had to sell the Buick Lesabre and even borrow some money from Jake Tyrell?"

"Stop, Mama," I cried. "I don't wanna hear any more of this dirt."

"Two thousand bucks. That's what your daddy had to shell

out to keep things quiet, and save our reputation, and maybe keep from spending the rest of his life behind bars. And you used to wonder why I have such regard for Jake and Phoebe Tyrell."

"I said stop, Mama."

"And, of course, he blamed it all on the whiskey, and said she lured him on when he offered her a ride home from work, and they stopped by some bar for a few nips, and one excuse after the next. She lured him on. Yeah, sure, as if this was the first time he'd been caught fooling around with chickens."

I got up and said, "I'm leaving this very minute, Mama."

"Your daddy was a disturbed man, sugar, and the sooner you accept that, the better."

"That's not true, Mama," I blatted again as I searched for the car keys in my bag. "Daddy was a good person and wouldn've ever done anything vile to anybody."

"Tell that to Miss Sandy Alexander if you ever run into her, or any of the other fillies who knew Buck Crawford when he was on the prowl."

"Then why in hell didn't you kick him out?" I asked more calmly. "Just tell me that, Mama. If Daddy was so rotten, why'd you put up with him?"

She started trying to maneuver her bulky self up from the glider, and stuck out her chubby pink hand, and said, "Here, sugar, help me up. Drank all that tea and now nature's calling."

Then, when she was finally on her feet, she said, "Why didn't I send your daddy packing? I'll tell you why. 'Cause other guys weren't exactly knocking at my door, and 'cause I had you two girls to raise, and 'cause money don't grow on trees, you know."

I held the screen door open for her, then asked, "Why do you have to tell me all this ugly stuff, Mama?"

She turned around for a second, and I noticed she's now huffin' and puffin' and wiping her eyes with a clump of her wrinkled muumuu. " 'Cause I wanna protect you, precious, and not see you hurt anymore the way I was. Ain't that the right of any mother who loves and worries about her daughter? You know you and Gladys are all I have on this earth—all I've ever had—and sometimes I think you forget that I'm still your mama."

More tears came to her swollen eyes, and when she just stood there staring at me with that helpless look on her sad face, what else could I do but reach out, and hug her tight, and say, "I never forget that, Mama, and you oughta know me and Gladys love you as much as you love us."

"I just want you to open your eyes a little more to reality, Loretta," she sobbed as I patted her on the back. "You ain't gettin' any younger, honey, and I just don't wanna see you make any more bad mistakes."

"I know, Mama. I know how much you care," I said.

After the shock of Vernon and Sally, it takes a lot these days to break me down, so when I got home, I tried to just put out of my mind all that garbage Mama had spewed about Daddy and concentrate on the chocolate enchiladas I'd decided to serve Mary Jane and Sam and a new fella at the shelter when they came over to watch an Astros game. Oh, the enchiladas are not really stuffed with chocolate, which would be really weird. What I do is dip tortillas in a hot chile sauce flavored with Mexican chocolate, then stuff them with Jack cheese and onions and bake them with more of the sauce. It's an authentic Mexican dish, and the flavor's not to be believed.

Anyway, no matter how much attention I paid to fixin' the sauce in my large cast-iron skillet, I just couldn't stop thinking about what Mama had told me about Daddy and that Sandy somebody. Not that I believed a word of the filthy story, but it did make me remember one time when Mama had to go up to visit her brother, my uncle Howard, in Austin, and I came home sick from high school around noon, and, much to my surprise, there was Daddy in just his jeans and undershirt sitting on the sofa with a strange chubby young lady with kinda mussed-up blond hair wearing a real flowery zip tank. Of course they both jumped up when they saw me, and all Daddy said at first was "Princess!" with this worried look on his face. Then, after I told him I had an upset stomach, he introduced me to this gal whose name I've forgotten, and said she worked at some nursery, and explained that they were both taking a long lunch hour to talk about what could be done to help Daddy's tomatoes. I remember wondering why they weren't out in the garden instead of on the sofa, but I'd already upchucked once at school, and my tummy was still awfully sour, and the woman seemed nice enough, and yeah, I knew how much Daddy loved his tomato plants, so I didn't give it much more thought.

Well, the more tortillas I stuffed and arranged in the baking dish, the more I realized Daddy just might have diddled around once or twice in those days like any normal male would do, but certainly not to the disgusting extent Mama would have me believe. And why wouldn't he have, considering the way Mama was always hounding him and finding fault over the least little thing. Take the time they were going to the Art Car Parade with the Willards and another couple, and Mama was wearing one of her floral tunics, and I overheard her lightin' into Daddy over the suspenders he needed to hold up the bunker pants he wore below his large stomach.

"I swear, Buck," was something like she bellowed, "looks like you're wearing overalls and going to a hog killin' instead of a downtown parade where people dress respectful."

"Whadda you want, Cub?" he shot back at her. "You want my britches to fall down in the middle of the street?"

"All you gotta do is put on a belt and wear 'em up, and I've told you that a thousand times. Why can't you just put on a damn belt and wear the pants up?"

"Yeah, you can say that in your comfortable muumuu," he muttered.

"That's right, Buck," she went on, "just wear those stupid suspenders and have Bonnie and Jasper and everybody else think we're trash. You do that and let 'em all tell each other we're nothing but common white trash."

That's just one of the little incidents that was running through my mind as I poured the remaining spicy chocolate sauce over the stuffed tortillas. Something else I thought about while I got the dish ready to be baked later on was how Mama insisted they get twin beds after they had their bedroom re-painted and got some new furniture. Okay, so I guess it does make lots more sense for two fatsos not to sleep together in a double bed, but I remember Gladys asking Mama at the time why they didn't buy a king-size bed, and Mama snapping, "Because, young lady, those beds and big sheets and pillow cases cost a small fortune, and money don't grown on trees, you know." Lord, who could blame Daddy for maybe cattin' around a little bit after that kind of treatment at home?

Those enchiladas looked so good I came within an inch of my life popping one in the toaster oven and eating it as a snack, but instead, all I did was taste that rich chocolate sauce with my finger—a couple of times, in fact—then cover the dish with plastic and put it in the fridge. One last thing that did dawn on me was how much Daddy would have loved my en-chiladas. Daddy may not have really known that much about food and cooking, but, like with everything else, he did know what was good and what was bad.

20

Queen for a Day

Glorious Bounty. That's the name Billy Po suggested for my catering business, and I gotta agree with him it sounds really high class and professional. And since the catering is up and running more every week, I finally bit the bullet, and took out a loan, and bought a small house up in the Heights. Yep, I sure did and am as happy over it as a lizard in the sun. Two bedrooms, good computer space, a nice patio out back, fenced-in yard for the dogs, and, best of all, a big kitchen where I can now do my cooking without too many problems. All thanks to Lester at Bluebird, who's involved with renovating some of those historic houses in the neighborhood north of the Loop, and heard that the old woman who lived in this house had died, and told me her son up in Missouri was anxious to get rid of the place quick. Oh, sure, the house needs a little fixin' up—pretty scuffy wood floors, lots of mildew damage in the bathroom, aqua walls in the living room that need repainting, cracked Formica kitchen counters, things like that—but Lester says I got it for a song and dance, and I was able to put down a minimum on the mortgage, which gives you some idea of the bucks I've been saving from catering and bartending at the grill. Yeah, I gave up the shelter not long after the breakup with Vernon. I mean, Sally being there, and sick of having to deal with those vile abuse cases, and the time I need for cooking during the day, and all that. I do miss the animals, but I got my hands full with Sugar and Spice and the cat I took in, and . . . well, I just figured it was the best move to make while I get my life back together. To tell the truth, I'd probably also give up Bluebird if I didn't enjoy all the people I meet there so much and didn't feel it would be unfair to Lester after he's been so good to me.

What else I've done is hire a young crackerjack girl named Angel to work with me part-time on the catering. Second-generation Mexican who answered my ad in the paper and knows as much about Southern food as Tex-Mex. Worried me a little at first when she said her daddy was in jail for robbing a 7-Eleven and she needed to help out her mama, but I'm a pretty good judge of character, and she's sweet and dependable as can be, and I don't have to pay her much to prep things in the kitchen and do setups at parties and receptions and what have you. Angel's guacamole and chicken-fried steaks and broccoli casserole are nearly as good as mine, and I gotta say nobody in the state of Texas can fix *pan de campo* as crisp as hers.

Something else I like about Angel is the way nothing seems to rattle her when we get in a jam. Take this big job Billy Po hired me to do at Mutual Savings a couple of weeks ago—$1,000 plus food costs, and no strings attached, if you know what I mean. Cocktail reception for one hundred thrown by the president of the bank himself. Beer cheese with sesame crackers, tiny deviled crab cakes, sausage-on-the-stick with picante sauce, Cajun popcorn, tamale hash, and some nutty fingers. We worked two whole days on that food, and Rosemary, bless her heart, offered to help us load up Angel's Dodge Caravan in the afternoon, and everything went fine till we got to the bank's delivery deck and a guy giving us a hand trips on a metal step at the elevator and spills the entire container of beer cheese all over the concrete. Well, I said the big wigs would just have to do without beer cheese at their party and I'd try to explain to Billy Po, but before I knew it, Angel's on her BlackBerry and back in the van, and races to a Kroger down the street for cheese and beer and onions and a grater and what have you, and all I can say is that by seven o'clock there's a big bowl of perfect beer cheese on the buffet for people to spread on crackers—all thanks to Angel's gumption and know-how.

Just wish I was having as much luck with my love life as I am with the catering. Here's a good example. At that same bank shindig, I was heating up a few more crab cakes back in the small service kitchen when Billy Po showed up with a good-looking dude by the name of Jerome Webster who's got lots of black curly hair and was wearing a double-breasted blue blazer and silky red tie and looked like he might belong to Bay Oaks Country Club. Maybe in his early forties, and I also noticed he wasn't wearing a wedding ring.

"Jerome's a management executive with Hilton," Billy Po says, "and he's been raving about the crab cakes and insists on meeting the genius who made them."

"Why, thank you, sir," I say as we shake hands and he seems to give me the once-over.

"They're really quite exceptional," he says in this high-class Texas accent I've heard at church and in shops over at the Galleria. "Friends tell me mine are pretty good, but I must say they can't compare with these—like none I've ever tasted."

"Thanks," I say again. "So you're also a cook?"

"Oh, heavens, no." He laughs. "Not really, though I do like to fool around in the kitchen sometimes in my spare time. Mainly, though, we're always looking for ways to upgrade our catering in the hotels, and, as I say, I've never tasted crab cakes like the ones served today."

I thank him yet again, and wonder just what he was getting at. The answer comes when he asks in his deep voice, "Any chance you might share your secret?"

I laugh and tell him, "No real secret. Just plenty of fresh lump crabmeat, and some scallions and bell pepper, and Hellmann's mayonnaise, and not too much breading or handling the cakes too much, and . . . don't forget these crab cakes are deviled."

He gets a cute frown on his tanned face and says, "What's that?"

"Deviled," I repeat as I pull the tray outta the convection oven and arrange the little ovals on a platter. "Means they're real spicy with hot dry mustard and a few shakes of Tabasco."

"Well, I'll be damned," he says. "No wonder yours are so different. I never heard of deviled crab cakes."

"Oh, honey, I'm crazy about deviling lots of things—crab cakes, oysters, oxtails, and, of course, eggs. Gives 'em oomph, if you know what I mean."

"Hey," Billy Po says, "I better get back to the party and leave you two to discuss crab cakes. Don't hide anything from him, Loretta."

"Actually, Mr. Webster," I then say, "I gotta excuse myself too, and get these hot cakes on the buffet."

"Oh, sure, go right ahead," he says real politely after taking a sip of his drink.

Well, I was sure this handsome buck would follow us both out, but when I got back to the kitchen, there he still was picking at some leftover Cajun popcorn in a bowl on the counter.

"Oh, don't eat that!" I almost screamed. "It's awful cold. And, besides, you need to dip it in garlic mayonnaise for it to be really good."

"I think it's pretty good as is," he said, and suddenly I began to wonder if maybe I looked too heavy in the loose harlequin pants and metallic gold shirt I was wearing. "What's it called?"

"Cajun popcorn."

"But it's fried shrimp, isn't it?"

"Yeah, though over in Louisiana they usually use crawfish."

"Why's it called popcorn?"

"I have no earthly idea. Maybe 'cause people eat it fast as popcorn."

"What all's in it?"

I was now rinsing and drying some platters with a dishcloth and in a hurry to put out some more nutty fingers. "You do ask a lot of questions, Mr. Webster," I kidded him. "Sure you're not some hotshot chef out looking to steal recipes?"

He laughed and said, "Jerry. Call me Jerry. And no, I'm no recipe thief. I simply love good food and am always looking for new ideas."

"Okay, Jerry, there's everything in that battered popcorn except the kitchen stove."

"Like what?" he kept on.

"Like garlic and onion and a few hundred herbs and spices—and lots of love."

He smiled and asked, "Deep fried?"

"Yep, in peanut oil, but not too long—no more than about two minutes. Gotta be crisp on the outside but not over-cooked."

He pointed to the platter I was fixin' and then asked, "And what do you call those cookies with all the powdered sugar? I must have missed them on the buffet."

"Nutty fingers," I said as I held one up. "See, looks just like a finger studded with chopped pecans. Pretty, aren't they?"

He took it from my hand and popped it in his mouth and exclaimed, "Wow! These are something else. Utterly delicious. Boy, I would love to have that recipe."

"Oh, nothing to it, and I'd give it to you now if . . . Sorry,

Jerry, I'd love to talk food with you, but I really gotta keep an eye on that buffet out there."

"Sure thing," he said, "but I tell you what, Loretta. I'm really impressed with these dishes and wonder if we could continue this conversation sometime—maybe over lunch or at least a drink. Billy Po was telling me all about you and your cooking."

I had no idea how I was supposed to take that remark. I mean, I was pretty sure Billy Po would never be so stupid as to tell such a high-powered executive just how intimate we two had once been, so what tree was this Webster fella barking up? I asked myself. Recipes? A special catering job for one of the hotels? Maybe even some consulting work at Hilton? Or was it really possible a refined man like this might actually be trying to hit on Miss Loretta Nobody?

"Sure, Jerry," I finally said. "Just let me put these fingers out and check on the food, and I'll be back in a jiffy."

"You really take this work seriously," he said as I dashed out the door and noticed how he kept watching me.

"Sure, that's what I'm paid for."

When I got back, he then asked me if I knew where the Hilton off Sam Houston Parkway was, and when I said I had a pretty good idea, he wanted to know if I'd like to meet him there for lunch the next day—the very next day, mind you. Well, what I put on was my nice green ruffled minidress and high-heeled gold sandals, and when I pulled up to that Hilton, there he was dressed like a prince in a pair of neat khakis and a yellow tie and beautiful houndstooth jacket with the same kind of puffy handkerchief in the pocket that the man at the Riviera had in his pocket.

I don't know much about hotels, but I gotta say this one looked pretty snazzy to me—like some I'd seen in magazines. Big spacious lobby with shiny floors, and lots of trees and flowers in planters, and comfortable-looking chairs, and this really cool dining room overlooking a huge swimming pool, and waiters bowing and scraping around Jerry like he was the governor of Texas.

"Bloody Mary?" he asked as a waiter pulled out my chair for me, which made me feel real special. He then handed us both menus.

"Sure," I said, and in no time out came these fancy, tall crystal mugs with a little rib of celery stuck in the middle of the drinks.

"Great dress, by the way," he then kinda whispered, and I could almost feel his eyes working me over. "And, hey, how do you stay so thin doing all the cooking you do?"

Well, I almost fell out of my chair hearing that question I'd waited a lifetime for somebody to ask, but instead I just laughed at the compliment and awkwardly exclaimed, "Oh, for heaven's sake, I'm certainly not skinny by any means."

He laughed also and said, "All you gals say that, but seriously, you look like you stay in pretty good shape."

"Why, thank you, Jerry," I said just as, out of the blue, another waiter placed a tiny plate with four big sauced shrimp in front of us.

"Hope you don't mind being a guinea pig," Jerry then said. He laughed and reached over and touched me on the arm, which made me tingle. "Creole shrimp remoulade. It's a new recipe we're testing here before maybe putting it on the menu over at our flagship hotel in River Oaks, and I really would respect your honest opinion."

"I do a shrimp remoulade," I said before taking a bite and thinking how I'd love to eat at least a pound of good shrimp remoulade.

"I figured you probably did, and I like it almost as much as crab cakes."

He ate a shrimp, then leaned over, and I got a whiff of

what smelled like an expensive aftershave lotion, and for a second all I could think was how sexy his dark curly hair with little ringlets looked.

"Are there a few ground capers in this sauce?" I asked point-blank when I finished chewing.

"Well, I'll be damned!" he exclaimed as he grabbed my arm. "Pardon my language, but . . . you noticed! I was fairly sure yesterday that you really know your stuff, but this proves it."

I cracked a smile and said, "Oh, I just happen to love capers, and yeah, they really add something to this sauce."

"And you're being honest, Loretta?"

"Does a dog have fleas, honey? Of course I'm being honest. Why would I lie about something that important?"

"Any other suggestions?" he then asked.

"Could have a little more zip—at least for my taste."

"Really. It already has horseradish and Creole mustard."

"Paprika," I said. "I always put a couple of teaspoons of paprika in my remoulade sauce. Helps taste and color."

He now really blinked his eyes at me. "You're something, Loretta. I never thought of that."

"Oh, no big deal," I said as I thought about my stomach and risked eating the last shrimp. "Just something to think about. This sauce is fine, and do give my compliments to the chef about those capers."

Jerry leaned back in his chair like someone really in authority, and this big grin came over his sunny face, and he said in that really sexy accent, "I have a secret to confess."

For some reason, this kinda excited me, and I said, "And what could that be?"

He pointed at the menu and said, "Let's order first. If you like venison, we're quite proud of our venison enchiladas. Rich and delectable."

Needless to say, just the mention of the dish almost made

me drool, but I knew I couldn't take chances and was in no mood to give him any la-di-da about the weight problem and having to watch what I ate.

"Sounds wonderful," I said, "but I had a huge breakfast this morning, and what really intrigues me is this Caesar salad with anchovy croutons and toasted walnuts."

"Delicious and unusual," he said. "But are you sure that's all you want?"

"Positive," I replied with lots of conviction. "Now, what's this big secret you were going to tell me?"

He leaned back again and said, "Well, I have to confess that the remoulade sauce is not our chef's recipe."

"No kiddin'. Whose is it?"

"My partner's, and he's very proud of it."

"Your partner?" I asked. "Are all you Hilton execs this crazy about food? If so, I'm impressed."

He took another bite, and gave me a strange look, and waited a second, and finally said, "Not my business partner, Loretta. My domestic partner." He then laughed. "Everybody around here knows Sonny."

"Oh, you two got a little private business going on the side."

He looked at me real close for a while, like he's thinking hard, then leaned back over and touched my arm again and said, "Loretta, Sonny's my boyfriend—almost ten years now."

Well, a feather could have knocked me to kingdom come, and all I could do was sit real still and finally say, "Oh."

"Yes, Sonny's the one who does most of the cooking around the house, and this isn't the first of his recipes we've tested for our Houston hotels. Last night I told him all about your deviled crab cakes."

"Oh, really?" I sorta mumbled as I reached for the glass of white wine the waiter had poured and began to feel like a fool.

"Sonny's actually an interior designer and on the board of the Houston Symphony, but he's also a phenomenal cook who comes up with great ideas for us. And, in fact, I'm sure he'd love to meet you sometime and, you know . . . talk food."

"Sure," I managed to utter.

"And let me also ask you, Loretta. Any chance you might be free from time to time to consult with our food and beverage manager and toss around a few ideas? As I said, we're always trying to upgrade our food service, and we often hire professionals like yourself to talk with our kitchen staff and make suggestions—like those incredible deviled crab cakes and the nutty fingers."

For a moment, my head was sorta spinning after what all he'd just said, and yeah, I did feel like a jerk—and, you know, pretty shocked. But, hell, I said to myself. So the guy's gay. If I'm not used to surprise and disappointment by now, I never will be, so I looked Jerry straight in the eyes and told him, "Sure, honey, that could be interesting . . . real interesting."

Domestic partner. Boyfriend. Interior designer. Ten years together. I gotta say I really know how to pick 'em. Yep, Loretta dummy, you sho know how to pick 'em. And thanks a lot, Billy Po—you bastard. And when I told Mary Jane all about it, she just laughed her head off and hugged me and said, "Good Lord, Let, who'll you come up with next?"

21

SKUNK EGGS

There's an article in the food section of today's *Chronicle* on Houston entertaining, and guess what's mentioned in black and white? Yep, Glorious Bounty—along with my name. Don't know whether I was more thrilled about that or the fact that the gym scales read 144 this morning. Geronimo! Means I've now lost 136 pounds in all and only have about 15 to go to reach my goal—though, to tell the truth, I'd probably settle for 135 if I could feel comfortable in a size 10. Yeah, I feel pretty proud of myself because, all modesty aside, how many gals who cook part-time for a living and love booze and beer and wine the way I do can knock off 136 pounds? And to hell with what sickies like Mama and Gladys and Vernon Parrish and Sally McDonald, and anybody else, think. Dr. Ellis says most of my blood work looks good—cholesterol, hypertension, thyroid, sugar, all that stuff—and the only thing I need to do is increase my potassium and iron supplements to prevent anemia. I gotta confess I did have a couple more injections to tighten up a little loose skin on my left thigh and upper arms, but since I'm still lifting weights and running two miles on the StairMaster, that should be the end of the needles.

Poor Rosemary. She works out even more than me but just

can't seem to get below 175 no matter what she does. I do think she eats more than she pretends 'cause she's always bringing me something to taste she's fixed for Bear, and, I gotta say, her monkey bread and pecan tassies are almost as good as mine. Whatever, from what she was telling me the other day, fat's now the least of her problems. First, they found a bad tumor in her chocolate Lab's kidney, and, from what the vet says, it don't look like Emma's gonna make it much longer. Of course Rosemary's beside herself 'cause she's had that dog since she was a puppy and loves her as much as I do Sugar and Spice. Then there's Mr. Bear Dillard. Not that I have much sympathy after what happened that night at Ziggy's, but apparently Bear's now behind bars for setting another man on fire. Yep, that's what she said: set a man on fire, for heaven's sake. The jerk was drunk again, and got pissed off at some buddy he was hanging out with after a ball game, and dumped a bottle of tequila over the guy, and set him on fire with a cigarette lighter. Burns all over his face and neck and ears and hands, Rosemary says, and if somebody hadn't called the cops and helped put out the fire, the man would probably be dead as a doornail. Judge set bail at $100,000 and since, of course, Bear couldn't come up with that kind of dough, he's locked away in the clink till his trial.

"Honey, don't you think you better wash your hands of Bear?" I asked her while we sat on mats lifting kettlebells. "Just sounds like real trouble to me."

"But he swears he's not guilty," she said.

"How can he not be guilty if he douses the goddamn guy with tequila, then torches him? That's pretty rough stuff, you know."

"Bear says the man came at him with a bolt cutter, so it was self-defense."

"Yeah," was all I said.

"I gotta believe him, Let."

"All I'm telling you, Rosey, is, like my daddy used to say, sometimes it's better to spray for fleas before a dog comes in the house—if you know what I mean."

"What about you and Vernon?"

"That was different. I didn't have a warning in the world how really screwed up he is."

"What about when he kept criticizing the way you weren't eating enough? Skin and bones and all that?"

"Listen, Rosey, Vernon's a sick guy. We all know that now. And I mean, how's a gal supposed to suspect a man's crazy only about fat women? You of all people should understand that."

"I don't think Bear really gives a damn what I look like."

"Sister, I wouldn't bet my socks on that. You forget I was married to Lyman, who eventually learned he'd bitten off more than he could chew. Yeah, one wants 'em thin, the other fat. Go figure. Sometimes I think you just can't win and that my mean mama's right about men."

Rosemary puts down her bells, and dabs her sweatband with a towel, and looks real sad.

"Let, I don't know what to do about Bear," she says. "He seems crazy about me sometimes, and he really can be a sweet person when he's not drinking too much."

I also drop my bells to the mat, and dry my head, then say, "For God's sake, Rosey, Bear just about burned somebody to smithereens, and is in jail, and you're wondering what to do."

Now I notice she has her head down and is wiping her eyes.

"You still don't understand, Let. Bear's the first man who's ever given me the time of day . . . who's ever looked at me twice . . . and I figure I gotta stick by him—don't you think?"

I reach over and hug her and say, "I know, honey. Remember I been through pretty much of the same crap myself, but I also know comes a time when we gals gotta take the bull by the horns and protect ourselves."

She just sits there with her head down, and I can hear her sobbing a little, and she says, "You know, Let, sometimes I wonder if it's worth going through the hell we fat girls have to go through to lead a normal life like everybody else. Don't you ever wanna just throw in the towel, and go back to your old ways, and at least . . . have some fun?"

I hug her again and say, "Not on your life, Rosey, and neither do you, and I don't wanna hear any more of that shit. I have fun now, lots of fun, and all we need is to stick by our guns and meet the right guy who'll treat us with a little love and respect. That's what I think, or rather, that's what I know!"

"I guess you're right, Let," she says as she finally raises her head and sniffles, "but I do get so discouraged and depressed sometimes when I try so hard, then look at the scales and saggy skin on my thighs, and then Bear acts up the way he does, and—"

"Hush up, Rosey," I interrupt. "You're on the road, gal, and you look better every week, and one day when we have some good luck and are settled down with a good man and maybe some kids and all that, we'll both look back at all this and just howl. We gotta believe that, Rosey."

Even after that little pep talk, I didn't think for a minute Rosemary was about to stop seeing Bear even if he did manage to worm his way out of almost roasting a man alive. Of course I really can't criticize anybody about anything, not after I was stupid enough to let Lyman drag me to the Lone Star last weekend—something I didn't have the guts to tell even Rosemary. First time I'd seen him since that day at the apartment, and the first time he'd been at Ziggy's in well over a year. And the truth is, if I hadn't gone over to the bar for a quick beer after we'd wrapped up the first set, I might've not even recognized the dope there by himself decked out like nobody's business in this crazy red floral vest, and a white shirt with black sleeve garters that covered up his lizard, and a pair of canvas pants, and really weird green boots shiny as glass.

"Hi, Let," he said like he'd seen me just yesterday. "Lemme buy you a brew, hon."

"Well, looka here who's just off the riverboat," I kidded as I stared at his ridiculous outfit, and popped one of the garters, and held a finger up to Joey for a Shiner.

"Got dressed up just to come over and listen to ya play, Let. You were really great on 'Wicked Ways.'"

"Where'd you find these duds, Bozo?" I asked.

"Over at Horizons in the strip mall on Griggs. Pretty cool, don't you think?"

Me, I was wearing black tights and a sexy, cropped green leather lace-up vest that showed lots of cleavage, and I noticed Lyman was working me over like he'd never seen me before.

"Boy, hon, I gotta say you're looking really fine."

"Yeah, sure," I said as I took a big slug of beer, "but I havn't got time to hang around here and gotta see my boss about something before the final set. See you, sport."

"Hey, hold yo horses, Bubbles."

I snapped my head back around, and glared at him, and said real quiet and slow, "Don't call me that name, Lyman. Don't you ever call me that name again, you hear? Nobody calls me that name anymore. Get it?"

"Okay, okay. Don't get ya dander up, honey. Just trying to be friendly. And say, I ran into Sam and Cha Cha at Lucky Strike, and she tells me you got a new house."

I kept looking at him hard and said, "Listen, Lyman, nobody invited you to show up here tonight, and I'm in no mood to discuss houses, and I'm sure you can find plenty of other goddamn chicks to hit on around here."

He grabbed my arm real tight and said, "I don't wanna hit on any other chicks, Let. I told ya last time I saw ya I've changed, and I have, and I came over here tonight just to see ya, and listen to ya blow, and maybe take ya over to Lone Star for a Frito pie or something when ya finish up so we can talk where it's quiet."

"I told you I don't eat things like Frito pie anymore," I said, "and we got nothing to talk about, Buster."

"Yeah we do, Let. Some important things—at least to me."

"Like what?"

"Like a new job I been offered making three hundred a week at Adobe Grill over in Bellaire, and I need ya advice, hon."

"What kinda job?"

"Day manager."

I looked him square in the eyes and said, "Who you think you're kiddin', bub? You couldn't manage a Burger King."

"That's what I wanted to ask you about, Let. I been to school."

I thought I must not've heard him right, but before I could ask him to repeat what he said, I saw Joey waving his cell in the air and saying Buzzy was looking for me.

"I gotta go, Lyman," I sorta snapped before I swilled the rest of my suds.

"One hour, hon," he then said. "Let's run over to Lone Star when you're finished for just an hour so we can grab a bite and I can tell ya about school and the job and some other things. Okay, Let? Just one hour. That ain't asking too much, is it?"

I reckoned I'd probably rue the day if I agreed to go with him, but yeah, he really had my curiosity up big, and yeah, I knew I had to eat something after we finished the gig, so what I said was, "You on that Hog or in the same truck?"

He got this real proud smile on his face and said, "Now I gotta used Dodge Charger with custom caps—in great condition."

"Good for you," I said as I got off the stool. "Okay, one

hour after we wrap. But I'll follow you over there. Okay? And all I can eat's a salad."

Well, I'll be damned if the sucker wasn't telling the truth about going to school for three months—some business night school over near Rice. And, from what he said, he'd sure enough landed this day job at some blue-plate grill, and was planning to quit the muffler shop, and . . . says he's determined to improve his life and do something more respectable. Shocked the hell out of me, but I gotta say I have to hand it to him.

"You know all about food, hon," he then said as he knocked off a big platter of chicken-fried steak with skunk eggs, "and I don't know much, and I was just wondering if ya think I can handle it."

I handed him my fork and said, "Gimme a tiny taste of that meat. This chicken Caesar tonight ain't nothing to write home about."

"Sure thing, hon. You need to eat more than that."

"I said tiny, not that big hunk. You forget this ain't the old Loretta."

"Just leave whatcha don't want," he said as I ended up eating the whole damn piece of meat. "And nothing much wrong with the old Loretta."

"Yeah, sure," I said sarcastically. "Anyway, you don't have to be a cook to manage a meat-and-three like that. Any moron knows that, Lyman. All they're looking for is somebody to supervise things, and keep an eye on supplies, and maybe do a little bookkeeping, and I guess they taught you business stuff like that at the school."

"Yeah," he says, "but what about dealing with the customers? I ain't that good with people, ya know."

"Sure you are, Bozo. Look at the way you always put up with Mama, and finagled us better seats at Minute Maid and Aero games, and . . . you got us this booth tonight. I mean, it's not like you're gonna be working somewhere like the Riviera."

"What's that?"

"Never mind."

"So ya really think so, Let? I know you shoot straight with me, and I could always trust what you think, and I just don't wanna fuck up."

"Sure you can. Give it a shot. You'll probably love it, and it's a hell of a lot better than welding mufflers the rest of your goddamn life. Now, I gotta get outta here, bub. Gym in the morning."

Since I'd finished my Shiner, I reached over and took a sip of his Bud and was fishing around in my bag for the car keys.

"Before you go, hon, can I ask you one other question?" he then said.

"Shoot," I answered kinda impatiently.

"You still seeing that same guy ya mentioned that day at the apartment?"

I looked at him real serious, and noticed he'd spilt some gravy on that fancy red vest, and said, "Bub, I don't think that's any of your dang business, do you?"

"Just asking, hon. Ya don't have to bite my head off."

"Lyman, don't you think it's a little late for you to be worrying about your fat gal's love life?"

He grabbed the check, and reached into his back pocket for his billfold, and said, "Goddammit, Let, I told you what a jackass I was, and how sorry I been about everything, and just wish we could be close again. I never been as close to anybody as I was to you, hon. That's the truth."

"Yeah, sure, till I blew up like a blimp," I said as I began to slide out of the booth and wondered again why in hell I was there.

"Can't a guy make one big mistake, Let? And besides, ya

size was never really that bigga problem with me. I just handled everything wrong"

"Yeah. Well, thanks for the salad, bub, and good luck with
that new job."

"I'll call ya later on, hon, if that's okay."

"Yeah, sure," was all I said.

Back home, I flipped on the TV and there was Bobby Flay
again, this time showing President Obama, of all people, how
to grill steaks on the lawn of the White House. Okay, so I was
impressed, and Bobby could put his shoes under my bed any-
time he wants, and yeah, he's got this spice rub that makes the
crispiest and most delicious hamburgers I ever put in my
mouth. But what drives me up the wall . . . what really pisses
me off about Bobby is the uppity way he's always talking about
grilling being a male thing—like we gals don't have the know-
how to grill even a goddamn piece of chicken as well as the
next guy. Well, there he was going on and on with the president of the United States about how every man has his own
special technique for grilling steaks, and I'd had enough of that
crap, so I just cut him off and decided to get in bed with this
new Italian cookbook I'd ordered on the Internet. I mean, the
truth is, I could go on that show myself and teach macho
Bobby a thing or two about grilling or roasting or baking or
just about anything else that has to do with turning out good
food.

All of which got me to thinking more about Lyman and
what all he'd said at Lone Star. Okay, so Lyman's got his faults,
and ain't gonna win no personality contests, and nearly
screwed up my life at a time when I could have used a little
moral support. But one thing I gotta admit is that the guy always appreciated my intelligence and abilities, and that even
when I got too much for him to handle, he never made any
bones about carrying on with that tramp Tiffany—which is
more than I can say for Vernon and all his sneakiness. I gotta

also say, in all honesty, that maybe I didn't have the right to expect so much of Lyman once I'd blown up to a 280-pound blob. Not that Lyman ever set any bonfires in the sack like Vernon or even Billy Po could, but, then, the more I thought about it, the more I wondered if sex is actually all it's drummed up to be and whether what matters most between two people is sharing fun times and working out problems together and . . . mutual respect. Something else I realized also impressed me was that Lyman had apparently enrolled in that business night school and snagged that grill job smack on his own without any nagging or help from me or anybody else, which must mean the guy's grown up quite a bit and really is trying to take on some responsibility. Oh, I ain't about to drag Lyman back into my life at this point and be chummy chummy the way he seems to want, but I decided I do have a better opinion of him and don't guess it would do any harm to have a bite with him from time to time and hear how he's developing in that new job. At least we now have something interesting in common we can talk about.

22

MAN IN THE MOON

Something happened just recently that upset me to no end, and reminded me how cruel children can be, and maybe explains why I've never been crazy about the idea of having kids myself. Was on my way to Central Market on Westheimer to pick up more staples for a couple of pound cakes I needed to bake for a wedding reception at Christ Episcopal, and when I came to a stoplight at Elmwood Elementary School, I noticed through the chain-link fence around the playground half a dozen or so young children playing on swings, and climbing up and down a jungle gym, and tossing a big yellow ball. Then what caught my eye at the far end of the yard near the fence was a small chubby girl all by herself who seemed to be drawing something in the grassy dirt with a stick. I don't know what came over me, but in a split second I turned down the street next to the school instead of going straight, and parked the car near where the child was squatted, and went up to the fence. I'd say she was about seven or eight, and her long brown hair was tied back in a short ponytail with a pink ribbon, and she was wearing a loose print tunic and stretch leggings like the ones Mama bought for me at Sears when I was about that same age. Her neck and cheeks were puffy but smooth as silk, and I could see there were already tiny creases in the fat inside her elbows and around her wrists like I used to have. Made me shiver.

"Hey there," I said as I grabbed the link fence and gave her a big smile. "Whatcha drawing?"

"The man in the moon," she answered without any concern whatsoever over who I might be.

"Oh, yeah, I see one of his eyes."

"That's his nose," she corrected me.

"Oh, yeah, it sure is. I can tell now."

Across the yard, I could see and hear the other children romping and screaming, and at one point a girl in a red jumper yelled in our direction, "Hey, Dumpy, who's that?"

"None of your beeswax," she hollered back loud like she was mad.

"What's your name, sugar?" I then asked.

"Norma Sue," she answered without looking up.

"Well, Norma Sue, my name's Loretta."

"Hi," she said as she kept on scratching in the ground.

"That's a pretty ribbon in your hair. Did your mama get you that ribbon?"

"Un-huh," she mumbled.

"And where'd you get those pretty leggings?"

"My mama."

"Don't you wanna play with the other children over there?"

She waited a few seconds, then almost whispered in a sad voice, "They don't like me."

"Oh, Norma Sue, I don't believe that for one minute—not a pretty little girl like you."

"They call me names and throw the ball real hard at me," she said.

"What kind of names?"

"Dumpy, and Miss Piggy, and Moo Moo."

I gotta say another chill went down my spine when I heard that, and all I wanted to do was somehow break through the fence, and hug that poor child, and somehow explain that things wouldn't always be like that. Instead, I just said, "They don't really mean it, Norma Sue. They're just playing. Have you told your teacher?"

"No," she mumbled again as she kept drawing her man in the moon.

"Why not?"

"I dunno."

"Well, lemme tell you something, precious. Look at me." She finally raised her head and stared at me with her big shiny eyes that were almost green. "When I was a little girl like you, my friends used to call me names like that too. Did you know that?"

She didn't say anything, then went back to her stick-drawing.

"And do you know what I'd do when they'd call me names and not be nice to me? What I'd do, Norma Sue, was pick out somebody who was being mean and say, 'You got a crooked nose,' or 'You got skinny legs,' or something like that. And do you know what, Norma Sue? When I said that, they'd stop being mean and let me play with them."

For a minute, she didn't say anything, like she was thinking over what I'd said. Then she looked up again at me and said, "Abigail'd hit me or throw the ball at me."

"No, she wouldn't, sugar, and if she did, what you'd do is just laugh at her, and tell her again she's got skinny legs, and then she'd stop. I promise you."

This time she looked in the direction of the other children like she was really thinking hard, and after a long while a big grin came over her face and she dropped the stick.

"Now, Norma Sue, why don't you just run over there, and

remember what a pretty girl you are, and swing in one of those swings, and ask your friends if they know how to draw a man in the moon in the dirt? Why don't you do that now?"

For a while longer, she stared at the ground, then looked at the other kids, then back at me, then, without saying good-bye or anything, started walking fast toward the group. Myself, I watched as she said something to one of the girls and finally took a seat in one of the swings, and when there didn't seem to be any commotion, I got back in the car, and unwrapped a Nips, and turned on the ignition. Like I say, it takes a lot these days to make me cry, but when I thought about what had just happened, and remembered how I was bullied as a child, and realized I'd just made up all that stuff about the crooked nose and skinny legs, I grabbed the steering wheel, and put my head down for a moment, and sobbed like a baby.

Of course nothing perks me up more than cooking, so after I'd finished my shopping, I headed straight back to the house to meet Angel and work on the pound cakes—one plain, one chocolate. Now, like I say, Angel knows plenty about Southern cooking, but when it comes to pound cake . . . well, I'm as finicky about pound cake as Mama is, and I could tell right from the start I was gonna have to teach the girl a thing or two if the cakes were gonna turn out rich and fluffy and crusty the way I like 'em.

"Honey, that butter and sugar aren't creamy enough," I say when she stopped beating them in the mixer while I blended vanilla and almond and lemon extracts into a cup of whole milk. "Cream the hell out of 'em."

"Why?" she asks.

"'Cause if you don't, the batter's gonna be greasy."

"Why?"

"I have no earthly idea," I say. "I ain't no scientist. Just know it will be."

Next I go through the messy hell of sifting the flour three

separate times while she keeps beating and scraping the batter down the sides of the mixer bowl.

"I've never sifted flour for anything that many times," she comments with lots of surprise.

"It's a pain in the ass, honey, but it's one reason my cake has such a fine texture. You'll see."

So now she starts breaking the eggs one at a time into the batter, then I begin gradually dumping in flour and pouring milk, and when she lets the mixer keep running too long, I have to scream, "Stop, honey! Cut if off! That's enough."

"But my batter's much smoother than this," she complains.

"And I bet your cake sinks when it cools and isn't very light."

"Yeah, sometimes. Why's that?" she asks like she's a little frustrated.

"Gluten," I say. "Mama once explained to me all about this sticky stuff in flour called gluten, and if you overbeat the batter, the gluten makes the cake tough and heavy. Don't ask me why."

Angel holds the heavy bowl while I scrape the batter in one of the Bundt pans she's sprayed with Pam, and when we're through, I bang the pan down on the counter a couple of times.

"Why'd you do that?" she asks, and I gotta say I love her curiosity.

"Gets rid of any air bubbles," I say. "Don't want any holes in your crumb, do you?"

"How do you know all these things, Loretta?"

"Practice and experience, honey," I say. "After you've baked a hundred pound cakes the way I have, you'll get the hang of it too."

Just as Angel was rinsing the mixer bowl and beaters so we could start the chocolate batter, my cell rang, and it was Mary Jane, and I never heard her more excited.

"Let, you ready for a double blast?" she almost screamed.

"Shoot," I said.

"Well, I couldn't wait to call and tell you that Sam finally popped the question last night."

"You gotta be kiddin'," I yelled. "Oh, MJ, that's wonderful, honey, really wonderful."

"Well, Let, he was almost obliged to, if you wanna know the truth."

"Whadda you mean, gal?"

"Whadda you think I mean? I saw Dr. Braun yesterday, and he gave me the exciting news, Let."

"You mean . . . ?"

"Yeah, honey. I'm gonna be a mama."

"Well, I'll be goddamned," I said. "Hold everything, gal, till I go back in the kitchen a minute. Angel and I are making pound cakes."

Angel was now drying the bowl and beaters, and I asked her, "Honey, I gotta take this call. Think you can handle that other batter for the chocolate one by yourself? Like we just did, except add a cup of cocoa powder after the eggs."

"Sure, I can," she said.

When I got back on the phone, I could hardly shut Mary Jane up long enough to ask when they planned to tie the knot.

"Soon as possible," she explained, "and you'll never guess where we wanna get married."

"Riverside Methodist, I figure."

"Nope. None of that crap. We wanna have the ceremony and reception at Ziggy's, and I've already talked with Buzzy, and he says he could open up on a Sunday, and Daddy, bless his sweet heart, finally said he'd pay for it all if that's what we really want. Flowers, open bar, food—the whole caboodle."

"Mary Jane, that's the wildest thing I've ever heard."

"And that's not all," she said. "You know we gotta have music, Let, and me and Sam . . . well, we were talking, and do you know what we'd love, honey? What we'd love more than anything in this world is for you and maybe a couple of the other guys in the band to play for us. Think that might be possible, Let? No big deal. Just maybe something romantic, then country stuff afterwards for the reception and some dancing. Daddy could pay you."

Well, I almost' dropped the phone, and said, "We never done anything like that before, Cha, but I guess we could if I can get a few together."

"Oh, please say yes, Let," she begged. "It'd mean so much to us."

"Hold on, MJ," I said as I moved back into the kitchen to see how Angel was doing and noticed she had the oven set at 350 degrees.

"Honey, cut that oven down to 325 degrees," I said. "You don't wanna burn those cakes up."

"I've always baked mine at 350 degrees," she kinda grumbled.

"Just do what I say, Angel—350 degrees'll make the cakes too dry. Take my word. Do 325 for exactly one hour and ten minutes—not a second longer. That'll give us perfect cakes."

I then reminded her not to overbeat the batter once she'd added the eggs and cocoa, then went back in the living room and said to Mary Jane, "Lemme check with Tricksy and Matt and see what they say about playing. Maybe Tricksy could even do the wedding march solo on keyboard, and . . . hey, Venus is crazy about you two, so maybe she'd be willing to sing a few songs."

"Oh, Let, that would be so super," she said in a high-pitched voice. "Like I say, Daddy could pay y'all something, and we could hold off the date till . . ."

"Oh, stop it, Mary Jane," I interrupted her. "It's your goddamn wedding, for heaven's sake, and we're all friends, and just lemme see who I can round up for a special gig."

23

FADED FLOWERS

Okay, so I'm a jerk. I've been laid up here in Methodist Hospital on an IV for the past two days and, believe me, if I ever forget what a jerk I've been, there's always Mama and Gladys and Lester and Dr. Ellis and some others to remind me. Anemia and something they call a mild heart arrhythmia—all brought on by low iron and potassium and vitamin B12, along with stress and fatigue and alcohol and Lord knows what else. What happened was I first got this sudden shortness of breath and leg cramps working out with Rosemary, then later that same night at Bluebird, I felt real thirsty and sweaty and so dizzy that Lester finally forced me in the car and drove me to emergency.

"I warned you, young lady, you were overdoing it," Dr. Ellis told me early the next morning. "It's not that serious now, and once we get your nutrients and fluids stabilized, you should be okay. But no more weight loss—not one ounce. Is that understood? You've got to be more sensible from now on."

Of course that lecture was nothing compared to the criticism and rantings of Mama and Gladys, who were both real teary when they first got to the hospital and must have thought I wasn't long for this world.

"Sugar, you gotta get rid of that thing around your stomach," Mama started bitching after she'd calmed down. "I just knew something awful like this was bound to happen. It's not natural, and I've told you so a hundred times."

"Please don't start again, Mama," I said like I meant it. "I had a long talk with the doctor, and the band's not the problem."

"Honey, I think you've just taken on too much—the club and slinging drinks till the wee hours and catering that food all over town," said Gladys, whose copper blouse was so tight and stretched I could see the pale flesh of her gross stomach between two buttons when she leaned back in the chair to get a deep breath.

"And Loretta, whadda you expect, honey, when you get yourself tangled up with somebody like that good-for-nothing you were seeing so long?" Mama chimed in as she sat nibbling on a Mr. Goodbar she'd pulled out of her pocketbook.

"I've told you, Mama, that's none of your business," I snapped at her.

"Is that the man you never introduced us to?" Gladys then asked before I could say anything more.

"It certainly was," Mama answered, "and we've yet to get so much as a peep in the way of an explanation. Of course, as you know, my dear, Loretta doesn't let us know any of her friends."

"Why didn't you ever let us meet him, sis?" Gladys went on, and I noticed again how she could hardly catch her breath. "I mean, your own mama and sister."

Mama took another bite of her candy, then licked chocolate off her finger, and said, "Trash. Because she was embarrassed to introduce us to trash. That's the only reason I can come up with."

For a while, I just lay there with the goddamn needle in my arm and two electrodes stuck on my chest, and what I "and we just wanted to drop by to see if you're okay. It's been too damn long, hon. Hope you don't mind."

I just kept staring at them both, then cracked a smile and finally say, "I gotta say you guys got guts."

"Oh, don't talk like that, gal," Vernon says next, and I now notice he is wearing the tan longhorn shirt I gave him for his birthday. "Saw your name in the paper. Sounds like you're big-time now, doll."

"Are you really sick, hon?" Sally asks as she puts her hand on my arm and looks at the IV.

For a moment, I thought about telling them both to get the hell out, but then I realized how childish and rude that would be, and how I was raised better than that, so I answer, "No, no, no, I just wore myself down a little bit, and was dehydrated, and will be outta here tomorrow fit as a fiddle."

You look fine, Let," Vernon then says. "And, hey, I hear you got a new house."

"Yeah," I say. "And how's Daisy doing?"

"Daisy's fine, and big as a horse, and misses you."

Sally then squeezes my arm and says, "We've all really missed you lots, hon. Shelter's just not the same without ya, and I really miss you on those bad abuse cases."

"You still checking out at Foodarama?" I ask her just to be polite.

"Shit, no, hon," she answers in her crude way. "Had my fill of that place."

"Know what, gal?" Vernon changed the subject. "Minnie over at 20 Carats was telling us just the other night how you promised her your mud pie recipe and that she's still waiting."

"And Vernon here was telling Buddy Richards at Lucky Strike not long ago 'bout the night you pissed everybody off by slamming two doubles and a turkey in a row."

She let out a big laugh, which made the flesh on her neck

wanted to scream out was, "Because you both look li
popotamus, and I'm humiliated for anybody to see yc
why." Instead, of course, I kept my reason to myself and
told them if they were through raking me over the
needed some rest and would appreciate a little pea
quiet.

"Well, I just hope this teaches you a good lesson,
lady, and that you'll soon come to your senses," Mama l
as she reached for Gladys's hand to help pull her up fror
chair.

"They say you'll be leaving tomorrow," Gladys then
"and I don't need to tell you, sis, that if you don't feel u
being in that new house all by yourself, you know me
Rufus and the kids would love for you to stay with us till y
get yourself together."

"I'm fine, just fine, so stop worrying about me," I said a
thought how all I needed was that madhouse full of spoiler
rotten kids to really drive me up the wall.

And I would have been fine if, not thirty minutes afte
they left, who should appear out of the blue at the door and
shock the hell out of me but . . . Sally and Vernon. She was
wearing one of her pastel muumuus and had a big grin on her
face, and though she looked fatter than ever, I had to admit her
skin was still smooth and tight as an eggshell and she didn't
have any of those little crevices next to her nose like the ones
I've developed since I took off the weight. Vernon was handsome as ever and carrying a bunch of flowers wrapped in plastic. Myself, I felt my heart starting to pound and didn't know
whether it was from seeing Vernon again or just nerves.

"Hey, doll," is all he says as he hands me the flowers, which
look a little wilted.

"Thanks," I say as I smelled them and tucked them next to
me on the bed.

"Mary Jane told us you were in the hospital," Sally says,

wobble, then went on to say, "And I was telling Vernon at Spanish Café the other day it's high time we just showed up one night at Ziggy's to hear Loretta blow some Wynonna Judd and Stevie Earle, and do some line dancing, and maybe ride the bull the way we all used to."

"Doll, remember that time we all watched Cha Cha Baxter rack up five points for the Babes?" Vernon now asks. "Well, did she tell you how she jammed three Hellcats at the derby last month and ended up scoring a whoppin' nine points?"

I wait a minute, then say, "No, Mary Jane didn't mention none of that to me. All Mary Jane's told me lately is she and Sam are gonna get hitched."

Sally gets another big grin on her puffy face and says, "Yeah, isn't that wonderful? And a little one on the way. We're all so excited for them."

"How's Zach, by the way?" I ask.

Her smile disappears fast, and she says, "Oh, I ain't seen Zach in ages. Who needs all his crap?"

Well, by this time, my brain's going a mile a minute as I think about all their comments, so I say, "Sounds like you two've been real busy."

They both stay silent for a minute, then Vernon finally says, "Yeah, doll, we get around—that is, when I ain't working my friggin' ass off."

"But like Vern was saying just the other night, Let, it's just not the same without you around, and we want you to know that."

Now I felt this churning in the pit of my stomach, like I might be nauseated or disgusted, so I say, "Goddammit, you both know where I work and when I play."

Vernon grabs the big armadillo belt buckle on his jeans, and lowers his head too, and says, "Yeah, doll, and I was telling Sal the other day how we gotta go to Ziggy's one night. We just don't want you to be mad. We all had lots of good times together, ya know, and . . . we just want us all to be good friends like we've always been."

"Yeah," I say. "One big happy family. Right?"

Sally then looked like she was ready to turn on the waterworks, and before Vernon can answer, she almost sobs, "We all make mistakes, honey, and we didn't come up here to upset you, not with you not feeling good and all, and . . ."

"Oh, cut the crap, Sal," I interrupted. "You know me better than that. Like I said, there's nothing bad wrong with me, and I'm a big girl—maybe no longer big as you two would like, but a tough gal—and, after all, I ain't been exactly sitting around twiddling my thumbs—if you know what I mean."

"Glad to hear that, doll," Vernon mumbles, like he doesn't care one way or the other.

"Okay," I went on, "Mama and Gladys were here right before you, and I'm pretty tired, and think you two better leave."

"Yeah, gal, we're outta here lickety-split," Vernon says as he leans over and pecks me on the forehead. "Gotta get back to work, myself. Can I give you a ring sometimes? And maybe we'll drop by the bar one night or show up at the club for a gig."

"Sure," I say as I watch Sally waddle out the door with Vernon's hand on her flabby waist. "Thanks again for the flowers."

After they left, I lay there and didn't know whether I felt hurt or a little jealous or just confused. Then, the more I thought about it, the more I realized I was simply mad—mad as a hornet. Oh, I guess I can deal with Vernon getting his kicks with fatties from time to time, and Sally cheating on her best friend for a little nooky, and even the two jerks ignoring me when they find something better to do. But what I won't stand for is them rubbing it all in my face like it's . . . normal and expecting me to forgive everything and play along like I'm just a good egg and am around when they need help or wanna have some real fun. Well, goddammit, Loretta Craw-ford's not dumb. I do have feelings, in case they don't know it, and yeah, I can be hurt and humiliated as much as the next gal. I mean, after all, I've gone through too much hell with the weight battle to put up with this crap, so all I gotta say to Buster Parrish and Fat Sally is, when they're around me from now on, they better . . . buckle their saddles tight.

24

CANINE BEREAVEMENT

I feel so sorry for poor Rosemary. Like we feared, her dog Emma had to be put down because of that kidney tumor, and, along with the weight problem and Bear being in jail, it's been almost more than she can take. Of course Rosemary's a pretty strong gal, and when it came to the actual procedure for Emma, there was never any question that Rosey would stick by the dog till the bitter end and hold her while the vet did the injection. I stood there with her and watched Emma go to sleep so peacefully, and I gotta say it wasn't the first time I wondered why in hell the same humane thing can't be done for people who have a terminal disease and don't wanna suffer. Me and Vernon once had a bad argument about this, and he called me crazy for talking like that, but, then, we all know how much Mr. Parrish cares about others' pain.

Anyway, when Rosemary said she was buying a small urn for Emma's ashes and may eventually bury her in the backyard, I told her I thought we should have a bereavement luncheon at my place and invite a group of dog lovers and their dogs. I mean, everybody in the South has bereavements after funerals, so I figured, why not have one to celebrate Emma's life and show Rosemary how much we all care? I even suggested she bring along Emma's urn, and we'd have a little display of Emma's photographs, and Rosey could tell a few stories about the dog, and I'd whip up something to serve on a nice buffet.

"That's so sweet of you, Let," she sobbed, "but don't you think some people will think that's all sorta corny?"

"I do not," I exclaimed without giving it a second thought. "Everybody there will be a dog lover, and anybody who thinks it's a corny idea can just stay home. Let me handle it."

"On one condition, hon," she said, perking up. "That you let me help with the cooking."

Well, we had the shindig this past Sunday, and even though I sometimes thought I'd bitten off more than I could chew, I gotta say it not only did Rosemary worlds of good but taught me a few more lessons about catering. Of course Mary Jane and Sam were there with Nugget, Cha Cha's golden retriever mix we rescued from a disgusting pen at a house out in Pasadena. Eileen and Harry Silvers came with their poodle, Zizi, and Venus with her Yorkshire, Macho. Lester and his wife, Bambi, brought Grindel, a beagle mix they adopted from the shelter. And with one of Rosemary's friend's corgi, and a shepherd mix, and a spaniel, plus Sugar and Spice, we had nine dogs in all. What we didn't have were any children since I'd made it clear to everyone that things would probably be hectic enough without a bunch of screaming kids fooling with the dogs and demanding attention.

At first, I planned to do just a big pot of son-of-a-bitch stew with coleslaw and cornbread, but when I thought about dogs running around the house and thirteen people trying to deal with bowls of soupy stew sloshing all over the place, I realized the idea was stupid. Then I remembered an extra turkey breast in the fridge I'd roasted as backup for a bank cocktail buffet but didn't need, as well as half a baked ham shank I'd kept to make sandwiches and nibble on. Wham! It dawned on me: a sumptuous turkey and ham casserole with mushrooms

and cheese and water chestnuts and sherry. The perfect bereavement dish. And with that I could do my baked cheese
grits, and my congealed pickled peach and pecan salad, and
some buttermilk biscuits, and maybe a simple bowl of am-
brosia and some cookies. Everything but the grits and biscuits
done in advance, easy to serve and eat, no mess, and who doesn't
love a great casserole and grits and congealed salad?

"You have to let me fix dessert," Rosemary volunteered on
the phone. "What about my caramel layer cake? It'll take my
mind off my sadness and worries."

Frankly, I thought a frosted layer cake would be a little
heavy after the other food, but of course I thanked Rosey pro-
fusely and said it would be the highlight of the get-together.
Like I say, Rosemary's a damn good cook, and I know exactly
what she meant about cooking being the perfect distraction
when you're upset.

So that took care of the menu for the buffet. Next, I had to
think about something special for the dogs, and what I came
up with was soup bones I could get from my butcher, Homer,
at Central Market. A bone for each dog, which they'd love and
might keep 'em quiet in the yard while we humans ate and listened to Rosemary talk about Emma.

Well, I was up bright and early, and while everybody else
went to church or whatever they do on Sunday morning, I
was chopping turkey and ham and mushrooms for the casserole and mixing chopped pickled peaches and pecans with
cream cheese for the salad that had to congeal in the fridge at
least two hours. I also decided to go ahead and mix all the dry
ingredients and shortening for the biscuits so all I'd have to do
would be add buttermilk at the last minute, cut 'em out, and
bake 'em. That left only the cheese grits, which I knew could
be boiled in advance, then mixed with butter and sour cream
and eggs and cheddar and a little garlic and seasonings, scraped
into a big baking dish, and stuck in the oven with the casserole

to get nice and golden by the time everybody arrived. All simple enough, until, that is, I reached up in the cabinet for my special stone-ground grits, and opened the sack, and noticed black specs scattered among the tiny cream-colored grains. Bugs! I knew in one second they were goddamn bugs, even though I'd wrapped the sack tight in not one but two plastic bags. For a few moments, I just stared at the filthy critters, and the more I stared, the more a feeling of panic came over me.

The problem was, of course, I got hooked on stone-ground grits when Central Market began carrying Anderson's from Tennessee a few years ago, and now can't abide those blanched, gritty, bland commercial brands that never get creamy enough no matter how long you cook 'em. Normally, I would have just jumped in the car, driven to the store, and bought another sack, but I knew the market doesn't open till noon on Sundays and that there wasn't another supermarket in town that carries any variety of stone-ground grits. The only person I was sure would have a bag was Sally since she's the one who first raved about the grits to me, but I told myself hell could freeze over before I'd ask her.

"Mama," I said in a frantic voice on the phone, "I'm having a few people over for a dog bereavement, and wanna bake some cheese grits, and was wondering if you have any of those wonderful Anderson stone-ground grits I once brought you."

"Whadda you mean a dog bereavement?" Mama asked right off the bat.

"My friend Rosemary's Lab died and some of us are having a bereavement lunch for her," I explained.

"Why, that's the most ridiculous thing I've ever heard," she huffed. "Have you lost your mind, sugar?"

"Mama, I found bugs in my grits, and I don't have time this morning for your criticism, so could you please just see if you have a sack of those grits?"

"Did you have 'em in the refrigerator?"

"No, Mama, they were wrapped real tight in plastic up in the cabinet, if you must know. I don't have that much room in the fridge."

"Then it serves you right, young lady," she kept on. "If you don't know by now to keep grits and cornmeal and flour refrigerated, you deserve bugs."

"Please, Mama," I begged impatiently, "I don't have time for your lectures this morning, so could you just tell me yes or no whether you got any stone-ground?"

"I do not," she stated flatly, "and what's more, honey, I think you highly overate those fancy grits that cost a fortune. All I got's a box of plain old Quaker grits and don't see why you gotta make such a to-do. Grits is grits."

I wasn't about to get into an argument with Mama about grits, so all I did was thank her, and say I couldn't talk, and try to think who besides Sally might have a sack of Anderson. I remembered Eileen Silvers telling me about some shrimp and grits she fixed for Harry's thirty-fifth birthday party, but wouldn't you know, she said she always uses quick grits. Same with Rosemary. Mary Jane did have some Anderson, then, when she checked, discovered there wasn't even a cup left in the bag. Couldn't reach Angel on the phone, and Bambi had never even heard of stone-ground grits. Ditto the new fella who works at the shelter, Andy. And since I don't think dear Venus can fry bacon, I didn't even bother calling her.

Now, when I set my mind on doing something right, not even the Good Lord can change it, and if I had to eat my pride and humiliate myself to get some of those goddamn grits, I finally decided to do just that.

"Sally, this is Loretta," I said kinda cold like we were no more than casual acquaintances. "I don't have time to explain, but the store's closed and I was wondering if you got a sack of those Anderson grits."

"I reckon I do, honey," she answered real sugary-like. "I'm

just back from church, but lemme check. When do you need 'em?"

"Right now," I said. "I'll pay you for 'em, or get you another bag tomorrow."

I could hear the TV in the background and wondered if she'd really gone to early church and if Vernon was there.

"I sure do, honey," she then said, "and I'll bring 'em right over."

"I can drive over and get 'em."

"No, no, hon," she snorted sorta nervously. "I gotta go by the nursery for some topsoil and can drop 'em off on the way."

"Sal, I'm really in a big rush for those grits," I said, again without explaining.

"Be there in fifteen minutes."

And she was, decked out in jeans and a flimsy lavender tee that made her look big as a heifer and her messy hair now down on her flabby neck. Since I didn't invite her in, I'm sure she thought I was rude, but I figured I no longer owe Sally one blessed thing but a bag of grits, and besides, I knew those grits had to be boiled and stirred at least thirty minutes before going into the oven and I didn't have a minute to spare if the food was gonna be ready by twelve-thirty. So I simply thanked her, and once more offered to pay for the grits, and told her again I was in a hurry, and that was that. Oh, she must have wondered what in hell was going on as she backed her Cavalier out the drive, but, like I say, I didn't feel like I had to give either her or Vernon so much as the time of day.

Around noon, Rosemary shows up in a pretty pink sundress carrying a spectacular caramel cake and an envelope, and when I ask kinda sheepishly, "Where's Emma?" she breaks down standing in the kitchen and cries, "She's out in the car, Let—in that awful container."

I'm still stirring the grits, but when I see what a state she's in, I stop for a moment, and give her a big hug, and tell her I'll go get the urn if she'll keep stirring the pot. Well, what I find on the front seat of her Chevy Equinox is not really an urn but a shiny, heavy wooden box with a nice picture of the Lab on the top that looks like it's been somehow etched on a small marble tile. I bring the box inside, and place it smack in the middle of my small entrance table with a vase of wild flowers, and exclaim over and over to Rosemary how beautiful it is and how good the photo of Emma is. Of course what's worrying me are the grits, so I take the wooden spoon myself, and when the grits look really creamy and feel perfectly smooth, I take the pot off the heat, and stir in the butter till it's melted. Then I ask Rosemary to add the sour cream and cheese and eggs and seasonings while I stir, and scrape everything into the baking dish, and finally stick it in the oven next to the casserole. Next, Rosey and I glance at the photos of Emma in the envelope, and when we've picked out the best ones, we arrange them carefully around the cremation box on the table, which seems to make Rosemary real happy.

I'm not tootin' my own horn or anything, but I gotta say the buffet we set up on my dining room table with a blue-checkered cloth and some fresh daisies couldn't have looked more beautiful. Used my large, glazed, tobacco-spit pottery dish for the casserole, and with the crusty, buttered bread crumb topping, it was appetizing enough to be photographed for a food magazine. For the grits, I'd decided to sprinkle extra Parmesan over the top, so they were not only soft and creamy inside but a crispy golden brown outside. The congealed salad I fixed in a glass mold the shape of a pinecone, so when I turned it out on a plain white platter lined with leaves of romaine, the peaches and pecans could be clearly seen suspended in the lemony aspic in an interesting design. This time my hot buttermilk biscuits were as high and fluffy as Mama's, and next to the cloth-lined straw basket I had a big slab of the sweetest local country butter in the state of Texas, which I buy every weekend at the farmers' market out off Eldridge Parkway. We transferred Rosemary's yummy cake to the cut-crystal plate with tiny legs I remember my grandmamma using for birthday parties, and to tell the truth, I wondered how in hell I was gonna get through that lunch without cuttin' myself more than just a sliver of that mouthwatering caramel layer cake.

I wish I could say everything went smoothly after people arrived; everything did go pretty well till we heard lots of growling and yelping out back and caught Venus's small Yorkshire trying to snatch a huge bone away from Reinhard Cullen's shepherd, Reno. Then, while everybody was eating and Rosemary was telling an incredible story about Emma once saving a cat's life, Zizi the poodle got bored and whined and begged to get up in Eileen's lap and lick her plate. And then Grindel wandered into the house and howled till Lester picked pieces of turkey and ham off his plate and tossed them to the hound. And Spice dropped his bone in the living room and began sniffing and trying to hump Booker Polk's corgi, Dixie. And the next thing I hear is Mary Jane screaming at Nugget, who's got his muddy front paws up on the buffet table trying to get to the food, and the caramel cake is just a few inches from being dragged to the floor.

Well, much as we all love dogs, eventually we had to put most of these in their separate cars so everybody could enjoy Rosemary's cake, and I had to admit to myself that this was my first and last canine bereavement affair. I think it did do Rosey's heart good to see Emma honored by so many nice people, and I know it did my heart good when I went to clear off the buffet and noticed there wasn't so much as a morsel of food left. What did kinda shock me and tick me off was when I also noticed those folks had managed to knock off that whole goddamn cake while I was busy in the kitchen, meaning the only taste I got was a small gob of caramel icing scraped off the plate with my finger.

25

FIRE POWER

Plateau. That's the word Dr. Ellis keeps using to describe what he hopes will happen to my weight once my metabolism has changed completely. The way he explains it, my body will tell me when I'm at the right weight, and when I reach that plateau, my craving for food should be less and less and the only challenge will be maintaining that ideal weight. Well, I've been at about 138 for some time now, so guess I've plateaued, like he said, and shouldn't lose another pound unless I'm asking for more trouble. I can live with that, I think, especially since the other day I slipped into a size 12 denim jumper without sucking in as much as a tiny breath. And yeah, I gotta say my mental attitude about myself gets better every day, though frankly, sometimes I have to ask myself if I'm really much better off than when I was a fatty. Also wish Dr. Ellis was more on target about my appetite. Sure, it's still pretty much under control, even with the temptations involved in all the catering, but I'd be lying if I said I don't think about food most of the time and could wolf down a plate of barbecue, or big wedge of my chocolate-butterscotch pie, or half a keg of suds in no time if my willpower wasn't so strong and I wasn't still determined to meet the right man.

Speaking of which, leave it to me to get involved with another weirdo who makes Lyman and Vernon and Mr. Jerome
Webster and a couple of others look almost normal. Cordell's
his name. Cordell Hines, and the way I met Cordell was Rudy
brought him into Bluebird one slow night after selling him a
new set of wheels down at Folger's—a Buick Enclave with
Bose sound system and climate control leather seats and lots of
other snazzy extras. Nice-looking fella about Rudy's age with
wavy blond hair and a cute mustache and one ear pierced with
a diamond and wearing a tan seersucker jacket over a black
tee. Turns out he owns this big store over near the Galleria
called Bayou Electronics, and also turns out he don't drink just
Jack Daniel's but the really premium Gentleman Jack at twelve
bucks a shot—on the rocks. I mean, I could tell in a jiffy the
man had style. I also noticed he was wearing a wedding ring,
but then so does Billy Po Cahill.

"Loretta here also blows a mean sax on weekends in the
band out at Ziggy's," Rudy told Cordell at one point when I
served another round.

"Hey," Cordell said to me, "we used to go over there to
have chili dogs and dance after shootin', and come to think of
it, there was this real heavy gal called Bubbles who played sax
that everybody was crazy about. Must have been before your
time, but maybe you know her."

Well, if anybody had made that comment six months ago
before I worked up my new confidence, I would've just played
dumb, but ever since the breakup with Vernon, I've stopped all
that cover-up and decided to come clean with friends, and so
all I did without blinking was smile and look him straight in
the eyes, and say, "You're looking at her, cowboy."

"You're Bubbles?" Cordell asked with shock on his face.

"You were fat?" Rudy stammered before I could explain.
"You never mentioned that to anybody."

"Guilty as charged, boys, though Bubbles Crawford is long

gone," I said kinda proudly as I mopped the bar with my sponge and replaced their napkins. "Was 280 smackaroos at my worst."

"I don't believe it," Rudy went on. "Never would have guessed you were ever that heavy, gal."

"Not just heavy, buster, but the size of a giant armadillo."

"I'll be a son of a bitch," Rudy added. "You must've gone on one hell of a diet."

"Long story, and I won't bore you."

Then, to show off real crazily, I laughed, and stood back from the bar, and struck a glamorous pose, and said, "La-di-da! The new Loretta!"

They both had their eyes glued on me, and in a while Cordell said, "Great pair of boots."

"Thanks. Full quill ostrich. I splurged."

"Mind if I ask where you got 'em?"

"City Buckaroo on Navigation. Best boots in Houston—ladies and gents."

"Bet they're comfortable as hell."

"Soft as a baby's butt."

"Come on, sweetheart, show us a little more leg," Rudy then teased.

"Behave yourself, bub," I said as I pulled down on my silver suede mini and heard Dolly order two margaritas for the floor.

Rudy turned to Cordell and said, "In case I didn't tell you, Loretta's known around here as the Ice Babe."

I chuckled out loud and said, "And don't you forget it, big boy." Actually, Rudy's really a good guy, and the more I get to know him, the more I like him.

Well, business started to pick up after a while, so I had to stop most of the small talk and take care of other customers. But there was something about Cordell that really caught my fancy, and, lo and behold, when he showed up again by himself pretty early the very next night, I figured something good was bound to happen.

"Said to myself driving home that I bet you can mix one hell of a J.D. Manhattan," was his only excuse for coming back.

"Straight up or on the rocks?" I ask as he works me over with his eyes, and I wonder if I look okay in my cropped leather vest.

"Neat," he answers like he knows what he's talking about. "And Rudy tells me you're also one hell of a cook and even do some catering on the side when you're not working here."

"Yeah, but sorta the other way around now the way business has been going," I say. "And if Rudy don't stop telling my secrets, one day I'm gonna take my gun and blow his goddamn head off."

"You shoot?" he asks next.

"I got a gun, if that's what you mean. Beretta 92 automatic."

"Legal?"

"Sure, I got a permit."

"Ever shoot for fun?"

"Whadda you mean?"

"You know, shoot at a firing range with friends just for practice and to have a good time."

"Heavens, no," I say. "Only shootin' I ever done was when I bought the gun and had to hit a target at the gun shop to apply for the permit. But I sure ain't no sharpshooter, if that's what you're wondering."

He takes a big sip of his drink, and gets this serious look on his pinkish face, and asks next, "You married?"

I arrange a stack of swizzle sticks in a glass and answer with a big smile, "You don't beat around the bush, do you, cowboy? But naw, I'm divorced." I then point to his ring and say, "I see you're hitched."

"Separated," he says. "Four months now, and soon I'll be taking your same road."

"Any kids?"

"Yeah, one boy. That's a big problem."

"Sorry," I kinda mutter.

"Just the way the cookie crumbles sometimes," he says, and I now notice how his nails look bitten. "Anyway, shootin's lots of fun and keeps you in practice."

"Lord, I barely passed the test when I applied for the permit," I tell him.

"That's normal," he says. "All you need's practice."

"To tell you the truth, guns sorta scare me. My husband used to shoot birds, and even that bothered the hell out of me—for more reasons than one."

"That's just 'cause you feel insecure with 'em, and that can be dangerous, you know—in case you ever need to really protect yourself."

He points to his drink and says, "That's one great Manhattan. What's your formula?"

"Three parts whiskey to two parts sweet vermouth, dash of bitters, and wanna know the secret? A quick squirt of dry vermouth."

"I'll be damned," he says like he's impressed. "Hey, mind if I make a friendly proposal?"

I cock my head playfully and say, "Watch it, bub. Remember you're talking to the Ice Babe."

He laughs and says, "Naw, no hanky-panky. Was just wondering if maybe you'd like to go shootin' one night with me and a couple of friends over at Fire Power on Memorial. We shoot about a hundred rounds apiece, then usually go grab a pizza and brew at a great place called Pizza Pronto. Lots of fun, and we're home by ten."

I don't know exactly what it was about Cordell I found so fascinating—and, okay, sexy—but one thing I felt was that the guy respected me and I could trust him to treat me like a real lady. Oh, the idea of going somewhere and shootin' guns just for the fun of it didn't exactly turn me on, but at least it was something different, and me and Vernon never did anything really insane like that, and so without giving it much more thought I said, "Sure, bub, why not? Just remember I ain't no Annie Oakley and I gotta watch what I eat and drink."

And, sure enough, we made a date for Friday, and I cleared things with Buzzy and the band at Ziggy's, and at around seven I showed up in jeans and red pony tee and suede boots with my Beretta in a satchel at this cinder block building on Memorial with the name Fire Power painted across the front. Inside, more guns and rifles in glass cases than I ever knew existed, and waiting near the check-in counter were Cordell in a striped shirt and khakis, and another guy named Randy in a polo shirt and a young, right heavy gal called Dee Dee wearing jeans and a devil-logo tee. Turns out the two are married; Randy's a Continental Airlines pilot based in Houston, and she's a lab technician at Methodist Hospital.

"I told Randy and Dee Dee here we got a greenhorn on our hands tonight," Cordell kids as he seemed to be studying the tight carpenter jeans and black suede boots I was wearing.

"Don't worry, honey," Dee Dee says. "I shot like a blind billy goat before Randy and Cordell shaped me up."

"Got any ammo?" Cordell then asks me as we go up to the counter to get paper targets, and I notice all this racket in the next room.

"Just this one clip," I tell him.

"Okay, you'll need at least fifty rounds," he says with real authority. "And we also gotta rent you some safety glasses and ear protectors."

Can't deny I felt like a jerk at first, but after we'd gotten all the ammunition, and moved into the room where the noise of guns at six separate ranges was earsplitting, and put on the glasses and protectors, and attached a target to the cable, I started to get the hang of it all. Then Cordell pushed a button that sent the target flying down about twenty feet, took aim with his S&W .38-caliber revolver, and blasted holes mostly in the black circle on the target.

"Doing good, sport," yelled Randy, who attached his target next, fired his .38 a few times, and hit one bull's-eye in the small, red center circle.

"You got it, boy!" Dee Dee screamed over all the noise from the other ranges, and before long she too was shootin' in the black with her .45 automatic like a real pro. I did notice when she bent down at one point, and her tee rode up over her jeans, she had a pretty hefty handlebar around her waist.

My turn next, so I gripped the Baretta with both hands the way I'd been taught at the gun shop, lined up the bull's-eye in my site, pulled the trigger, felt the gun kick like hell, and hit only the white outer circle.

"Try again, honey," Cordell blatted patiently, "and this time put your left foot forward and your right one back, take a deep breath, and hold it till you fire."

I did like he said but still hit only the white. So what he now does is step behind me, and force my right arm out really stiff while holding me around the waist with his left hand, and tell me to take aim and pull the trigger very slow. The gun kicks like hell again, but this time I hit smack in the black and they all cheer me on.

Well, this goes on for, I'd say, about forty-five minutes with each of us taking turns, and even though I never did hit a bull's-eye, I gotta admit that, yeah, I got better and better, and the better I shot the more fun I had. Then, when time came to leave and pay, and I tried to hand Cordell some money at the counter while Randy was settling up for himself and Dee Dee, he just looked at me kinda serious and said, "Next time I'm at Bluebird, you can fix me a couple of those great Manhattans on the house, okay?" That was awfully nice and considerate, I thought, but you know, what also impressed the hell out of me was how good Cordell smelled—soap, maybe aftershave, something kinda fresh and clean that reminded me of pine needles. First noticed it when he was close to me at the shootin' range, and now again when he whispered to me about the Manhattans, and . . . yeah, I gotta say that sort of thing really turns me on.

In any case, the four of us next went to this pizza place, and when they asked what all I like on top of mine, I didn't hesitate a minute to tell them it made no difference since I could eat only one slice and preferred to drink most of my calories.

"Loretta ain't got much stomach left and has to watch what she eats," Cordell tells the other two, like my condition was just a normal fact of life and didn't mean a thing to him.

"Gastric bypass?" Dee Dee asks nonchalantly.

"No. Banded gastroplasty. Silicone ring," I explain kinda nervously.

"Oh yeah," she goes on, "we do more and more lab work for that at Methodist." She then laughed, and grabbed a handful of fat around her middle, and said, "I ain't far off from having that procedure myself."

"Over my dead body," Randy barks playfully as he hugs her. "Hey," he then says, "we got a stewardess on the Buenos Aires flight who also had her stomach tied. Eats like a sparrow."

"How much you lose?" Dee Dee asks.

I wait a second like I'm figuring, then say, "Exactly 142 pounds."

"Yikes!" Randy blurts out.

Cordell was sitting close to me in the booth, and he pops my arm like he's known me forever and says to the other two, "What you don't know is Miss Loretta here is also a certified masochist. Guess what she does when she's not mixing drinks at Bluebird or playing saxophone at Ziggy's club."

They look puzzled, so Cordell now nudges my leg under the table and says like he's proud, "Tell 'em, babe. Tell 'em what you do for a living to help keep your weight off."

I laugh and say, "I cook. I love to cook and even do some catering."

Then we all laugh out loud, and I tell them a little bit about Glorious Bounty, and what suddenly dawns on me . . . what really strikes me is, I'm actually talking openly with no embarrassment about my weight and surgery—with strangers, no less—and nobody seems to give much of a damn one way or the other. And when this huge pizza arrives loaded with cheese and sausage and pepperoni and peppers and mush-rooms and Lord knows what other goodies, I take my one slice while the others dive in, and don't have to make excuses for not having another one, and just relax with my pizza and beer and new boyfriend and his shootin' pals. Kinda crazy, in a way, and yeah, I was dying for another wedge of that pizza, but I had to say to myself I was actually pretty happy for the first time in ages.

26

BEDROOM BOOTS

Sometimes I wonder exactly what I do to deserve all the punishment I get. I mean, I'm pretty good to Mama, and I work hard and pay my taxes, and care about animal welfare, and go through almighty hell to lose 142 hideous pounds to be healthy and attractive, and whadda I get but a lotta lip and heartbreak and . . . freaky stuff. What's funny is it always just creeps up on me with no warning when everything seems to be going so good.

Take this latest episode with Cordell. First, let me say that Cordell Hines is not a bad person. In fact, he's one of the most polite and respectful and classy men I've ever met—somebody who seems cut out to be a good husband and father and all around normal guy. Of course, all this was running through my head when we split up with Randy and Dee Dee at Pizza Pronto, and he puts his arm around me in the parking lot, and asks real nice if I'd like to follow him to his apartment on Woodway not far from his store in the Galleria for some music and a nightcap. Oh sure, I knew exactly what he had on his mind. I'm not dumb. And he even made some funny remark about the Ice Babe maybe thawing out before the night was over. But the truth is that I was as taken by Cordell as he apparently was by me, and I remembered even thinking back at the shootin' range that this considerate and fun-loving guy could put his shoes under my bed any time he liked.

Well, I'd have been more on target if I'd been thinking how I could put *my* shoes under *his* bed. Lemme explain.

When we got back to Cordell's really cool apartment with expensive-looking, modern furniture and a huge thin-screen TV and big-time sound system that made it clear he was in the electronics business, he told me this was all temporary while his divorce was going through. Then he offers me a drink or beer or anything I want, and puts on a CD of Gatemouth Brown, and we sit on the sofa, and when "Flippin' Out" comes on, I start bobbing my crossed leg and pretending to play this great tenor sax solo on my knee.

"Hey, girl," Cordell says after a while, "why don't you let me pull off those boots so you can put your feet up and get comfortable?"

I thought that was real considerate, so I held my boots up, and he pulled 'em off, and I just prayed my feet didn't stink. Then I stretched my legs out on the glass and steel coffee table and wiggled my feet to the beat of the music.

"Suede?" he says as he rubs one boot and then kinda sniffs it.

"Yeah. City Buckaroo. Pretty expensive, but they're so soft inside I don't even have to wear any sockettes."

"You usually wear sockettes?" he asks.

"Sure I do, most of the time."

"What size shoe you wear?"

I wonder why he cares but say, "Usually a nine, but these boots felt just fine in an eight and a half."

"Good size foot," he mutters as he reaches down and squeezes my left one. "High arches, I see."

"Pretty average now, I think. Used to wear a goddamn ten when I was so heavy."

"Wow!" he declares. "My wife, Angie, wears a nine and a half but has short toes."

"Oh, is Angie heavyset?"

"No, thin as a reed."

I wadn't sure how nosy I should be about his private life, but finally say, "You two must've had some serious differences."

He waits a few seconds, then answers, "Yeah, I guess you could say that. Angie thinks I'm the only one with problems, but, you know, as the old saying goes, it always takes two to tango."

"And she has the boy, I take it."

"Yeah, but I drop by and see Cody a couple of times a week. I take it you have no kids yourself."

"Naw, never got that far," I answer.

Well, I tell him a few things about me and Lyman, and he asks me some questions about the way me and Angel set up buffet receptions, and he fixes us both another drink, and all this time I'm wondering why in hell he's still kneeled at the coffee table and not making some sort of move on me. I mean, there I was on the sofa with my big boobs in the tight red tee, and yeah, I admit I was ready for a little action, and the only thing I could figure was Cordell was just trying to be a Southern gentleman and waiting for the right moment to play his cards. Shit, by now Vernon would have had me back in the sack going to town like gangbusters.

"Have I told you you got really beautiful feet?" he says at one point as he stroked my left foot up and down with his fingers.

I just laugh, and wiggle both feet, and say, "Thanks. That's sweet. Nobody's ever told me that before."

"Want a foot massage?" he then asks.

"Sure, why not?" I sorta mumble as I sip my Scotch and soda.

With which he begins rubbing and kneading and fingering first my left foot, then the right.

"Umm," I moan with my eyes half-closed the way I used to do when Daddy would give me a neck and shoulder massage.

"Feel good?" he asks, and when he leans down and kisses my right big toe real gently, I notice he's breathing heavy.

"Hell, yes," I mutter, and I gotta say it did feel sexy, and I got this sudden quiver that raced up my left leg to my stomach.

"Great nails," he says next. "Ever polish 'em?"

"Yeah, when I wear sandals in summer."

"What color?"

"Oh, red, pink, sometimes purple—depends on what I'm wearing."

"What kind of sandals?"

I now open my eyes wide and ask, "You really wanna know?"

"Sure."

"Oh, you know: platforms, gladiators, Mary Janes, plain old flip-flops—I got a lotta sandals."

"Umm," I hear him kinda groan as he keeps massaging, and before I know it, he is sucking on my left big toe and groaning even louder.

"Hey, bub," I finally say, "what's so great about my piggies and nails and shoes and all that?"

He don't look up and keeps staring at my feet like he's in some kinda trance. "I just like attractive feet, and gal, you got two beauties. Does that bother you?"

Well, I am pretty much at a loss for words, but finally say, "Never gave my feet that much thought, to tell the truth."

"Great-looking feet really excite me," he says right out before sucking my toe again. "Hope you don't think I'm crazy or anything."

And with that he finally gets up real fast, and I can't help but notice the huge bulge in his khakis, which, yeah, turns me on to no end. Then, before I can say another word, he's on the sofa kissing me all over my neck and face and lips, and I'm groping and squeezing and fondling him like the wild woman I can be. For a few minutes, I figured all the foot stuff was over and things would now move along more normally, but what I notice next is the whole time he's working me over like mad with his lips and really getting me churning inside, he keeps reaching down to my foot with one hand and manipulating it like some lunatic. I mean, any other fella would have been grabbing my boobs and all over my thighs and butt and privates, but all Cordell seemed to care about were my goddamn feet. And you know what suddenly dawned on me? What dawned on me was I think I could have been heavy and fat and gross as a whale and it wouldn't have made a particle of difference to this guy.

"Let's go back and stretch out," he sorta pants as he takes my hand and pulls me up and toward the bedroom before I can even grab my drink. Then we both strip off to our underclothes like maniacs. Now, what Cordell did next should have shocked and maybe scared me and sent me running for the door, but, like I said, I was so hot to trot with this really nice stud that all I could think about was trying to please him, no matter what. And what he did next was reach into a bureau drawer, and take out a pair of glittery black mesh women's stockings, and hold them up, and ask, "What would you say, pet, to slipping these on for me? I think they'd really look great on those beautiful feet of yours, and . . . would you mind, baby?"

Well, by then I was starting to catch on to what was really happening, and I remembered seeing on some TV program or reading in a magazine about men with weird sexual hang-ups. Oh, I thought about asking why in hell he had stockings in his apartment but decided to just play along with him and let him have his kicks any way he wanted. Also figured it could be pretty intriguing.

"Sure," I agree as I lift my right leg up from the bed and wiggle my toes again.

He simply holds one stocking a second, then hands it to me, and says, "Mind putting it on yourself? I'd really like to watch you put it on yourself."

So I take the damn stockings, and pull 'em tight up my legs, and watch as he rubs the erection in his jockeys and breathes heavy like he's been jogging a mile. Then he squeezes and licks and sucks my toes again, and before I know it, he's ripped off my panties and his shorts, and is kneeling on the bed in front of me with his big tool between my feet, and begging me to rub it back and forth with my toes. Well, I gotta say I never saw any guy so excited and thought he was going to explode right then and there when, all of a sudden, he jumps on top of me, and starts humping like there's no tomorrow, and yeah, drives me so crazy I let out a few screams. Wadn't till it was all over that I looked down and realized he'd been holding my left foot in his hand the whole time we were going at it. Go figure.

I guess I was hoping for too much when I thought there might be at least a little romance after things had cooled off, because the truth is I ended up feeling more like a piece of meat than anything else. Oh, like I said, there's nothing mean and crude and disrespectful about Cordell, and I sure wadn't expecting instant moonlight and magnolias with a man going through a divorce. You might even say I got exactly what I bargained for—not including, of course, all the goddamn footsie stuff. But it would have been nice to have him cuddle for a while, or to hear him say something besides, "Girl, you sho ain't no ice babe, I can tell you that," while he's pulling his shorts back on and laughing, or, for God's sake, to give me a little peck on the cheek. Instead, what he does after I've gotten dressed is reach in a drawer in the living room and hand me a small box.

"You got an iPod?" he asks as he opens the box.

"Why, heavens no," I answer. "But my girlfriend does."

"Well, girl, now you do too. Best one we carry in the store. All you have to do now is rip some Gatemouth and Travis and Nitty Gritty on it, and plug it in your ear, and you got music for cooking and the gym and anything else you want."

Naturally I thank him over and over, and when he don't mention maybe having another drink or listening to some more music, I tell him I better be making tracks since I got gym at the crack of dawn and Angel is due so we can begin work for a small reception at the Sculpture Garden. Of course I kept expecting him to mention the footsie thing and maybe try to explain it. Not a peep, and what's really weird is I don't think Cordell finds one thing the least bit abnormal about his perversion—like Vernon and his attraction to fat.

Okay, he finally did peck me on the lips at the door, and told me he had a great time shootin' and playing around, and reminded me I owed him a couple of Manhattans next time he was in the bar. Sure, I wouldn't mind seeing him again, but let's just say I ain't exactly holding my breath to have another piggy massage. Boy, do I know how to pick 'em, but like my daddy used to say, live and learn.

27

WICKED WAYS

This past Sunday at Mary Jane and Sam's wedding, I not only ate barbecue for the first time in ages but also smoked the first cigarette in my life. Or rather, I took a few puffs of Venus's Camel when she told me it might calm me down. Not that I ever actually looked down on anybody who smokes. I mean, after all, Mama smokes like a chimney, and I was always used to Sally smoking, and Billy Po likes his cigars, and of course Venus smokes, and come to think of it, I know right many people who still smoke. I guess I never smoked for the same reason I never did pot or coke or any other drugs. Health—pure and simple. Yeah, I heard all that stuff about how smoking helps keep weight off, so you'd think I'd be the first one to take up the nasty habit. But I never did. All I did was eat.

In any case, the reason I took my first puffs at the wedding was because I don't think I've ever been so humiliated and shocked and upset. Oh, it had nothing to do with the wedding at Ziggy's itself, which started at eleven and couldn't have been more beautiful. Mary Jane had invited almost everybody— Sally and the other workers at the shelter, all the Rhinestone rollergirls and their husbands or dates, Rosemary, Lyman, Lester, Vernon, even sweet Rudy from Bluebird. She also wanted to invite Mama for my sake, but when I told her what an ordeal that would be since Mama wouldn't know many people and would probably just gripe and complain, she understood my problem. And she was right about her daddy sparing no expense on the flowers and decorations and food and open bar and, yeah, the honorarium he insisted on paying me and Tricksy and Matt and Venus for the music. Nothing like a formal church wedding, and of course Buzzy supervised everything. Mary Jane was dressed in a simple yellow and white halter dress with a starburst pin and some baby's breath in her curly brown hair, and Sam wore a metallic sports jacket with a rose in the lapel and a longhorn shirt with a thin bolo tie and some good-looking bunker pants. But most people were in real nice leather jeans and pony tees and embroidered vests and skin boots and comfortable things like that.

Mary Jane was born and raised a Methodist, but she picked some preacher at the Congregational church named Pete Ledbetter she met through the shelter and is crazy about to do the ceremony—which I don't think made her mama and daddy any too happy. Tricksy did play the wedding march on keyboard, then, after all the official stuff was over, the three of us in the band struck up "Baby, Now That I've Found You" for Mary Jane and Sam to slow dance to, and Venus sang "Stand By Your Man" with my sax backup, and soon everybody was on the dance floor having a good time. That's when I first noticed Sally and Vernon dancing together, her in this tacky red-and-yellow-checkered tunic that just made her look fatter than ever and him in a V-notch crew shirt and leather jeans with wide suspenders. And that's also when I noticed Lyman go up and cut in on them, and then at least try to dance with Sally for a few minutes, and then begin shaking hands with Vernon like they were being introduced for the first time. Next, the three of them stepped off the floor and started talking and laughing real chummy-like. Who the hell knows what all they were saying, but it did piss me off and made me feel kinda weird and helpless and, yeah, a little jealous.

When Mary Jane and her daddy decided they wanted to serve pit-cooked barbecue at the reception in old-fashioned Southern tradition just the way I did when me and Lyman got married, I reminded 'em nobody would do a better buffet than the guys at Pink Pig Caterers, and I was right. Brisket, back ribs, links, sweet potatoes, beans, coleslaw, dirty rice, jalapeño cornbread, peach cobbler—enough food to feed a goddamn herd of cowboys. So after Buzzy banged on a steel steam-table lid with a big serving spoon, and we stopped the music, and everybody bowed their heads while Pete Ledbetter blessed the marriage and offered up thanks, the crowd lined up at the long table like a flock of hungry vultures and dug in—Tricksy and Matt and Venus included. Lyman did come up to me and offered to fix me a plate without so much as mentioning meeting Vernon, but when I told him I couldn't be tempted and might just pick at the barbecue later on, he patted me on my back and went to stand in line while I moved to the bar for a bourbon and water. I still don't know why Cha Cha had to invite both Lyman and Vernon, but sometimes she just don't think.

I gotta say everything was fine, and lots of people complimented me on the music and begged for more after lunch, and I was pretty calm till Sally and Vernon finally wandered over with small plates in their hands and asked if I'd sit down with them at a table for a few minutes. They both looked like ducks peeping at thunder, but I tried to remember that I have manners, and I couldn't help but be curious about what in hell they wanted now, so I played along.

"Still eating like a bird, I see," Vernon tried to joke as I plopped down my drink and Sally took a spoonful of her cobbler à la mode.

"Yep," was all I said.

"Don't Cha Cha look great?" Sally muttered between bites. "We're so damn happy for her and Sam—and to see so many of the old gang."

"Yeah," I said.

"Hey, gal, there still ain't nobody who blows 'Wicked Ways' like you do," he said as he leaned back and pulled on one of his suspenders that I noticed had faces of dogs all over them.

"Thanks."

"Y'all gonna play some more when everybody's finished eating?" he asked next, kinda nervously.

"Yeah," I said, "but Mary Jane promised Buzzy we'd all be outta here by three."

"Any chance Venus might do 'Jesus' for some line dancing?" he asked as Sally kept on gobbling her cobbler and ice cream.

I already felt uncomfortable with all this boring chitchat, so I reached down to rub my aqua tank, then took a big sip of my drink, and said, "Listen, you two, I gotta talk with Mary Jane's parents and Lester and some other people, so why don't you tell me if you got something on your minds?"

For a minute they both sat with their heads down, then Vernon put his arm around Sally's shoulder and said, "We do have something to tell ya, hon."

Sally wiped ice cream off her mouth with a paper napkin, and raised her puffy eyes, and almost whispered, "Let, we wanted you to hear it from us first, and we thought this would be the perfect time and place."

"Shoot," I said, thinking maybe Vernon had been laid off at Freedom Computers, or one of them might be changing jobs or moving out of town, or the two were in cahoots on a new business, or something like that.

She then got this big grin on her face, and glanced over at him, and said in this real syrupy voice, "Hon, what we got to tell you is me and Vernon . . . well, me and Vernon, we're gonna get married."

I won't say somebody could've knocked me down with a feather, 'cause the truth is I really thought she was kiddin'.

"Yeah, well, good luck." I laughed as I took another slug of bourbon.

Vernon then looked up and said, "Sal's serious, Let. We wouldn't hurt you for the world, but we been talking about it for a long time, and these things just happen, and all we can pray is you'll be happy for us and always be our good friend."

I just sat there and stared at them with my eyes wide open like a big bird, then finally said, "I don't think you're bull-shittin', are you? You're really not puttin' me on."

"No, hon. No bullshit," Sally mumbled.

"Well, I'll be goddamned" was all I could say then as I began to churn inside. "Miracles can still happen, I guess."

"They sure can, Let, and Vern even says I remind him lots of his Mona."

"He does, does he?"

Vernon then took her pudgy hand, and gave her this sick-ening look, and said, "It's not just that. Sal and I gradually real-ized just how much we got in common and how compatible we are in so many ways."

I glared at him and said, "I bet you are. Yeah, I bet you really are. And when does this earth-shaking event take place, Buster?"

"Don't be like that, doll, please," he grumbled.

"We ain't set a date yet," Sally answered. "But considering everything's that happened . . . I mean, you and Vern, and me and you being such good friends, and everything . . . we did think it was right for you to be the first person we told. Some of our friends might be a little surprised, you know."

"Yeah, I'd say you could be right on target there. And I gotta also give you two credit for having guts—real guts."

"Just hope you can always be our best friend," Vernon then said as he reached over and grabbed my arm. "You're a special gal and always will be, hon."

"Yeah, bub. One big happy family. Right?"

"Oh, Let," Sally whined.

Now I really did feel a little nauseated and dizzy, so what I did when I saw Venus in her sequin sheath at the buffet was tell them I needed to eat something before the next gig, and excused myself politely, and marched straight to the steel container of steaming brisket, and without really thinking forked a few slices on a plate, along with a couple of ribs and some slaw and a piece of cornbread.

"Hey, girl," Venus said as I dove into the barbecue standing right there on the floor. "Ain't you overdoing it?"

"I gotta eat," I think I said, though, come to think about it, I can't remember whether I really enjoyed the food or not.

"I know, child, but you don't have to go crazy," she kinda scolded me. "You know what can happen, honey."

"I've just had the goddamn shock of my life, Venus," I said as I gnawed on a rib and noticed Rudy talking to Rosemary not far away. "The shock of my life."

She just looked at me with her big, shiny, dark eyes and asked, "What's wrong, child?"

"Sally and Vernon. That's what's wrong and sick and perverted."

"Whatcha talking about, girl?"

"You won't believe it. You simply won't believe it. Nobody would believe it."

"Believe what, Loretta? Did they say something real ugly?"

I remember I was right on the verge of telling her what had happened when, in a split second, I began burping, and got that familiar burning sensation in my throat, and knew I was in trouble.

"I gotta go outside, Venus," I said real frantic-like as I put my plate down on the table, and hoped nobody was watching, and headed for the exit behind the bandstand.

"Wait up, child, and I'll go with you," she almost hollered after me.

How I made it to the exit without upchucking right there in front of everybody I don't know, but the second I got to the parking lot I started heaving and puking like I'd been poisoned, and by the time I felt Venus's hands on my waist from behind, I was crying and shaking and gasping for breath.

"I warned you, honey. You okay? You okay?" she kept asking. "You know you can't eat like that. Why'd you do it, child?"

"They're gettin' married, Venus," I sobbed as I tried to brace myself against a car. "Sally and Vernon just told me they're planning to get married."

She reached down in her cleavage for her Camels and matches and lit one up. "You gotta be kiddin', girl."

"I'm not kiddin', Venus. That's what they just told me— right to my face."

"Now, calm down, girl," she then said when she saw me shivering like a lunatic, and hugged me. "Just take a deep breath, hon, and calm down."

"Can you believe it, Venus? Him marrying that fat pig— my guy and my best friend getting married?"

She then puts the cigarette between her glossy red lips, and takes both my arms, and shakes me hard. "Pull yourself together, Loretta. You gotta pull yourself together. It ain't the end of the world, ya know."

"After all I been through, and now this." I kept crying like I'd been stabbed or something.

"Here, gal, take a puff of this and don't argue with me," she then says as she holds the cigarette up to my face.

"You know I don't smoke."

"No matter, child," she insists. "Just take a puff, and it may calm you down."

So I did, and inhaled, and coughed. Then I took another one, and felt a little dizzy, but this time I didn't cough, and it tasted pretty good, and yeah, was kinda relaxing, so I took another one.

"That's enough, girl," she says as she takes the weed, and draws on it again, and lets out a little laugh. "I don't wanna be accused of corrupting youth."

"Bastards," I say as I reach in the back pocket of my jeans for a Kleenex. "It's so sick."

"To hell with 'em," Venus mumbles. "Believe me, girl, I been through that kinda crap more than once myself, and . . . you can't let it get to you and start punishing yourself."

"Makes me feel like such a moron—a real fool."

"Loretta, hon, you ain't no fool," she says as she hugs me again, then asks, "You okay now, child? Remember, we promised Mary Jane we'd also do 'Finger on the Trigger' just for her and Sam. Feel up to it?"

I wipe my eyes again and say, "Shit, yes. How's my face look?"

"Almost pretty as this black girl's," she kids as I hug her back.

"You're a good friend, Venus."

"Oh, get on with you, girl."

28

MEAT LOAF MADNESS

Like I say, nothing takes my mind off personal problems like shelling a mess of butter beans, or sticking my hands in a bowl of dough, or mixing ingredients for a good casserole. Yeah, it can still be frustrating as hell not being able to eat the way I used to, but when things go right it's really something how fooling around with food and cooking and just tasting a beautiful dish can be the most satisfying experience I know. Take my drive home from Mary Jane's wedding. I could have sat there and cursed and bawled and felt sorry for myself over Vernon and Sally. Instead, I made myself concentrate on the two meat loaves and creamed succotash and tomato and olive aspic and chess pie me and Angel were fixin' to prep for a socialite's small birthday luncheon for eight the next day out in Cloverleaf. In fact, I decided I wouldn't even wait on Angel to start chopping and mixing everything for the meat loaves, which would not only give me something to do but allow the flavors of the unbaked loaves more time to meld in the fridge. And why two loaves for only eight guests? For the simple reason that I've learned never to take chances with possible accidents or big appetites—that's why.

Now, if I say so myself, my meat loaf's the best on earth,

mainly because it has no less than four different meats including a local bulk pork sausage that's got just the right amount of
fat to add flavor and keep the loaf moist. I also use minimum
bread filler for binding, and drape bacon slices over the top for
even more flavor and moisture, and, for crispiness on the sides,
I wouldn't dream of baking my loaf any way except free-form.
Bobby Flay and Paula Deen and Emeril and all those other
hotshots on TV fix meat loaves, but I've yet to see one I can't
find a bad flaw with. Mary Jane once called me "Houston's
Meat Loaf Queen," and Billy Po loves my meat loaf so much
he even said I should go on the food channel myself just to
show everybody what perfection's all about.

In any case, much as I was looking forward to changing
clothes and prepping for Mrs. Wainwright's luncheon after the
shock about Vernon and Sally, I knew it was gonnna be a bad
afternoon the second I opened the front door, and didn't hear
Sugar and Spice howling, and saw the sausage wrapper all
shredded on the living room rug. What I'd done was leave the
roll of sausage on the kitchen counter to thaw while I was at
the wedding. Don't ask me how one of the dogs managed to
reach up that far, or how the rascals chewed that heavy plastic
wrapper open, or why they hadn't vomited all over the floor
after wolfing down a whole pound of raw sausage. Of course it
would have been pointless to punish them, and all they did
when they saw me was sit and stare with big haloes around
their shaggy heads.

"Angel," I said when I called her cell, "the dogs have eaten
up all the sausage for the meat loaves, so could you stop by
Kroger and get another roll of Schwan's? Oh, please don't ask
me how, honey. They just did, and it's not been a great day for
me, so please just get the sausage and come over as soon as you
can so we can get to work."

Of course the second I got off the phone, I felt guilty the

way I'd been so snappy with Angel, but by then I'd started thinking about Vernon and Sally again and feeling like I'd been slammed in the butt with a baseball bat or something. I mean, I knew now Vernon was a sick man, and Sally was desperate to grab any guy who needed his firecracker lit, but . . . the two of them actually getting married, and thinking they can make a go of it, and maybe having babies? It was more than I could imagine, and just the idea nauseated me.

For a moment there, I couldn't seem to find my big chef's knife to chop the onions and bell peppers and celery and other veggies, then, all of a sudden, I noticed it right there next to the chopping board. That's how confused I was.

All that hell I went through to lose weight, I thought to myself, and where'd it get me except up shit's creek without a paddle?

I don't know whether I was sad or just tearing up from the onions, but soon everything seemed blurred as I chopped away at the mushrooms and garlic and pushed them over with the onions and celery and peppers. Then, like a lummox, I must have somehow beared down too hard on the handle of the cutting board stupidly sticking over the edge of the counter because, in a split second, the board flipped up and that whole goddamn pile of vegetables went flying all over the counter and stove and floor. I don't remember what filth spewed out of my mouth, but soon I heard the dogs yelping, and felt myself churning inside again, and was down on my hands and knees really crying my eyes out and trying to clean up all the mess with my fingertips and a sponge and wondering if I shouldn't just stop cooking altogether. No wonder Lyman and Vernon got rid of me, I figured. If I can't even chop vegetables for a meat loaf without screwing up, who says I got much more to offer than the Tiffanys and Sallys of this world?

"Angel, it's me again," I practically sobbed on the phone as I tried to pull myself together. "Also get a pound of mushrooms—oysters or shiitakes, if they have 'em. No, no, I'm fine. Just seems like nothing's going right today."

What I really wanted next was a cold beer and something to eat, but when I remembered what had happened with the barbecue at the wedding, I wised up fast about fixin' even a few pimento cheese crackers, and put on a Clint Black CD, and plopped down on the sofa with a bottle of Big Red to wait on Angel. That calmed me down a little while, till I started wondering how things might have turned out for me and Vernon if I'd let well enough alone when the scales read 175, or if I'd cooked him more tasty meals at home instead of going to all those restaurants, or if I'd been more of a wild woman when he wanted to play. Then I said to hell with him, and realized again he or no other man was worth my changing one thing about my new life, and decided to go back in the kitchen and chop some more vegetables and garlic and herbs and to hell also with the mushrooms till Angel showed up.

Normally, I would've sautéed all the veggies and herbs in butter before mixing them with the meats, but I've learned to improvise to save time when there's a problem, so decided just to go ahead and mix the ground beef and pork and veal with the various seasonings and deal with the sausage and mushrooms later on. I also usually improvise when I add mustard and Worcestershire and Tabasco and other things to my meat loaf. I'm sure Rachael and Paula and Bobby would have a conniption and say the meat loaf won't taste the same every time, but the truth is I don't want my meat loaf to always taste the same, and who the hell ever learns anything new if they don't experiment. And something else: Unlike some of those TV chefs, I mix meat loaf with my hands and am convinced if I don't, the texture won't be right. I mean, what's the big deal about sanitation and simply washing your hands?

Anyway, there I was squishing all that meat in the bowl between my fingers, which always feels so wonderful, when Clint

starts singing "Killin' Time" and I remember the afternoon
Vernon helped me make gumbo and burned the roux. Song
tells about a guy who's lost his gal and is now trying to lose
himself in the bottle just to kill time and forget. Well, I gotta
say I knew exactly how sad he felt, and if I hadn't had more
willpower and determination to get over this mess, not to
mention two meat loaves to fix, for two cents I think I
would've reached up in my cabinet, and grabbed that bottle of
Jim Beam, and poured myself at least four good shots—
straight. Besides, 'bout the time I'd added a speck more
ketchup to the meat, I heard Angel yell "Yoohoo" at the door.

I guess my face must have been a little puffy and my eyes
watery, 'cause the first thing Angel said when she saw me was,
"Are you okay, hon?"

Me and Angel never make a habit of discussing our intimate lives in any detail, so all I answered was, "Yeah, girl, I'm
fine, give or take the dogs gobbling up my one pound of
sausage, and me scattering a mound of chopped vegetables to
kingdom come, and . . . dealing with a couple of jerks at my
friend Mary Jane's wedding."

"Sorry to hear about that," she said as she opened some
gelatin to soften in a little V8 juice for the aspic while I
chopped mushrooms and heated butter in a skillet for sautéing
all the vegetables for the meat loaf mixture. "Did something
go wrong at the wedding?"

I began stirring the veggies real slow, and noticed that
wonderful smell of butter and onions, and answered without
thinking, "No, Angel, something went wrong with my life, if
you must know."

Angel's got dark hair that's almost in ringlets, as well as the
most beautiful green eyes I've ever seen, and she also happens
to be one of those lucky young women who can eat like a
horse and never gain an ounce—which is really odd considering her Mexican heritage and the way most of those gals tend

to get fat even in their twenties. I did tell her all about my weight problem and surgery not long after we met. Angel can talk a blue streak when it comes to food and cooking, but only on rare occasions had I heard her mention much about her life except her no-good father in the clink and a boyfriend who works at a boot factory and loves to go to Comets games.

"What are you talking about, Loretta?" she then asked as she heated more V8 juice in a saucepan next to my skillet, and I could smell her same cheap perfume she wears all the time.

I scraped the veggies and herbs into the bowl of meat, and added some bread crumbs I'd soaked in a little heavy cream, and began to mix everything again with my hands. "Lemme ask you a question, girl," I said.

"Sure," she muttered while she doctored up the gelatin mixture in her big bowl with grated onion and vinegar and Worcestershire and a couple of other seasonings and stuck it in the fridge to thicken.

"How serious are you about that guy you've told me about—if you don't mind me asking?"

"Who, Earl?" she asked like she wasn't too interested.

"Yeah, the one you say you've hitched up with."

"Where's the corn for the succotash?" she then asked, looking around the kitchen for the ears.

"In the fridge," I pointed out. "I cleaned and scraped the cobs before I left this morning. And the limas are in there too—shelled."

She sorta laughed. "Oh, Earl and I are pretty serious 'bout each other. Think he'd like to tie the knot with me, in fact."

I kept mixing the meats, which just didn't feel right. "Gal, I wouldn't get my heart too set on it," I then said kinda boldly.

"Whadda you mean?" she asked with real surprise.

"Burned, honey. You can get your ass burned bad and your heart broken to smithereens, you know. Take it from me, guys can be real jerks, and I ain't just talking 'bout the one I married."

"Oh, Earl's not like that, Loretta," she said as she started peeling and chopping two tomatoes. "He really cares about me."

"What are those tomatoes for?" I asked suddenly.

"The succotash."

"I don't put tomatoes in my succotash."

"You don't? It's a trick we Mexicans use in lots of creamed dishes to balance things up. You hardly know they're there, but the acid really does wonders to offset the rich cream. My mama taught me that years ago."

I thought for a moment about what she was suggesting, then said, "I'll be damned. Okay, let's give it a try. Can't do much harm." I gotta say I was more impressed than ever with Angel's know-how.

"You must've had a real bad experience," she then went on. "Was it the computer guy you mentioned meeting after that stomach operation you had?"

"Yeah, Vernon," I stammered. "A real SOB who wouldn't give a gal like you a second glance—if you wanna know the truth."

She jiggled the aspic to see if it was thickening, then turned and looked at me. "Whadda you mean?"

"Honey, you're not fat enough for Vernon. I wasn't fat enough. No gal's fat enough for a sick guy like Vernon—except my fat friend Sally, that is. And now I learn today the two are gettin' married."

Angel looked puzzled as she started chopping olives and celery to go into the aspic. "Is he heavyset?"

"Not in the least, and that's part of what's so sick."

"So the man just likes tubbies."

"Does he ever," I said as I kept trying to shape half my meat mixture into a perfect oval loaf and feeling like I might choke up again. "And Vernon was out the door when I was no longer tubby enough for him. Just wanted you to know what kind of stunts these guys can pull on a gal out of the blue."

"I gotta say that is pretty sick," she commented in a disgusted tone, "but Earl's nothing like that, Loretta. He couldn't be a more normal dude."

"Yeah," I cracked sarcastically. "They're all normal dudes. Boy, do I have stories I could tell." I pressed and patted and manipulated the soft loaf in my hands, then swore, "Goddammit, why won't this firm up and hold together? Never had this much trouble."

Angel reached over and stuck a finger in the loaf. "How many eggs did you use?"

Eggs. The second she mentioned them, I felt another shudder when I realized I'd totally forgotten to add any eggs to the mixture. And when this latest goof dawned on me, I suddenly lost all control, and bellowed "Shit!" and wondered again out loud if I just shouldn't stop cooking, and flung the whole lump of meat back into the bowl with the rest.

"Hey, gal." Angel tried to console me when she saw I was on the verge of bawling, putting her arm around my shoulder like she'd never done. "What's the big deal? I forget crap like that all the time, and you've just got lots on your mind."

"So stupid," I blurted. "It was so goddamn stupid to forget the eggs."

Within seconds, Angel had beaten three eggs in a small bowl and dumped them over the meat, and this time when I mixed everything together again, the two loaves finally felt exactly right and formed into perfect compact ovals. This calmed me down again, and made me think straight, and after I'd covered the loaves with plastic and put them in the fridge to ripen up overnight, I glanced at Angel as she fingered the aspic again and said, "Forgive my rotten mood, hon, and forget all my bullshit. I'm sure Earl's a great guy."

29

CHILIROO

This morning Mary Jane called on my cell at the gym to tell me the shocking news that Billy Po Cahill had been shot dead and I could read about it in the paper. Not many details, but apparently Billy Po had also been carrying on with some filly who worked in the service department of his Cadillac dealer, and when the gal's husband got wind of it, he marched over to Billy Po's house in Bellaire and blew his brains out with a shotgun just as Billy Po was pulling into his driveway. Sounds like really a mess, and when I called Margo Whitaker at Hawthorn Presbyterian to see if she knew anything more, all she said was how nobody at the church could believe what had happened and that she'd heard Sissy Cahill was so beside herself that one of Billy Po's sons had to take her to the hospital to be sedated. I hate to imagine what the folks at Mutual Savings are thinking and saying. Myself, I cried my eyes out all morning long.

Of course I know from firsthand experience about the stunts Billy Po could pull when he needed his firecracker lit, but I never, ever thought the man was crazy enough to hit on low-class trash like this hussy he was involved with. Boy, that was just plain down stupid. I mean, look how careful he'd been when he was dallying even with me before we became just good business friends. It's so sad and really breaks my heart. Billy Po always treated me with respect and had lots of faith in me, and I really liked the guy, and the truth is that without Billy Po's help and contacts, I wouldn't be half where I am now with the catering.

Take this chiliroo I did for the Dewitts a few weeks ago at their mansion in River Oaks. Okay, so the job almost ended up a disaster through no fault of my own. I still got my foot in an important door, and turned out one hell of a meal, and walked away with 5,500 big ones, and it was all because Billy Po recommended me to Mr. Clinton Dewitt. Now, Mr. Dewitt from Austin's not only the president of Century Petroleum in Houston and one of the richest oilers around, but he also happens to love chili as much as oil itself and prides himself on the Sunday chiliroos he and his wife Rose Ann throw twice a year on their enormous outdoor patio for exactly seventy-five friends. At least that's what Billy Po told me, and since Mr. Dewitt's big time at Mutual Savings and deals with everybody at the bank, Billy Po would have known.

Anyway, I'd always heard and read about those big shindigs all over River Oaks and would have given my eyeteeth to cater one. Then one day Billy Po calls and says this Clinton Dewitt tells him he's all upset 'cause the regular caterer for his chiliroos got thrown off a horse and died, and he needs somebody to handle the job.

"Bub," I told Billy Po, "I'll put my bowl o' red up against any in the whole state of Texas."

"But can you do chili and all the extras for seventy-five?" he asked.

"Honey, if you can do chili for eight or ten the way me and my mama always did, you can do it for seventy-five so long as the kitchen's big enough," I answered. "All I'll need's a little help on the prep."

Of course nothing would do, but I had to have an official

interview with Mr. Clinton Dewitt and his wife, Rose Ann, and was also expected to bring along some of my chili for them to taste. Well, Mrs. Dewitt's maybe forty-five, and thin as a rail, and there she is at this white stucco mansion in the middle of the day decked out in spanking-clean white ducks and what looks like a multicolored designer silk blouse and the biggest diamond ring I've ever seen and not a strand of blond hair out of place. Nice enough, I suppose, with that Austin twang, and when we go in the kitchen, I can't believe what I see. Granite countertops, Viking gas range with eight burners and a griddle in the middle, real sleek Sub-Zero refrigerator, two wide copper sinks, built-in microwave and rotisserie oven, two dishwashers, splashback Mexican tiles, and, best of all, a goddamn see-through glass wine cooler along an entire wall. What's also pretty obvious to me by the looks of the eyes on the range and the shiny pots and pans hanging on hooks over a butcher-block island is there ain't been a meal cooked in this kitchen in a coon's age. All for show, or as Lester says when a group of big shots sometime come in Bluebird and start flashing fifty-dollar bills, "Vulgar new money." Whatever, Mrs. Dewitt hands me an expensive All-Clad saucepan that I swear has never touched the stove, and I scrape my container of chili into the pot, and put it on to heat slowly.

Soon Mr. Dewitt appears in a pair of yellow slacks and a blue-and-white-striped polo shirt with his initials monogrammed on one sleeve, and anybody can see from his belly and jowls that the man doesn't miss many meals. Midfifties, I'd say, balding on top, a chubby pink face with thick black eyebrows, and after he says, "Howdy. Smells good" in his deep voice, the three of us pull up tall stools around the island so they can taste my chili. May be some put-on the way he dresses, but not the way he talks.

"See you do chunk chili," he says kinda suspiciously as he

looks at the small cubes of beef in his bowl and sprinkles some chopped onions and grated cheddar over the top before even tasting the chili.

"Yeah," I say. "Classic bowl o' red. Beef's browned first in a little suet."

He then pushes everything around with his spoon and asks, "Where're the beans?"

"I don't put beans in my chili," I tell him. "Authentic Texas bowl o' red doesn't have beans."

"I don't care what you call it, little lady, but I like beans in my chili, and my friends like beans, and I betta tell you you're dealing with a bunch of real chiliheads at this chiliroo."

"What I do is serve big bowls of spicy pintos on the side," I say, "and if people want beans, they can add 'em."

"Clint really does love beans in his chili," Mrs. Dewitt chimes in as she takes a tiny bite and raises her thin eyebrows like she might be surprised.

"Up in Austin we always served chili with beans at our chiliroos," he goes on while still just dipping his spoon in and out of his bowl, "and we've never thrown one down here that didn't have beans in the chili."

On one hand, I could tell the man was going to be pretty obstinate about the goddamn beans, but on the other, it really impressed me how he cared this much about the matter. What I wadn't about to do was make him mad and have him tell me to get lost, so what I said with as much gumption as I could drum up was, "Mr. Dewitt, why don't you just taste my chili, and if you still want beans, it's easy as pie for me to put some in."

He finally eats a big spoonful, and chews for a few seconds, and his eyes open wide. Next he takes another bite, and chews even longer like he's thinking real serious about what he's tasting, and finally gets this big smile on his face.

"Sister, I always shoot straight, and I know good chili from bad, and I gotta say that's some of the best damn chili I've ever put in my mouth," he announces like an authority.

"Why, thank you, Mr. Dewitt," I say real calm so I don't let on how relieved I am.

"Yep, you got it down pat," he goes on as he spoons more from the pot into his bowl and adds more onions and cheese. "Whatta you think, pun'kin?" he asks his wife.

"Perfectly delicious," she sorta purrs in her high-class manner, though she seems trying to resist eating more.

"Just the right amount of cumin and oregano, I can tell," he adds, "and with that zing you got the chile peppers right on the button—three-alarm, I'd say."

"Plus paprika and Tabasco and guess what? Beer," I inform him. "But wanna know my real secret? A little bit of bitter chocolate."

"Chocolate!" he exclaims.

"Yep, chocolate."

"How much?" he asks real excited.

"That's my little secret, Mr. Dewitt," I tease him as I chuckle.

"Well, I'll be damned."

"I'm so glad it's not too soupy," Mrs. Dewitt says next. "Just thick enough."

"Masa harina?" he asks.

"My, my, Mr. Dewitt," I try to compliment him, "I can tell you do know your bowl o' red."

He finishes up the bowl and lets out this crude laugh. "Don't fix any myself, but I warned you, sister, you're dealing with real chiliheads around this house."

"So you've decided you like it without the beans?" I ask.

He wipes his mouth on the linen napkin like he's just eaten Russian caviar instead of plain old Texas chili. "Now, I ain't saying that by a long shot, Loretta, 'cause for me chili's not chili without beans. But I got an open mind, and, besides, you say you also fix a big pot of pintos on the side?"

"Yeah, I do, spiced up with jalapeños."

"What else you serve with your chili?"

"Anything you want," I tell him in a real confident tone. "Guacamole, coleslaw, rice, tacos, sour cream, red pepper vinegar, and maybe some corn tortillas my Mexican helper makes—just tell me whatcha like."

"And beer?" Mrs. Dewitt asks.

"Sure. You can't eat a bowl o' red without plenty of beer."

"Our bartenders also serve lots of margaritas at our chiliroos," he says. "Things can get pretty lively." He lets out another big laugh.

"Sounds good to me," I say.

"And you can handle seventy-five, Billy Po Cahill tells me?"

"That's what I'm in business for, Mr. Dewitt," I tell him like I'm an old hand at this kind of job.

"Then I'd say, young lady, we got a deal," he says as he cleans the last morsel from his bowl. "And who knows, from what I just tasted, you might even make us all beanless chili hounds." Once again, he bursts into another belly laugh, then looks at Mrs. Dewitt. "Honey, you work out the details with Loretta. Buddy Elwood's expecting me over at the club, and we got nine holes to play."

Well, the details first involved the most greenbacks I ever made in my life, and it was Mrs. Dewitt who asked if "$5,500 plus expenses would be acceptable"—the same whopping fee she said they paid the other caterer. I just sorta nodded my head yes like I was used to this kind of money. I then told her I figured I should fix four five-gallon pots of chili just to play it safe, but that since I couldn't deal with that many pots in my own kitchen, I'd have to do the cooking in hers—if that was okay. No problem. What was a problem were the pots themselves. Mrs. Dewitt seemed a little surprised that I don't own four five-gallon chili pots, and since all she has is one small All-Clad pot, I said I'd have to rent the big pots from a kitchen supply house the way any caterer would do for a big job like this.

"Oh, that's what Prissy used to always do," she says, "and I'm getting a little tired of having to worry about chili pots round here, so why don't you just go to Neiman Marcus, and buy the pots you need, and they can put it on my charge."

Would be nice, I said to myself, just as it would be nice to have the stacks and stacks of beautiful hand-painted earthen-ware bowls she was planning to use for the chili. In any case, we got everything straight, and decided what would be on the menu, and the only problem left was who in hell I was gonna get to help me and Angel fix all that food. I mean, it's not like I'm set up yet with a full staff to do major prep work, or know the ropes about hiring more help at the last minute for one big job. So 'bout the only option I had was to call Rosemary and Mary Jane and also a gal in the band who loves to cook, and beg them to help me out in this emergency, and offer to pay 'em to just peel and chop and stir and do things like that. What I prayed was I hadn't bitten off more than I could chew.

Just as I thought, my friends couldn't have been nicer, and we showed up at the mansion after early church with tons of stuff in Angel's van, and everybody worked their butts off doing what I told 'em. By middle of the afternoon we had four big pots of chili simmering on that giant stove, and bowls of guacamole and beans and slaw and tacos and I don't know what else ready to go on the buffet, and black skillets of jala-peño cornbread in the two ovens. Outside on the huge patio were big round tables with red checkered tablecloths and um-brellas, and it seemed like waiters and bartenders were every-where going about their business. Even a small combo at one end playing country. What was really weird was seeing all these servants in formal uniforms when most of the Dewitts' guests couldn't have been more casually dressed in real colorful slacks and ritzy tees and polos and Bermuda shorts and even sandals. And boy, can these people wandering around down the booze and beer—especially margaritas in crystal glasses with thin stems like some I've seen at Williams-Sonoma. Of course Mr. Dewitt himself was playing the big enchalada he wanted to be, though, to be frank, I think he looked like a jerk wearing a monogrammed green blazer and pair of red Bermuda shorts and what looked like real expensive alligator loafers with no socks at a goddamn chili party.

Whatever, time comes to serve the chili, and the guests seem to be feeling their oats, and nothing will do but for Mr. Dewitt to ring a crazy cowbell he's got on the patio, and bellow "Chili time!" and wheel one of the big, piping-hot pots on a metal wagon from the kitchen across the sandstones to the long buffet table already covered with food. I did ask him if this wadn't pretty risky business, but nobody questions Mr. Clinton Dewitt, and all me and Rosemary and Angel and even Mrs. Dewitt could do was hold our breath. Well, he made it past the first two tables while everybody watched and cheered, but just as he reached the third table, one wheel of the cart must've hit an uneven stone, and the big chili pot started wobbling, and before anybody could steady it or do anything, the whole goddamn pot fell backwards and every ounce of that boiling hot chili went spilling and splashing all over Mr. Dewitt's jacket and shorts and bare legs and feet and also in the laps of a real snooty-looking couple sitting at the table.

I gotta say I don't think I ever heard anybody on God's green earth howl as loud as poor Mr. Dewitt did, and for a few minutes there was real chaos at that chiliroo. Biggest mess I ever saw, and Mr. Dewitt was so doubled over in pain that all a couple of his buddies and one waiter could do was grab him and help him back to a stool in the kitchen so me and Mary

Jane and Mrs. Dewitt could try to wipe him off with wet towels and see how bad he was burned.

"Where's Leroy Finch?" Mrs. Dewitt screamed at the crowd peering from the patio. "Somebody get Leroy!"

Soon a handsome, middle-aged man in beige slacks and a denim longhorn shirt rushed up, and it was pretty obvious he was a doctor by the way he inspected Mr. Dewitt's legs and feet and pulled off his saturated Bermudas down to his boxer underwear right there in the middle of the kitchen.

"Clint, honey, are you okay?" Mrs. Dewitt kept squealing at her husband as he made awful faces when the doctor so much as touched his legs or thighs. "You hurt much, sweetheart? Are you okay?"

"Oh, simmer down, Rose Ann," he muttered real gruff-like in a weak voice, "and you women go look after the folks. Leroy'll take care of me."

"You got some bad burns, Clint," the doctor finally said as he pulled a tiny cell phone out of his pants pocket. "I'm calling EMC and gettin' you to emergency. These need to be treated, old buddy."

"Son of a bitch," Mr. Dewitt kinda moaned.

I'd been standing next to the doctor with a clean, wet towel in my hand, and when I noticed the blistered skin on Mr. Dewitt's tanned right knee and the top of his chubby feet, it was easy to see why he wadn't objecting to medical attention.

"Guess I should've listened to you, little lady," he then managed to gasp at me. "Hope you got plenty extra of that great chili."

That made me feel good and relieved, so I said, "Don't you worry about a thing, Mr. Dewitt. Just go get yourself taken care of, and we'll handle everything here."

And, goddammit, we did sorta take over after the ambulance arrived and took Mr. Dewitt and his wailing wife to some hospital. That uppity couple back on the patio were lucky the only damage done was to their designer jeans, and, mean as it sounds, I almost got a kick out of watching 'em hop off somewhere like chickens since, after all, they hadn't so much as glanced in the direction of the kitchen to see if their host was dead or alive.

"Excitement's over, folks," I yelled at the small crowd still gawking. "Mr. Dewitt's gonna be just fine, and soon as we clean up the mess, there'll be a whole new pot of chili."

Next I noticed a drain not far from where the chili was splattered all over the sandstones and figured there had to be a hose around somewhere. When a man pointed to one looped over a hook at the far end, I signaled for everybody to move back, and hosed all the chili down the drain, and, to tell the truth, I think they found the action pretty exciting and didn't mind the wet floor at all. Then me and the girls got a waiter and bartender to carry another pot of hot chili by the handles to the buffet table, and we warmed up the beans and corn-bread and tacos, and before long the combo was playing again and everybody was having fun and raving about my chili and other food like nothing had ever happened. Funny, but not one single person made any comment about the chili having no beans, and two guys even wanted my recipe—which, of course, I wouldn't give them. A couple of others also asked for my business card, and I gotta remember to have some of those printed up if I wanna be really professional.

Me and my gang were pooped after we cleaned up and got the kitchen and patio back in perfect shape, and after all that work, I rewarded myself by sitting down with the others and eating a whole bowl of my delicious chili and a few tacos with no repercussions whatsoever. I do think I shocked Mary Jane and Rosey when I asked one of the waiters for a puff of his cigarette to calm me down a little more, but boy, did that chiliroo teach me a thing or two about what big-time catering

is all about—especially when you're dealing with Houston's
finicky top brass who'll apparently shell out oodles to impress
one another. First time, in fact, I convinced myself I could
really make a go of Glorious Bounty if I hired more staff and
bought more equipment and really got my act together. Yeah,
poor Billy Po would have been proud of the way I handled
things at the Dewitts, and now he's gone. I should've called to
thank him again, and that's eatin' me up.

30

RAGING BULL

Can't say Mary Jane didn't warn me, but I still think it took a hell of a lot of nerve for Sally and Vernon to show up at Ziggy's with her and Sam Saturday night. The place was packed, and there the four of them sat at a front table slugging beer, and all I could think about while blowing backup to Venus's soulful version of "Chattahoochiee" was how much had changed since the time I felt so bad for fat Sally and made her join me and Vernon and the others for the roller derby and Ziggy's and the bull room. I guess what really dawned on me most was how I'm now the odd gal out and how my romantic life's not much better than it was when I was big as a whale. Maybe I'm just a goddamn fool.

But I don't let these things get me down, so when I blew my last solo, and ignored a couple of jerks calling out for Bubbles to play more, and finished the set, and Vernon almost begged me to have a bite with the four of them, I accepted if for no other reasons than to show them I still had manners and was in full control of myself. I also happened to be hungry as hell, so this time I decided to throw caution to the wind, and treat myself to the first Tex-Mex burger in ages, and order a double Wild Turkey and splash, and just pray my stomach would cooperate. What really surprised everybody was when I bummed a Marlboro from Sally and held it up kinda defiantly for her to light.

"When did you start smokin', doll?" Vernon asks like he's dumbfounded.

"Just once in a while," I reply casually. "Good for the digestion, and they say it helps keep the weight off." I glance at Sally to see her reaction, but she's now too busy pouring beer from the pitcher to notice.

Oh, I know I should've felt guilty about the greasy burger and cigarette, but nothing ever tasted so good, and the truth is I really didn't give a damn under the circumstances. I mean, Mary Jane and Sam all hitched up, and my old girlfriend planning to tie the knot with the one guy I really cared about, and me . . . I guess I was supposed to just marry my saxophone or something. Yeah, I gotta admit I was feeling kinda sorry for myself, so after I finished my burger and smoke and got bored with the chitchat, I was about to say adios and maybe have another drink with Buzzy at the bar when one of the strapping bucks drinking at the next table got up and came over to me.

"'Scuse me, darlin', for interrupting," he said in a strong Texas accent, "but me and my two buddies just wanna tell ya how great we think your playing was tonight—'specially 'Mama, Get the Hammer.'"

"Why, thank you, cowboy," I said.

Young, clean-cut-looking fella with sandy hair and wearing faded jeans and a maroon leather shirt with a Bud logo that showed off his husky build, but what really got my attention were his eyes, which were the lightest blue I think I've ever seen. I also noticed he wasn't wearing a wedding ring.

"Any chance you might be tootin' some more tonight?" he then asked. "Don't hear many country bands with a sax."

I laughed and said, "'Fraid not, bub. I'm blown out on country and leave it to my pals to finish up the R & B."

"Well, you play one hell of a horn, gal," he went on real friendly-like, "and me and my buddies just wanted to tell ya so."

"This your first time at the club?" I asked.

"First time in this room, yeah. We come over to ride the bull, but this time they tell us there's a wait for a bench, so we come in here for some hooch till things clear out a little back there."

"So you ride the bull?" I asked as I notice the way he's staring down at my silver fringe lace-up vest that does full justice to my boobs.

"You betcha I do," he said. "My record's eighteen seconds at full throttle."

"Eighteen seconds," I said. "You're a real buckaroo, ain't ya?"

He had this proud look on his face. "I hold on pretty good, I reckon."

All this time the four others hadn't uttered a peep, though I noticed Cha Cha had a strange look on her face while this guy talked. Then Vernon finally spoke up and said with a laugh as he pointed at me, "We ride, all except Loretta here, that is. She's chicken."

I snapped my head around, and glared at him, and said, "That was a long time ago, Buster. Try me today."

"Ya name's Loretta?" the man asked.

"You got it, bub," I answered as I really looked him over.

He reached out to shake my hand. "Virgil's mine. Virgil Hobbs. Please to make ya acquaintance."

I didn't have much alternative but to introduce him to the others, and I gotta say it did my heart good to see maybe a little jealous expression on Vernon's face as he stared at Virgil.

"Care to join us for a beer?" I then asked when he made no move to go back to his table.

"Don't mind if I do," he said as he reached over and pulled

his chair next to mine. "My teammates can live without me for a while."

"Teammates?" I asked before I signaled the waiter for another glass.

"Yeah, we race together. Cars."

"Whereabouts?" Sam asked.

"Mainly Motorsports Park, but we also do some NASCAR when we get sponsorship." He pointed to the BUD on his shirt. "Fort Worth, Talladega, Lowe's, and a couple of other tracks."

"I used to drag a dirt track up in Waco," Vernon said like he was trying to impress Virgil. "Modified Ford Taurus."

"Good car," Virgil said.

"Hey, we've been out to Motorsports a couple of times," Mary Jane piped in, "and once even went up to Fort Worth. Maybe we've watched you race."

"Could be," Virgil commented before turning back to me. "You also a fan, darlin'?"

"Just TV once in a while," I answered kinda awkward, "but I'd love to go to a racetrack sometime."

He popped me on the arm and laughed and said, "Gal, I'm sure that could be easily managed." He then gawked at me again with those blue eyes.

Turns out Virgil's originally from Beaumont and was a garage mechanic before his daddy got him interested in a Dodge Challenger he built for the track. And once Virgil drove that car and won a couple of races for his daddy over in Pasedena, he told us, the racing fuse was lit. Been driving professionally for lots of rich car owners ever since—going on fifteen years. And the way he talked about prize money, I figured Virgil must have a pretty nice nest egg himself by now.

"Had many wrecks?" Sam then asked him.

"Oh, we've all had our share of pileups, but I only been down bad one time—clipped dead right into the wall and ended up with a broken collarbone and a few ribs."

"Know what you mean." Mary Jane laughed. "I do roller derby over at the Thunderdome, and I cracked a collarbone once and had to wear a damn cast for a month."

"No shit," was Virgil's reaction.

"Remember that, hon?" she then reminded Sam.

He smiled and gave her a sweet look and said, "How could I forget? It ain't easy trying to hug a hunk of plaster."

Everybody pretended to laugh.

"Speaking of which," Virgil then said, "are you guys up to breaking a few bones on the bull with us? Should be some free benches by now."

Before Vernon or anybody else could make another snide remark about me being chicken, I spoke up without catching a breath and said, "Sure, bub, I'm game." Of course I prayed I wouldn't end up eating my words, but the truth is I now had my eyes set on Virgil, and no problem at all with the burger, and the bourbon was working its magic, and I had a few things to prove to my friends, so, hell, why not give it a shot?

"You all by yourself, darlin'?" Virgil then asked me.

"Yep" was all I said.

"Gotta count me out for the next seven months," Mary Jane bragged with a grin while patting her tummy.

"Congratulations," Virgil said like he meant it.

Vernon looked at Sally and asked, "Wanna have a go, hon?" She just nodded her head up and down like she wasn't sure.

Next, Virgil introduces us to his two pals, Clark and Bobby Lee. Clark lives in Houston, but Bobby Lee's from Dallas and down to test a Chevy Cobalt for some race at Motorsports. Well, soon the whole gang of us are perched on a bench back in the bull room slugging beer and yelling and waiting our turns for the bull with everybody else. Just like before, Sam and Vernon and Sally don't last more than a few seconds, and I still think Sally's making an embarrassing spectacle of her fat self.

Then Virgil mounts up wearing his cowboy hat, and the sucker bucks at least ten seconds, and raises his hat for more juice, and holds on a good four or five seconds more till he finally spills. Next, his two buddies make almost as good a go, and the crowd is wild cheering and whooping.

"Okay, Miss Loretta," Virgil said as he took my hand and pulled me up. "Show us whatcha got, gal."

I gotta say I was scared shitless at first while I tightened the laces on my vest and tucked my jeans in my boots, but I was never so determined to do anything as get on that bull, and when Virgil grabbed me around the waist to help me up and said, "Try to land on ya hands when you spill," that just upped my confidence even more.

So I steady myself in the saddle, and raise my arm, then hold the horn with both hands for dear life, and, whoooa, am flat on the floor in what seems like a split second. Yeah, the bucking was just as brutal as it looked, and I can't imagine how anybody could hold out for full throttle, but the truth is I really wadn't all that frightened while it was going on, and I guess I showed Vernon and the others I could be as tough as any roper, and Virgil hugged me when he helped me up like I'd just won a rodeo. Of course I'm not stupid and never forgot my gut for one minute, so when the others had another go, and Virgil and Clark and Bobby Lee bucked at least twice more, I just sat and watched and wondered what might be in store for me later on in the way of hanky-panky with Virgil. I admit I was also pretty looped by now, and though Clark and Bobby Lee neither one still had much to say, after his last go Bobby Lee did put his hand on my shoulder and say, "Keep at it, gal. Soon you'll be as good on the bull as ya are on the sax." In fact, for a second, I thought he might even be flirting with me.

"Me and Sal are 'bout ready for a pit stop," Mary Jane said

as the two got up, and she winked at me. "Wanna come along and powder ya nose?"

I figured she was trying to tell me something, so I also excused myself and teased Virgil kinda forward-like by saying, "Don't bust your ass, bub, while we're gone. We still got some serious drinking to do—if you reckon you can keep up."

"Darlin'," he kidded back as he stood up and pulled my chair out like a real gentleman, "I was ahead of you half an hour ago."

Back in the little girls' room, Mary Jane surprised me when she said in a very serious tone, "It's really none of our business, hon, but me and Sal both get bad vibes from those dudes out there and hope you don't plan on doing anything crazy."

"Whadda you mean?" I asked. "Virgil's a great guy and lots of fun."

"Just something not quite right about 'em," Sally said.

"Don't that Virgil seem a little pushy and full of himself to you, Let?" Mary Jane added as she put on lipstick at the cracked mirror.

"Why, they just love to ride the bull and kick up their heels," I said, "and Virgil couldn't be treating me more like a lady, so I don't know what y'all are talking about."

"Let, we're only saying we don't wanna see ya run into any trouble," Sally went on. "Those guys have had lots to drink, and they're here without gals, and we think they may just be out on the prowl and up to no good."

I finished drying my hands and checked my lipstick and mascara and then stared hard at Sally. "And, sister, you know all about how to deal with guys who drink too much and hit on broads, don't ya?"

She looked like I'd slapped her in the face, and all she can say is, "I know I deserve that, Let, and I guess you'll always be pissed off at me and Vernon, but you gotta believe me and

MJ when we say we worry about you and strangers like those fellas."

"Just promise us, hon, that you'll be careful if this Virgil comes on heavy like he seems to be doing," Mary Jane almost begged.

"Oh, for God's sake, woman, it's not like I'm gonna be raped and strangled by some weirdo maniac," I kinda growled. "Lemme have a little fun, okay?"

"Sure, Let," she said as Sally finished stuffing her tassled shirt in her jeans over all the fat. "Remember, hon, you're pretty tanked yourself, so just promise you'll watch your p's and q's."

I put my arm around her skinny waist as we went out the door and said, "Goddammit, Cha, I'm a big girl, so stop worrying your head off about me."

31

WILDCAT KICKBOXING

"Ya like to dance?" Virgil asked me as we all left the bull room and headed back into the club.

"Love to dance," I answered, "but for some goddamn reason, my boss around here don't allow members of the band to dance with customers on nights we're playing."

"You two-step?"

"You betcha, bub. My favorite."

"Then what say we go out to Cozy Coral?" he suggested.

"Never been, but this gal I work with at Bluebird's always talking about that place. Good as Dixie Stampede?"

"Hell of a lot better. Best two-steppers in the whole state of Texas."

"It's gettin' pretty late, you know."

"Shit, hon, they're just warming up at Cozy Coral. So whadda ya say?"

I turned around to the others following us and asked, "Hey, you guys, y'all wanna go dancing at Cozy Coral?"

Like I expected, Sally came up with her old song and dance about having to get up early for church, and since Vernon didn't make any move to coax her, I had a pretty good idea what was on his sick mind. Mary Jane said friends had invited them to lunch the next day before an Astros game, and when I looked around for Clark and Bobby Lee, I noticed they'd already meandered over to the bar and were talkin' up some chicks.

"Maybe we betta just tuck it in, cowboy," I then said to Virgil, though I did love his arm around my back and just hoped I didn't feel too fat to him. "We ain't exactly sober as a judge, you know, and I got some cooking to do tomorrow."

"Oh, come on, darlin'. I gotta time trial on a Camry tomorrow afternoon, so if I can go packin' tonight . . . whatta ya say to 'bout an hour of two-stepping?"

I gotta admit it didn't take much to convince me, 'cause the truth is my stomach felt just fine and I was raring to go if only to show Vernon and the others I got more spunk than all them put together. Of course Mary Jane sorta whispered, "Remember, hon, what we said," as they headed out, and I could have sworn Vernon just shook his head before he hugged me like a sister or somebody, but I'd made up my mind to go dancing with Virgil and to hell with what the others thought.

While I was telling them 'night, I noticed Virgil had gone over to talk with his buddies, and when he got back, he asked, "Mind driving? I came with them and they wanna hang out here a while."

I laughed and said, "You telling me to wheel a race car driver around? What I'll do is watch you drive my Ford Focus if you promise not to gun it over one hundred."

He was right about Cozy Coral. Huge dance floor with strobe lights, country music blaring from loud speakers with some kicker doing voice-over between numbers, and must've been a good hundred dudes in hats and gals in jeans or ruffled miniskirts and a few female couples two-stepping round and round in the same direction. Playing was "Firecracker," so before we go to the bar, Virgil grabs me and starts leading me in twirls and full turns and side steps and even triple two-steps. And I gotta say I followed him like a real pro.

"Hey, babe, you're damn good," he compliments me when he raises my arm and I do two double turns in a row. After a few more fast rounds, he says he's dry as a bone, so we amble over to the bar, and he orders two bourbons and water, and we plop down at one of the small tables at the edge of the floor to cool off and wipe our faces with a bandana he pulls out of his back pocket. He then tries to tell me something about his mama's Osgood pie, but the racket's so loud I can hardly hear him and, besides, what's really on my mind is slow dancing with him and feeling him hold me tight.

'Bout that time, on comes "If I Ain't Got It (You Don't Need It)," and suddenly standing at the table is this pretty hefty middle-aged guy and his chubby girlfriend, and he yells over the music to Virgil, "Hey, bronco, can I steal ya gal for one round and let ya have a go with my Polly here?"

That really caught me off guard, but Virgil explained later that everybody likes to mingle like that at Cozy Coral, and I had to admit that other guy was as good on his feet as Virgil and it was all lots of fun. After we did a couple of rounds, they finally put on a slow number, "Someday," with lots of acoustic guitar, which made Virgil hold out his arms to me and get a big smile on his face and pull me close like he was gonna smother me. Made me tingle all over when I felt his strong body pushing up against mine and noticed his real manly smell mixed with the liquor on his breath, and yeah, the way I pressed my boobs against him and stuck my knee between his legs, I think he knew he had a wild woman on his hands.

Anyway, by now we were both pretty smashed, so after we'd danced maybe a half hour more, he grabs me and squeezes and says, "Ya know I ain't got no wheels, so what say we get outta here, and you drop me off at my place, and if you're game, maybe we could even kick off our boots for a little while and have a nightcap?"

"You live alone?" I ask, and it dawns on me that neither one of us has yet so much as mentioned whether we ever been married or what. Also makes me shudder when he talks about kickin' off our boots, and I wonder if maybe I got another crazy Cordell on my hands.

"Yeah, all alone," he answers. "Bobby Lee's bunking at the house while he's in town, but Bobby Lee's a real night owl and don't usually get in till the rooster crows."

Guess it was pretty obvious I was hot to trot, so I didn't pay much mind to Bobby Lee or anything else as me and Virgil tottered arm in arm out to the car and he took over the wheel again. Next thing I know we're turning off Navigation onto a small road that goes up to the bayou, then Virgil pulls into a gravel drive that leads up to what I can make out as a real modern-looking, big house that's kinda secluded right on the water. Parked out front's a red Camaro with lots of trim, and when I ask if he races that, he laughs, and says nobody toots around town in wheels you race on the track, and makes me feel a little dumb. What I say to myself is I wish I had thirty-five or forty grand to shell out on a Camaro like his—not to mention what this house must have set him back. Then what Virgil does is hurry around the car and open my door like a real gentleman, and I just leave my bag on the seat and get out.

"A few fingers of hooch?" he asks when we go in this living room full of modern, light-wood furniture that looks sorta Scandinavian and expensive but not very practical.

"Yeah, with a big splash," I answer. "Great house you got here."

"Thanks, but no thanks to me," he says in a slurred voice.

"Whadda you mean?"

"What ya see, gal, is what I bought 'bout a year ago. Owners both killed in a plane crash, and I bought it furnished as is with all this modern shit. Not my style at all, but, ya know, I'm on the road a lot racing and ain't had much time to fool around with this place. What I like's just being private here on the water."

He picks up a stack of CDs on a table and asks, "Ya like Dwight Yoakam?"

"Love him. Best honky-tonk guitarist around, and he's also got one hell of a piano player in that band. I've soloed some of his stuff at the club."

While he was back in the kitchen fixin' drinks, I couldn't help but notice all the race car trophies and plaques and pyramids and other things on the stone mantel and small glass tables. There was also a framed picture of an older woman with salt-and-pepper hair next to the wood-framed sofa, and I figured this had to be his mama. For a second, it sounded like he was trying to say something to me or maybe talking to somebody on a phone, but I couldn't make it out 'cause of the music.

He then hands me my drink, but instead of plopping down next to me on the sofa, he puts his drink on the table, and holds out his arms while Yoakam sings "Ain't That Lonely Yet," and says, "How 'bout another turn, sugar?"

Well, there for a while, Virgil just held me tight as we shuffled back and forth and he'd break a little and look at me with those light blue eyes, which were now kinda glassy. Actually, it was pretty romantic, and I couldn't have felt more relaxed and liked and respected, and for the first time in ages I don't think I gave a second thought to being too fat. Then, things began to heat up when I noticed the hard bulge in Virgil's jeans and responded by grinding up against him like I knew he'd want, and in no time he'd let go of my right hand and was stroking and squeezing my breast so passionately I thought I'd go crazy.

"You're a frisky little heifer," he stammered as I let him

have his way and could hear him breathing hard even with the music playing.

I dug my nails into his shoulder and kinda moaned, "Yeah, I can be with a guy like you."

Then we started kissing real hard on the lips, and I could feel my whole body shiver when he ran his tongue up and down my neck, and he was just fiddling with the laces on my vest when, out of the blue, I thought I heard a car door slam outside.

"What was that?" I said as I suddenly pulled back and looked in the direction of the front door.

He kept on trying to kiss and grope at me like he'd heard nothing, but when I asked again if somebody was in the drive, he finally let go and muttered, "Probably just Bobby Lee."

"But you said he didn't come home till the crack of dawn."

"Oh, hon, ya never know what Bobby Lee's up to," was all he could say.

Now I felt a little uncomfortable, and went over to cut the music down, and was lacing up my vest when the door opened and, sure enough, there stood Bobby Lee with a big grin on his face.

"Mind if I join the party?" he said, and I could tell by his voice and the way he weaved into the room he was really smashed.

"Hey, sport," Virgil said as he tucked his shirt into his jeans and I sat back down on the sofa and sipped my drink. "You know where the hooch is."

Bobby Lee goes to the kitchen and comes back with what looks like a glass of vodka or gin. He then splashes some of his drink on his tee with a Frito logo when he plops down next to me, and I notice how strong his hairy arms look.

"Shit," he grunts as he slaps the drops off his front away from me. "Whatcha listening to?"

"Dwight Yoakam," I say, and I didn't know whether I was

more confused or nervous or pissed off over Bobby Lee just
showing up like that.

"You say ya dropped Clark off at his place?" Virgil asked
him from where he was standing behind the sofa.

"Yeah," he answered. "Town's dead as a flophouse on Sunday morning."

At first, Virgil's question didn't register, but since not one
word had been said till now about Bobby Lee dropping Clark
off anywhere, I wadn't so crocked I didn't suddenly realize this
was something they must've been talking about on the phone
when I thought I heard Virgil earlier back in the kitchen. Now
I was really mixed up and wondering what in hell was happening.

"Y'all been stirring the fire?" Bobby Lee asked as he put
his hand on my knee kinda easy and squeezed.

This did catch me off guard, so all I could think to say was,
"Just having a nightcap, bub, and listening to Yoakam do some
good honky-tonk."

Then from behind I felt Virgil's hands massaging my shoulders and heard him say, "No need to put on the dog 'round
Bobby Lee, darlin'. Bobby Lee's my buddy, and he likes to have
good a time as anybody else."

Next I feel Virgil's hand creeping down under my vest, but
before he can go much farther, I start to suspect something really weird's going on and try to get up.

"Not so fast, baby doll," he says more serious as he holds
my shoulders down and I feel Bobby Lee's hand groping my
thigh and smell his liquor breath.

"She's a little wildcat, ain't she?" Bobby Lee then says as he
reaches up for my breast.

"Yeah, Loretta likes a good time, don't ya, babe?" I now
feel his wet kisses again all over my neck, and this time they almost scare me.

"Stop it, you guys!" I finally say real loud as I fight to push their hands away and get up. "I don't know what this is all about, but I can tell y'all it ain't my scene."

"Sure it is, babe," Virgil says, and I can't believe he's actually trying to snatch the laces out of my vest. "You know you been beggin' for it all night, so why don't you just calm down and be nice to a guy and his buddy? We just wanna have a little fun, don't we?"

Up till now, I gotta say I was mainly confused and shocked and thinking here were two drunk guys just playing around. But then the more they went at me, and talked dirty, and acted like animals, the more scared I got and the more I realized they were up to ugly business.

"I'm outta here, you guys," I yell as I break Virgil's hold on my shoulders and jump up, but no sooner am I on my feet than Bobby Lee pulls me back down on the sofa with those strong hairy arms of his and tries to unbutton my jeans.

"Stop it, goddammit!" I shout, and with one mighty whack across his face, I send him reeling to the other end of the sofa.

He pulls himself back up and says, "You're a wild little filly, ain't you?"

"Naw," says Virgil, "she just a good prick teaser."

"That's not true, Virgil," I say as calmly as I can.

"Yeah, darlin', you can prick tease all night," he slurs on as he grabs me again, "and when the action picks up, you kinda change ya tune, don't ya?"

"That's a lie," I say. "I ain't like that."

"Naw, you little wildcats never are." He now kinda laughs as he rips the front of my vest open like some maniac. "You prick tease the hell out of a guy, then when time comes to whistle Dixie, ya wanna play tough. Well, sister, my buddy and I can show you how to play tough if that's what you want."

Don't ask me why I didn't just start screaming my lungs

out or reaching for objects to hit 'em with or throw at 'em the way most gals would have done. Instead, I gotta say I kept my wits about me, and it was like, in one split second, all protective instincts in my body lit up, and I remembered every lesson in kickboxing I'd been taught at the animal shelter and practiced over and over, and here was the threat I'd always been warned about. So when Virgil grabs me again real rough, I push him away, then land a stiff kick with my boots first at his thigh and next to the pit of his stomach, and this makes him tumble all over a chair and onto the floor. Next I feel Bobby Lee's arms around my waist from behind, and after I ram my elbows into him to break his hold, I turn around and kick him square in the groin and hear him howl as he bends over clutching his crotch.

This gave me just enough time to rush to the door, but by the time I reached my car, I could hear Virgil at the entrance bellowing, "Okay, babe, so you wanna play games in the car instead of the house?" How I fiddled so fast with the car door and glove compartment and towel around my gun I don't know, but by the time Virgil staggered to the drive and I saw Bobby Lee weaving right behind him, I was aiming the Beretta straight ahead at them and yelling, "Okay, you jerks, this goddamn thing's loaded and I know how to use it!"

Both of them stop dead in their tracks, and just stare a few seconds, and Virgil says, "Whatcha got there, babe?" He then starts walking toward me again.

"I'm warning you, buster," I repeat. "I know how to use this and I'll fire if you come one step closer."

"She's bullshittin', Virg." Bobby Lee garbles his words, and I notice he is still holding his crotch with one hand.

I aim the gun at the side of Virgil's boot and fire a shot. "That sound like bullshit?" I shout as he jumps back.

"Holy shit," he swears. "Just calm down, little lady. Calm

down, ya hear? You wanna hurt somebody and wake up neighbors across the water? We just thought ya wanted to have some fun. We don't want no trouble. Okay, darlin'?"

"She's fuckin' crazy, Virg," Bobby Lee mutters.

"Just get your asses back in that house," I tell 'em, "and thank your stars I don't call the police."

Then I slid across the seat still holding the gun, and locked the doors, and thanked my own stars that Virgil had left the keys in the ignition, and scratched outta there. Know what's funny? I thought I'd be all rattled and shaking, but the truth is I was calm as a lizard in the sun. Know what's not so funny? I wondered how good a kickboxer I would've been if I hadn't lost all that weight, and I also wondered what in hell would've happened if Vernon and Cordell hadn't taught me about guns.

Something else that wadn't too funny was when I was on Navigation, and suddenly noticed in my rearview mirror a cop car behind me, and my heart started thumping. Thank God I was driving only around forty, but who knew if I'd been weaving, and that's all I needed was to be stopped and given a breathalizer and slammed in the clink and my license taken away for six months. All the booze I'd been drinking, the gun on the seat, my laces still hanging out of my vest—I knew I wouldn't have a chance in hell if those lights started flashing and I was pulled over. Well, the cop seemed to follow me for maybe a mile, then, with my pulse really pounding, and my foot steady on the gas, and my eye on that mirror, I watched as he finally signaled a left turn and disappeared down a side street. There for a moment, breathing heavy and almost in a sweat, I didn't know whether to be more thankful for keeping my cool during the horror at the house or for escaping the damn cop.

When I got home, Sugar and Spice were barking and jumping all over me for attention and a Pup-Peroni treat they always expect, and after I'd let them out to pee, I cut on TV al-

most instinctively and had a craving myself for a snack. The
only thing on was a rerun of that silly *Iron Chef* I'd already seen
a hundred times, so I switched it right off, and put on Gatemouth Brown's "Texas Swing," and grabbed a box of Cheez-
Its in the cabinet. I've been addicted to Cheez-Its since I was a
child and remember when I could knock off a whole box
without blinking an eye. Then, after my surgery, I learned to
count out exactly ten crackers and limit myself to those when
I had a hunger panic—the same way I learned to ration anything I put in my mouth.

Well, I don't know what came over me, or whether I just
didn't give a damn anymore, but what I did was stick my hand
down in the bag, and take a big heap of crackers, and almost
shovel them in my mouth, chewing as fast as I could and tossing a few to the whining dogs who're never satisfied. Yeah, I
probably realized what I was doing as I just stood there at the
counter eating, but when it dawned on me not only that I
could have been raped pretty bad but also hauled off to jail for
drunk driving, the last thing that seemed to matter was feedin'
my face and doing whatever else I had to do to stop my hand
from shaking and my heart from racing like a time bomb ready
to explode. I guess I was already too tanked to reach for the
Jim Beam or even pop a Big Red, but I do know if I'd had a
pack of cigarettes in the house, I would've probably smoked
the whole goddamn pack.

Then, just as I was ramming my hand back into the crackers, I stopped all of a sudden, and stared long and hard at the
red box and white letters kinda in a daze, and, like a mad
woman, flung it through the air all the way into the living
room and let out a howl that sent the dogs running to the bedroom. Going through my mind at first was how I wanted to
blow Virgil's and Bobby Lee's brains out for treating me like a
piece of meat, and what in hell I would've done if the cop had
arrested me for DWI, and Vernon hugging me like a sister out-

side the bull room at Ziggy's, and lots of other things that
pissed me off. But the more I thought about everything, the
more I had to wonder just how much of this mess was really
my own fault and whether I wadn't foolin' anybody but myself. I mean, I had to admit I'd made some dumb decisions not
leveling with Vernon about the weight problem, and gettin'
mixed up with a bunch of crazy other guys who really didn't
respect me, and sometimes trying to be something I'm not,
and . . . just losing control of my life. My daddy used to call it
fallin' outta the saddle, and what Daddy would say is the only
thing to do when you fall outta the saddle is climb back up
and try to do better. Well, standing there in the kitchen listening to Gatemouth, that's exactly what I told myself I had to do.
I had to climb back up in the saddle and give it a better shot.

32

BUBBLES

Sorry to say I've put back on 7 pounds in the past couple of months, but, to tell the truth, too much else has been happening for me to worry about that. First, the catering's been going gangbusters, and I even had to lease the space of a deli that went belly-up over on Shepherd and get workers in there to install another stove and build some cabinets and work counters. Also traded my Ford for a much larger Chevy Blazer van. Best of all, I've actually hired Mary Jane and Rosemary to help me and Angel on major jobs, and they're as tickled pink as I am. And why not? They're both damn good cooks, and can be trusted like nobody else, and are learning to deal with suppliers and rentals as well as I can now. Rosemary don't make enough at CVS to keep body and soul together, and from what she tells me about Bear still being in the clink, she sure can't depend on him or anybody else to help her pay many bills. As for Cha Cha with a baby on the way, she's had to give up the roller derbies, and Sam says she's also better off chopping onions and decorating a dining room part-time than lifting 80-pound German shepherds and dealing with dangerous abuse cases at SPCA. Yeah, we gals make a great team, and so long as I watch my credit, I predict Glorious Bounty will be one of the classiest caterers in Houston in no time flat.

Know what jobs I've picked up? A fund-raising tent reception for one hundred at the Houston Zoo. A Cajun dinner for twenty-five doctors and their guests at the TMC—including a four-piece steel band those fat cats brought in from over in Lake Charles. Thanks to the wonderful Dewitts, my name's not only now spread all over River Oaks but Mr. Dewitt also wants me to cater some Tex-Mex shindig at Century Petroleum he's throwing for his associates coming down from Chicago and New York. And, to boot, who should call last week but that snazzy, gay Jerry Webster at Hilton, who'd seen another blurb on me in the paper and wanted to know if I was free to test some of the dishes on their new menus to the tune of three hundred dollars per hour. Not bad, I say, for a former fat girl with just a high school education and only a mean mama for a cooking teacher.

Speaking of Mama, she had another bad fall while she was pickling some squash, and this time it took the rescue squad and half the police department to hoist her up off the kitchen floor and get her to emergency. Nothing broken, thank the Lord, but me and Gladys are determined to talk her into selling her dilapidated house, and moving her out of that white trash neighborhood, and getting a nice condo apartment closer to downtown or near me in the Heights where I can keep a closer eye on her. Of course she's throwing one hissie after the next, and saying we'd both be happier if she was dead, and even threatening to take poison if we keep at her. But Mama ain't gettin' any younger, and she's sure not gonna take off any of that weight, and with all her health problems, something's simply gotta be done. We've told Mama we could probably get eighty or ninety grand for that house that she could use if she ever had to go into assisted living or something, but when we so much as mention that touchy subject, what she grumbles is,

"That's right, y'all are never gonna be happy till you stick me away in some home with a bunch of old geezers and watch me starve to death." Then she finally calms down like she usually does, and gets that sad look on her face, and stretches her arms out to one of us, and says, "Come here and give your old mama a big kiss."

Sally and Vernon didn't waste any time gettin' married at her Assembly of God church, and all I can say is I hope they're happy as bugs in a rug over in that house with Daisy and two cats and somebody's abandoned pet white rat Mary Jane said Sally dragged home from the shelter. At first, I told Mary Jane I had no intention of attending the ceremony, but then I changed my mind when I realized I have more manners and character than that and don't want everybody to think I'm just sour grapes. I gotta say Vernon was his same handsome self in a charcoal jacket and gray satin vest and lizard boots and the green bolo tie I once gave him, but, to be honest, all Sally's pink tunic dress with miles of red fringe and a wide red belt did was make her look like a bloated Barbie doll. I couldn've been more civil to them both and even let Vernon give me a peck on the cheek when it was all over. I do wish I'd had the gumption to tell him to drop dead when he was dumb enough to whisper to me at one point, "Seems like you put on a couple of pounds, hon, which makes you look real fine and healthy."

What I did drum up the gumption to do was tell that sweet Lester I'd have to give up working at Bluebird 'cause of the pressure from the catering. Oh, he understood, but I already do miss him and the other folks there, and yeah, I gotta confess I also miss all the guys trying to hit on me—for better or worse. Of course, after that awful episode with Virgil and Bobby Lee, I really tried to be more careful who I fooled around with, though, to tell the truth, I can't see it did much good or got me one bit closer to finding the right fella. Take old Rudy, for example. I really like Rudy and let him take me out again—this time to a romantic French bistro in Rice Village he likes—but as far as fun and games go . . . well, let's just say Rudy's bark's a hell of a lot more than his bite. Another good-looking hunk named Eugene could cut the mustard almost as good as Vernon and even brought me a potted camellia for the patio, but, wouldn't you know, turned out the bastard's married with three kids. Then there was Joey, whose rough hands reminded me of Daddy's. Big talker and big tipper who could out-two-step any roper in the state of Texas, and everything was going fine till we read in the *Chronicle* Joey's in jail for supposedly raping a fifteen-year-old over in Kirkwood Park. Like I always said, I know how to pick 'em.

So that sorta leaves me with . . . yeah, Lyman. This time the jerk just showed up late one night at Bluebird, and I couldn't believe how he was decked out pretty nice like Billy Po used to dress in a suit and tie and suede vest and all that. Sure, he'd been buggin' me from time to time on the phone and talking about his new apartment and how good things were going for him out at that Adobe Grill. But not till he came in the bar and told me he'd just been made full-time general manager of the place at double the salary did I start to think the guy maybe really had turned over a new leaf and was serious about making something of himself.

"Still got that stupid lizard on your arm?" I asked after I popped him a Bud and fixed two Beams for Dolly on the floor.

"Yeah, those don't come off so easy," he answered. "Kinda crazy of me to do that, wadn't it?"

"You still gotcha Hog?"

"Naw, hon, I sold that to Lance over at the shop when I got my Charger. Thought I told you that."

"Been out to Tinhorn lately?"

"'Bout a month ago, I reckon."

"Still the best goddamn ribs on earth."

"Wanna go one night?"

"Maybe," I answered as I kept thinking 'bout those ribs and brisket and links.

He took a few real quick slugs of his beer the way I remembered he always drinks for some weird reason.

"Let, can I ask you a question?" he then said.

"Why not?"

"Whatcha still working here for? I mean, I read in the paper 'bout ya gettin' big-time in the catering business and . . ."

"When did you start reading a newspaper?" I interrupted him kinda rude.

"Oh, don't be such a bitch, Let," he said real slow. "Now I do lotta things I used not to do."

"Sorry, bub," I apologized. "Anyway, 'cause I love working here, and meeting all the people, and Lester's the greatest, and can't beat the tips. May have to give it all up soon, though."

"Bet ya got lotta guys hittin' on ya here."

I just laughed and said, "I ain't been twiddling my thumbs, if that's what you wondering."

Well, the truth was I actually had been sorta twiddling my thumbs lately in the romance department and also making a few other decisions about my life after all I been through. Sure, I'm damn proud of my success at losing all the weight and gettin' Glorious Bounty off the ground and rollin', but one day I looked myself real hard in the mirror and asked . . . what I said was, "Loretta, you really ain't one bit happier than you were when you were fat, and you deserve more than what's been thrown at you by these whacky dudes." Oh, I don't think I ever expected a miracle after I went through so much hell to improve myself, but goddammit, a girl can take just so much letdown and other crap. I mean, nobody likes to feel cheated and humiliated and lonesome, and all I ever wanted was to meet some regular guy with a little bit of class who'd give me

some love and respect, and help me outta my rut, and just . . .
give a damn.

Okay, maybe I screwed up, but one thing I learned was, like
Mama's always said, it don't do any good punishing yourself
and wrecking your whole life just to be somebody you're not.
So yeah, I took Lyman up on his offer to go to Tinhorn BBQ,
and we both ordered ribs and a chopped brisket on jalapeño
bread and split a vinegar pie and guzzled ice-cold mugs of
Shiner, and I gotta say it was like I'd died and gone to heaven.
Didn't bother my stomach one iota, and if that means my band
has stretched a little bit, to hell with it. Not that I plan to start
piggin' out like that again every day, any more than I plan to
give up that stupid gym altogether—at least not yet. I'm not
crazy, but, like I've been telling Lyman, I ain't that far from
forty, and I intend to make up for some lost time and get my
life on the right track.

As for Lyman himself, he's not such a bad guy these days,
and we've had some fun bowling with Mary Jane and Sam and
taking in a couple of Astros games with Rosemary and this
new geek from Galveston she's met, and I even introduced
Lyman to footsie-boy Cordell Hines when we ran into him
one night over at Fire Power. I've also watched Lyman work
the floor at Adobe Grill and deal with the cook out there,
which got me wondering if maybe he might not one day
wanna learn more about the catering business. Who knows
what could happen? The thing about Lyman is the guy really
is crazy about me, and treats me good, and yeah, I gotta admit
. . . well, the truth is I'm pretty used to him and know what to
expect. Of course he ain't gonna break any records between
the sheets, and I know things are never gonna be moonlight
and magnolias with him, but hey, maybe that's what life's really
all about, and, besides, I can't worry about things like that with
everything else going on.

Take what happened at Ziggy's last week. 'Bout the same

time I told Lester I was gonna have to give up the job at Bluebird, I also told Buzzy I was gonna have to quit the band since
the catering can get real crazy on the weekends. So he calls me
back not long ago, and tells me how upset Venus and Tricksy
and the others have been without me and my horn, and how
regular customers are screaming at him about me not being
there, and how business is dropping off some, and what have
you.

"Sweetheart, they really miss you," he says, "and I mean, it's
like you're a real star. If it's more money you want . . ."

"Buzz, you know it ain't a question of more money," I try
to explain. "I miss the band more than you can imagine, but
it's just I'm so bogged down now in this new business on
weekends. . . ."

"I understand that, honey," he goes on, "but what you
don't realize is we got dozens of customers who show up just
to hear Bubbles solo and back up Venus and do her thing.
Don't that mean anything to you?"

"Buzz, you know how I hate that name."

"I know you do, Loretta, but Bubbles is who lots of people
still come to hear and . . . goddammit, Loretta, nobody blows
like you, and you really are missed, and all I'm asking is for you
to help me out of a jam—even if it's just every other weekend."

If Buzzy don't know anything else, he sure knows how to
make a gal feel special, and if I don't believe in nothing else, I
believe in being loyal to anybody who's helped me out when I
needed help. So when he begged me to play last weekend, and
said he'd even have Venus announce to the crowd the week
before that I'd be coming back, I told him okay and figured
Angel and the others could handle an early cocktail job we
had at the Sculpture Garden.

What I decided to wear was my black-wash flare jeans and
plunging checkerboard zip tank and ice pick snake boots, and

I even fixed my hair in a mussed half-up style. Lyman, bless his heart, got somebody to cover for him at the grill and picked me up in his Charger dressed in good-looking burnt orange cargo pants and a nice longhorn jacket. After he stopped at a 7–Eleven for me to get a pack of Camel Lights, we dropped by the Lone Star for a couple of snorts of bourbon and a Frito pie, and when we finally pulled up at Ziggy's, I couldn't believe the number of cars and trucks in the lot and knew it was gonna be a big night.

Well, right off the bat, we do "Texas on My Mind" to get dancers on the floor, then I back Venus up as usual on "Jesus, Take the Wheel," but when I blow a long solo in "Do You Love as Good as You Look," the crowd really goes wild clapping and whistling and yelling for a repeat. Gotta say it all sorta embarrassed me, but when I saw Lyman and Buzzy grinning over at the bar, I stepped back up to the mike, and nodded at Tricksy and Bobby for a downbeat, and gave 'em what they wanted for all it was worth. Everybody went crazy again, and I made a little bow, and most of the racket had almost stopped when I suddenly heard a guy holler, "Bubbles, you back for good, gal?"

For a second I cringed, but then I cracked a big smile, and held my sax up in the air, and shouted over the mike, "Yeah, cowboy, Bubbles is back!"

RECIPES FROM LORETTA'S KITCHEN

Pimento Cheese

1 pound extra-sharp cheddar cheese
1 (7-ounce) jar pimentos, drained
½ teaspoon freshly ground black pepper
Salt to taste
Cayenne pepper to taste
Worcestershire sauce to taste
⅔ cup mayonnaise

Finely grate the cheese into a mixing bowl. On a plate, mash the pimentos well with a fork till they're very pulpy, add them to the cheese along with the pepper, salt, cayenne, and Worcestershire, and mix till well blended. Using a fork, fold in the mayonnaise and mash well till the spread is smooth, adding a little more mayonnaise if it appears too dry or stiff. Scrape the spread into a jar or crock, cover well, and refrigerate for at least 2 hours before serving with crackers or using to make pimento cheese sandwiches. Keeps up to 1 week tightly covered in the refrigerator.

Makes about 3 cups.

Seafood Gumbo

½ pound bacon, cut into small pieces
¼ cup all-purpose flour
1 pound firm fresh okra, stems removed and pods cut into
    small rounds (about 5 cups)
1 large onion, chopped
½ medium green bell pepper, seeded and chopped
1 large celery rib, chopped
2½ cups canned tomatoes, drained
2 quarts chicken broth
¼ cup chopped fresh parsley leaves
1 teaspoon dried thyme, crumbled
1 bay leaf
Salt and freshly ground black pepper to taste
Tabasco sauce to taste
1 pound fresh medium shrimp, peeled and deveined
1 pound fresh claw crabmeat, picked over for shells and
    cartilage
1 pint small, fresh-shucked oysters
Boiled white rice

In a large, heavy pot, fry the bacon over moderate heat till
crisp, drain on paper towels, and reserve. Add the flour to the
bacon grease, reduce the heat to low, and whisk more and
more steadily for about 15 minutes or till the roux is light
brown, taking great care not to burn it. Add the okra and
cook, stirring, till the okra is slightly browned and the roux
dark brown.

Add the onion, bell pepper, and celery, stir well, cover, and let
cook 3 minutes. Add the tomatoes, broth, parsley, thyme, bay

leaf, salt and pepper, and Tabasco, bring to a boil, reduce the heat to low, and simmer, uncovered, for 2 hours, adding a little water if the liquid is too thick.

Add the shrimp, crabmeat, oysters, and reserved bacon, stir, return to a simmer, and cook about 15 minutes longer. Taste for seasoning, and serve the gumbo over rice in deep soup bowls.

Makes 6 servings.

Chocolate Enchiladas

8 tablespoons bacon drippings
5 tablespoons all-purpose flour
1 garlic clove, finely chopped
6 tablespoons pulp from boiled and seeded ancho or jalapeño
    chile pepper
1 quart hot water
Salt to taste
4 squares Mexican chocolate (available in specialty food
    shops), mashed
2 large onions, chopped
1 pound sharp cheddar cheese, grated
1 pound Jack white cheese, grated
1½ cups corn oil
10 to 12 tortillas

Preheat the oven to 350°F.

In a heavy skillet, heat the bacon drippings over low heat, add the flour, garlic, and chile pulp, and stir about 5 minutes. Add the hot water, stirring; then add the salt and chocolate, stirring constantly. Continue cooking till the sauce is medium-thick, then set aside.

In a bowl, combine the onions and cheeses and mix thoroughly. In another large skillet, heat the oil and add a tortilla just long enough to soften. Remove from the oil, dip in the chocolate sauce, fill with a little of the onion and cheese mixture, roll up neatly, and arrange in a large baking dish. Continue softening and rolling tortillas till the dish is full (one layer only). Sprinkle the remaining onion and cheese mixture over the tops, pour on enough of the sauce to fill half the dish, and bake about 20 minutes or till bubbling hot.

Makes 4 to 6 servings.

Deviled Crab Cakes

½ cup half-and-half
½ cup mayonnaise
1 large egg white
1½ teaspoons dry mustard
2 teaspoons Worcestershire sauce
2 teaspoons fresh lemon juice
Tabasco sauce to taste
2 scallions (part of green tops included), minced
1 small red bell pepper, seeded and minced
½ teaspoon salt
1 pound fresh lump crabmeat, picked over for shells and carti-
    lage
1 cup fine dry bread crumbs
1 tablespoon butter, melted
¼ cup peanut oil
2 tablespoons butter

In a bowl, whisk together the half-and-half, mayonnaise, and egg white till well blended. Add the dry mustard, Worcestershire, lemon juice, Tabasco, scallions, bell pepper, and salt and stir till well blended. Gently fold in the crabmeat and ½ cup of the bread crumbs till well blended.

Divide the mixture into 4 equal parts and shape each into an oval patty. In a small bowl, combine the remaining bread crumbs with the melted butter, mix well, and turn each patty in the mixture to coat lightly.

In a large, heavy skillet, heat the oil and the 2 tablespoons butter over moderate heat, add the crab cakes, and cook till lightly browned, about 3 minutes per side. Drain briefly on paper towels and serve immediately.

Makes 4 servings.

Turkey and Ham Casserole

6 tablespoons (¾ stick) butter
1 cup finely chopped onions
6 tablespoons all-purpose flour
1 teaspoon salt
½ teaspoon freshly ground black pepper
2½ cups milk
½ pound fresh mushrooms, sliced
5 tablespoons dry sherry
5 cups chopped cooked turkey breast
2 cups chopped cooked ham
Two 5-ounce cans water chestnuts, drained and sliced
1 cup shredded Swiss cheese
2 cups fresh bread crumbs
6 tablespoons (¾ stick) butter, melted

Preheat the oven to 400°F. Grease a large, shallow baking dish and set aside.

In a large, heavy skillet, melt 4 tablespoons of the butter over moderate heat, add the onions, and cook, stirring, till soft but not browned, about 3 minutes. Sprinkle the flour, salt, and pepper over the onions and stir about 2 minutes longer. Reduce the heat to low and gradually add the milk, stirring constantly till the mixture is thickened and smooth. Remove the pan from the heat.

In a small skillet, melt the remaining 2 tablespoons butter over moderate heat, add the mushrooms, and cook, stirring, till golden, about 5 minutes. Add the mushrooms to the milk mixture, then add the sherry, turkey, ham, and water chestnuts and stir till well blended. Spoon the mixture into the prepared baking dish and sprinkle the cheese over the top. In a small mixing bowl, combine the bread crumbs and melted butter, spoon the mixture evenly over the cheese, and bake till the casserole is lightly browned, about 35 minutes. Serve hot.

Makes at least 12 servings.

Meat Loaf Deluxe

5 tablespoons butter

½ pound large, fresh mushrooms, stems finely chopped and
   caps reserved

1 large onion, finely chopped

½ medium green bell pepper, seeded and finely chopped

2 celery ribs, finely chopped

2 garlic cloves, minced

½ teaspoon dried thyme, crumbled

½ teaspoon dried rosemary, crumbled

1 pound ground beef round

1 pound ground pork

1 pound ground veal

½ pound bulk pork sausage

1 tablespoon Dijon mustard

½ cup tomato ketchup

3 tablespoons Worcestershire sauce

½ teaspoon Tabasco sauce

Salt and freshly ground black pepper to taste

3 large eggs, beaten

1 cup bread crumbs soaked in ½ cup heavy cream

3 strips bacon

Pimento-stuffed green olives, cut in half, for garnish

Preheat the oven to 350°F.

In a medium skillet, melt 3 tablespoons of the butter over
moderate heat, add the mushroom stems, and cook, stirring,
about 5 minutes or till most of their liquid has evaporated. Stir
in the onion, bell pepper, celery, garlic, thyme, and rosemary,

reduce the heat to low, cover, and simmer about 15 minutes or till the vegetables are soft and the liquid has evaporated.

Place the meats in a large mixing bowl, add the sautéed vegetables, and mix lightly. Add the mustard, ketchup, Worcestershire, Tabasco, salt and pepper, eggs, and bread crumbs and mix with your hands till blended thoroughly. Shape the mixture into a firm, thick oval loaf, place in a shallow baking or gratin dish, drape bacon over the top, and bake 1 hour in the upper third of the oven. Remove the bacon strips and continue baking 15 to 20 minutes longer, depending on how thick the loaf is and how crusty you want the exterior to be.

Shortly before the meat loaf is removed from the oven, melt the remaining 2 tablespoons butter in a small skillet over moderate heat, add the reserved mushroom caps, and cook, stirring, about 2 minutes or till nicely glazed. Transfer the meat loaf to a large, heated platter, arrange olives over the top, and garnish the edges with the mushroom caps.

Makes 8 servings.

Texas Bowl o' Red (Chili)

1 (4-pound) lean beef chuck roast
½ cup corn oil
2 medium onions, chopped
1 medium green bell pepper, seeded and chopped
1 jalapeño chile pepper, seeded and chopped
5 garlic cloves, minced
½ cup tomato paste
1 (1-ounce) square semisweet chocolate, chopped
½ cup masa harina (corn flour)
½ cup chili powder (or to taste)
2 teaspoons ground cumin
2 teaspoons dried oregano
1 teaspoon paprika
Tabasco sauce to taste
2 cups canned beef broth
2 cups lager beer
Salt and freshly ground black pepper to taste

Trim excess fat from the meat and cut the meat into 1-inch cubes. In a large pot or casserole, heat the oil over moderate heat, add the meat, and cook, stirring, till it loses its red color. Add the onions, bell pepper, jalapeño, and garlic and stir till the vegetables soften, about 10 minutes. Add the tomato paste and chocolate and stir till the chocolate melts. Sprinkle the masa harina over the top and stir till the pieces of meat are evenly coated. Add the chili powder, cumin, oregano, paprika, and Tabasco and stir till well blended. Add the broth, beer, and salt and pepper and bring to a boil. Reduce the heat to low, cover, and simmer 3 to 4 hours or till the meat almost falls apart, adding a little more broth or beer if the chili seems too dry. Serve with pinto beans on the side.

Makes 8 to 10 servings.

Pinto Beans

1 pound dried pinto beans
1 large onion, chopped
½ pound salt pork

In a bowl, soak the beans for about 1 hour and drain. Add fresh water to cover by 2 inches and add the onion and salt pork. Bring to a boil, reduce the heat to low, and simmer about 2 hours or till tender.

Hummingbird Cake

For the Cake

3 cups all-purpose flour
2 cups sugar
1 teaspoon baking soda
1 teaspoon ground cinnamon
1 teaspoon salt
3 large eggs, beaten
1½ cups vegetable oil
1 (8-ounce) can crushed pineapple, undrained
2 cups chopped nuts (pecans, walnuts, or hazelnuts)
2 cups chopped bananas
1½ teaspoons pure vanilla extract

For the Icing

2 (8-ounce) packages cream cheese, at room temperature
½ pound (2 sticks) butter, at room temperature
2 (16-ounce) boxes confectioners' sugar, sifted
2 teaspoons pure vanilla extract

Preheat the oven to 350°F. Grease three 9-inch round cake pans with butter, dust the bottom and sides with flour, and set aside.

To make the cake, combine the flour, sugar, baking soda, cinnamon, and salt in a large bowl and stir till well blended. Add the eggs and oil and stir till the dry ingredients are moistened, taking care not to beat them. Stir in the pineapple, 1 cup of the nuts, the bananas, and vanilla. Divide the batter evenly among the prepared pans. Bake till a straw inserted into the center of the cakes comes out clean, 25 to 30 minutes. Let the cakes cool in the pans for 10 minutes, then turn them out onto racks to cool completely.

To make the icing, combine the cream cheese and butter in a large bowl and cream with an electric mixer till smooth. Add the confectioners' sugar, beat till light and fluffy, and stir in the vanilla. Spread the icing between the cakes stacked on a cake plate, ice the top and sides of the cake, and sprinkle the remaining nuts over the top.

Makes 10 to 12 servings.

Lemon Drop Cookies

½ cup (1 stick) butter, softened
¾ cup granulated sugar
1 large egg
1 teaspoon grated lemon rind
1 tablespoon heavy cream
1½ cups all-purpose flour
1 teaspoon baking powder
½ teaspoon salt
½ cup (one 6½-ounce package) pure lemon drop candy, very
    finely crushed

Preheat the oven to 350°F. Grease a large baking sheet and set aside.

In a large mixing bowl, cream the butter and sugar together with an electric mixer till light and fluffy, add the egg, and beat till well blended. Add the lemon rind and cream and stir till well blended. In a small mixing bowl, combine the flour, baking powder, and salt, mix well, add to the creamed mixture, and stir till well blended. Add the crushed candy and stir till well blended. Drop the batter by the teaspoon about 1 inch apart onto the prepared baking sheet and bake till lightly browned around the edges, about 10 minutes. Let the cookies cool completely before removing from the sheet.

Makes about 3 dozen cookies.

Jelly Treats

1½ cups (3 sticks) butter, at room temperature
1 cup sugar
4 large egg yolks
4 cups all-purpose flour
Strawberry, peach, and mint jelly or jam

Preheat the oven to 325°F.

In a large mixing bowl, cream the butter and sugar together with an electric mixer, add the egg yolks, and beat thoroughly. Gradually add the flour and mix till well blended and the batter is firm.

Roll pieces of the batter into small balls about the size of a large marble in the palms of your hands, place them on ungreased baking sheets about 1½ inches apart, press a fingertip in the center of each to make an indention, and bake till dull in color, about 10 minutes. Remove the cookies from the oven, spoon a dollop of jelly in the indentions, and continue baking till the cookies are just slightly browned, about 12 minutes more. Let cool till the jelly is fully set and store separated by sheets of wax paper in airtight containers.

Makes about 100 treats.

HUNGRY FOR HAPPINESS

James Villas

ABOUT THIS GUIDE

The suggested questions are included to enhance
your group's reading of James Villas's
Hungry for Happiness.

DISCUSSION QUESTIONS

1. Today, Houston is, in many respects, a very cosmopolitan American city, yet Loretta and her working-class family and friends might just as well be living in the rugged plains of West Texas. In what ways are the Southern heroine and her brood part of this society's fabric, and how are they misfits? Does Loretta ever give any indication of wanting to elevate her social status?

2. Texas women are generally perceived as strong, outspoken, and downright tough, and Loretta is certainly no exception. What might explain this phenomenon, and how is a "Texas gal" different from the South's proverbial "steel magnolia"?

3. Lots of people are loosely called "trash" in this novel. What's the meaning of the term in the context of the narrative, and just how derogatory is it?

4. Obesity is almost a way of life with Loretta's family. What has always prevented these individuals from trying to overcome the curse and improve their lives, and why is Loretta different from the others?

5. Why does Loretta tolerate a mother who, in many respects, is responsible for her daughter's unhappiness and seems to actually begrudge her happiness? What creates the bond between these two women?

6. Loretta's daddy remains a mysterious figure throughout the novel. What is the probable truth about him, and why is he so important to Loretta?

7. There seems to be a major change in the personality of Loretta's sister, Gladys, as well as in the two women's relationship. What might account for this?

8. Is Lyman's attraction to Loretta mainly sexual or psychological? Why does he try to get her back?

9. Vernon has a fetish for fat women. How might he have come by this irregularity, and is it a trait to be condemned? Are there actually more Vernons in this world than society cares to acknowledge?

10. Is Billy Po a character to be disparaged or admired, and what is his importance in the plot development?

11. Is weight loss Loretta's only goal, or are there other desperations from which she's trying to escape?

12. What does Loretta strive most to attain: good health, financial security, love, respect, self-esteem, or a stable family life?

13. Loretta's feelings about and reaction to children are ambiguous throughout the novel. Does she like children, and does she yearn to have any of her own like most women do? Is her devotion to Sugar and Spice and all animals simply a way to fulfill a powerful mother instinct?

14. Why and how are food and cooking so important to Loretta even after her diet is restricted? Could this passion be interpreted as a form of masochism? Can the argument be made that food is at once Loretta's downfall and salvation?

15. It's pretty obvious that Loretta will evolve into one of the city's most popular caterers. Will this professional

success bring her the happiness and respect she seeks, or are her emotional needs too strong to ignore?

16. Are there disappointments, frustrations, and desperations that Loretta can be said to share with all young women?

17. At the end, what is the likelihood that Loretta and Lyman will actually get back together? Is there any chance she would marry him again? If so, why?